If This Were a Love Story

Sara LaFontain

26 Trees Press, Tucson, Arizona

26 Trees Press
3661 N. Campbell Ave #379
Tucson, Arizona 85719
www.saralafontain.com

Publisher's Note: This is a work of fiction. Names, characters, places, and incidents are a product of the author's imagination. Locales and public names are sometimes used for atmospheric purposes. Any resemblance to actual people, living or dead, or to businesses, companies, events, institutions, or locales is completely coincidental.

Book Layout © 2017 BookDesignTemplates.com
Cover Design: Leigh McDonald
Editor: Amanda Slaybaugh

If This Were a Love Story/ Sara LaFontain -- 1st ed.
ISBN 978-1-7326857-5-8

To Connie and Rodney Williams
Thank you for being my family.

Chapter One

Midland, Texas, January 2016

The drunk tank was close enough to the front desk that she could hear her brother's arrival.

"I got a call about Nicole O'Connell?" Kenny's voice echoed down the corridor, his frustration and annoyance evident. Not surprising, considering it was three in the morning. But who else could she have called? Nobody, since her sister had abandoned her.

"You here to bail her out?" That was the cop on desk duty, the one who'd laughed while taking her mugshot. Asshole. They were all assholes, especially the one who arrested her. He could have let her off with a warning. It's not like anybody got hurt. Didn't police have more important things to waste taxpayer money on?

"Actually, I want to see who you have in there first."

Uh oh. He wasn't going to play along with her little white lie. Screw Kenny. She thought he was her ally. What was the point of having a favorite brother if he wasn't going to be supportive? And she hadn't done anything that wrong. She just miscalculated the number of drinks she'd consumed. Why all the fuss? Everyone did it.

Footsteps coming. Two sets. She wiped her eyes, glad of her waterproof mascara, and tried to put on a cheery smile. As soon as her brother came into view she rose to her feet, swaying slightly.

"Hi, Kenny. Thanks for coming! I'm ready to go home now. I owe you a huge favor for this. I'll babysit every Saturday night for the next two months to make it up to you." Her attempt at a bribe failed miserably.

Her brother, her sweet, loving big brother who was supposed to take care of her and protect her looked at her with such loathing in his eyes. "That's not Nicole O'Connell. Nicole is on her honeymoon in Europe. Amanda, what the hell were you thinking?"

🌲 🌲 🌲 🌲 🌲

"Sober enough to talk yet?" Kenny flipped on the light. Amanda blinked up at him. It was too early to deal with any of this nonsense. The events of the night before were still hazy. She couldn't quite remember why she had used her twin sister's name, or why she had been carrying Nikki's ID card to begin with. She remembered giggling a lot and falling over when they told her to walk a straight line. But that wasn't really her fault. How could anyone do that in high heels, especially after just wrecking their car? Having an airbag go off in their face would be enough to make anyone dizzy.

"No, go away." She tried to pull her pillow over her head to block the light, but he yanked it out of her hands.

"Last night you crashed your car, got a DWI, and dragged me out of bed to bail you out. You're not the one who gets to decide when we talk about this."

"You're not Dad."

"Want me to call him?"

"God, no. That would make everything worse." She sat up and threw the covers off, revealing her dress from last night. What, he couldn't lend her pajamas? Or an old T-shirt? Jerk. "Fine, we can talk. What is it? What is so important you can't let me sleep?"

"I did let you sleep, in my clean guest room, so you need to be nice to me. My children are downstairs. You want them to see their favorite aunt like this? What the hell is wrong with you?"

"I just had a little too much to drink. Who cares? Everybody does it, even you, Kenneth." Drinking was ingrained in their family culture. That's why she was so offended he kept acting like it was an issue. Pot, meet kettle, and all that.

"No, I drink occasionally. And I don't drive afterward. You knocked over a stop sign and totaled your car. You're lucky you didn't kill anybody, or yourself."

"It'd be better if I had." She said the words dramatically, even though she didn't mean them. She was trying to get a rise out of him. Her attempt didn't work. He just looked sad and frustrated.

"Something's gotten into you lately, Amanda. You're messing up your life. You're going to lose your job over this."

"Fucking morality clause. I don't drink at work. Who cares what I do on my free time?"

"Your bosses, obviously. And probably all the parents. You teach preschool, character matters. You might want to talk to Gina. Maybe she knows someone who can help you." His wife was an attorney, though she practiced corporate law. He was right. Amanda did need to talk to her, ask if she had any recommendations. This situation was undoubtedly the worst she'd ever been in. She'd have to face it—but later, when she got enough sleep.

"Whatever. I'll pay the fine. It can't be that big of a deal." Maybe if she said the words enough times, it would make them come true. *No big deal, it was nothing.*

"You need help, Amanda. You have a drinking problem."

"Yeah, I know. Two hands and only one mouth." She laughed at her own joke, but it didn't even earn her an eye-roll from her brother. If anything, his brow furrowed deeper.

"I don't think you're taking this seriously enough. It is. Remember how Aunt Cindy died? Drunk driver. If you think anybody in this family is going to have anything other than a come to Jesus meeting with you, you're sorely mistaken." How unfair, to dredge up such an ancient accident. Their aunt had been killed nearly fifteen years ago; it wasn't like anyone was still talking about that. It was tragic, of course, but Amanda's case was different. For one thing, she'd only hit a sign, not another vehicle. If there had been a car, she'd have seen it and stopped in time.

"Everybody in this family needs to mind their own business."

"That never happens, and you know it." His tone changed abruptly and became friendlier. "Anyway, sis, come downstairs. I made a fresh pot of coffee. You look like you could use a cup."

There—finally!—was the supportive brother she had been looking for. Not the judgmental jackass who had picked her up and yelled at her for the duration of the car ride back to his house when all she wanted to do was close her eyes and rest. Finally, Sweet Kenny appeared, ready to help treat her hangover, just like he had for years. Wasn't he the one who taught her and Nikki to take vitamin B and ibuprofen together with a liter of water and a strong coffee with extra sugar? It worked every time. Not that it really mattered. She wasn't very hungover—she was a smart drinker. Always one cup of water per alcoholic beverage. The technique meant she had to pee more often, but it made for better mornings. See? Being able to do that sort of thing while drinking proved she didn't have a problem. She was fine.

She followed her brother down to the living room and froze. Son of a bitch.

"You asshole! You're supposed to be on my side!" Her entire extended family was gathered in silence there. All of them. Her parents, weary and annoyed. Her Uncle Alan. Her frowning grandmother. Her brothers and their wives. And worst of all, three laptops were set up, with six faces: her cousin Cara, her sister Amy, and her damn twin-abandoning betrayer Nicole, all with their husbands.

"I am on your side. We're doing this for you, sis. This is an intervention."

"I do not have to put up with this," Amanda announced to the room. She turned to go back upstairs, but Kenny blocked her. He wrapped his arm around forcefully around her shoulders and led her to a chair.

"If you sit, I'll get you a coffee," he offered, but with a harsh bite behind the words.

"And if I should decline?"

"I'll make you sit, and you won't get any coffee."

"Do y'all see him threatening me with violence here?" Amanda asked the room, but not a single person said anything. "Fine! I'm sitting because I want to, not because Kenny told me to." She plopped herself down and crossed her arms. "And I'm still expecting that coffee."

Gina was the one who brought her a mug, black, no sugar. It was lukewarm, but she felt like she already stood on thin ice, so she wasn't going to complain. Instead, she scanned the room, assessed the level of anger and frustration in their faces, and tried to determine who might side with her here.

"Where's Trixie?" she asked when she noticed her aunt's absence. She took a mental note: Trixie opposed the intervention. She'd have to thank her later.

"She took all the kids to the playground down the street. They didn't need to be here for this," Dad said. Never mind, she wouldn't thank Trixie. She was on her own. Fine. She could face this. She was strong. Tired, but strong.

She shaped her mouth into a falsely cheerful smile and turned to the laptop harboring the image of her traitorous twin. "Good morning Nikki. How's France?"

"It'd be more fun if I wasn't getting a criminal record at home while away. This is not how I want to spend my honeymoon, Me-me." Nicole didn't smile back, but at least she used their mutual nickname for each other. She couldn't be too mad if she was still calling her twin by an affectionate term.

"I'm sure it's not," Amanda started to offer a false apology, but then she scrutinized the screen more closely. "Did you cut your hair?"

"There was this funky salon . . ." Nicole ducked her head and had the grace to look guilty. They always talked about it before getting haircuts. How can you be identical twins if you don't look identical? They weren't like their stupid older brothers, Sideburns and No-Sideburns. Also beer gut and no-beer-gut, but best not to point that out.

"Looks good." She lied and turned to the other computers, ignoring the family members physically present. "Amy, you're looking remarkably well for a woman on bed rest." Slight exaggeration. Amy's skin was sallow, and not just from poor lighting. Amy obviously knew it too, since she raised one middle finger and mouthed a particularly horrible insult. At least one of her sisters wasn't changing.

"Can we talk about this DWI?" Cara spoke up. "I have things to do today."

"Sorry to interrupt your busy Sunday," Amanda replied. "We don't need to do this. I'm fine. I made a tiny mistake. Nobody got hurt."

"Sweetheart, you aren't fine. You drink too much. You have a problem." This, from her mother? Her own mother, the woman who claimed to love all of her children equally no matter what?

Perhaps Amanda took things a step too far when she told them all to go fuck themselves.

Chapter Two

Ferry's Landing, Minnesota, May 2016

Nothing felt better than pounding on the drums in front of a cheering crowd. Nothing. Except maybe making eye contact with a hot blonde woman while doing so. Yeah, that felt pretty damn good too.

When the set ended, Everett Ryan wiped away his sweat and headed to the watercooler at the end of the bar. He needed a drink. As he gulped the water down, a manicured hand suddenly appeared on his arm and electricity shot through his skin.

"Nice muscles. You've been banging on those drums all night. Makes me wonder if there's anything else you like to bang all night?"

It was the hot blonde, and she would have been even sexier with that Southern accent, if she hadn't been slurring her words so badly. Damn, what a shame.

"Sometimes." He pried her fingers off his bicep.

"You look like a man who knows what he's doing." She tried to touch him again and he stepped back. He'd have been more susceptible to her flirtations if he had thought she could actually see him. She could hardly keep her eyes open.

"Sometimes," he replied again and scanned the room. She must be here with friends. Nobody came to a bar like this one alone. Unless they were a tourist and unaware of the bar's reputation. Shit. With that accent, she must be a tourist. Still, he had hope that there was a group of other southerners around here somewhere. "Where are your friends?"

"Oh, Sugar, I'm here all by myself. But I might not leave alone."

Everett closed his eyes and swore under his breath. He couldn't walk away from someone so intoxicated. Shore Leave wasn't the kind of establishment that was safe for a pretty girl, drunk and on her own.

The blonde swayed and for a second he worried she might fall over. He caught her with one arm. It brought his face closer to hers, and that's when he realized he'd seen those eyes before. He recognized those dark pools with long thick lashes—they looked exactly like her sister's eyes. He'd known her sister for years, and that meant he also knew her cousin—her cousin who had told him to keep a lookout on the ferry for a certain new summer employee who never showed up. Double shit. Now he'd definitely have to be the one to take care of her. Those were the obligations created by small-town living.

"Where are you staying tonight?" he asked, hoping she was able to form a coherent answer.

"There's a motel down the street," she waved vaguely in the opposite direction of the nearest lodging. "Unless you'd rather go back to your place . . ."

"How about I take you back to your motel? Get you into bed." Not the way it sounded though.

She giggled and started acting coy. "Oh, my goodness, I don't know about that! You're a stranger. Stranger danger, right?"

"Tell you what. If I can guess your last name, will you trust me enough to let me get you out of here?"

Her hand was back on his arm. "With these muscles? Sugar, if you can guess my last name, you can do whatever you want with me."

"O'Connell. Let's go."

She gasped loudly. "Oh my god, you must be psychic! Quick, tell me what I'm thinking right now!"

"I'm not psychic, I know you. Or your family, at least. Come on, I'll take you to your room." He'd have to come back for his drums later. This night was getting longer and longer, and he still had to be up before sunrise tomorrow.

"Hold your horses, you lovely man. I need to settle my tab." That was an unexpectedly lucid statement. He was amazed she still had the presence of mind to worry about her credit card.

"Here, you sit, I'll handle it," he said, pushing her down on an empty stool. He wasn't positive she'd be able to keep herself upright on it, but he figured it was a short enough time to be worth the risk. If she passed out, she was more likely to crash forward on to the bar rather than backward off the stool anyway.

A brief chat and a 25% tip got her card back from the bartender and an assurance that his drum kit would remain unmolested on the stage, even if he didn't make it back before closing time. He glanced at the card before he signed. Amanda. Good to know. When he made it back to her, another man—or more accurately, a predator—had taken his place.

"You bothering my girl there?" Everett asked him, trying to sound protective but not quite threatening. He didn't want to get involved in a fight—not without Duncan around. He could take on a few people on his own, but it was always better with his older brother's help. His bandmates, currently doing shots with a small cluster of fans, would surely jump in, but they were not the ideal backup. Two of them were too scrawny, and the other couldn't take a hit.

"Your girl? We were just talking about going back to my place," the man said. He draped an arm over Amanda's shoulder with his hand hovering in close proximity to her breast. Her eyes were half-closed and from the way she slumped over he could tell she wasn't going to stay conscious much longer.

"You're taking my girl back to your place? Forget it. Walk away, right now." Everett stood well over six-feet-tall, and spending more than a decade slinging crates on the docks had made him broad and powerful. He flexed, looked the man up and down, and grinned, showing all of his teeth. If it came down to it, he'd have to let the guy throw the first punch. That was the way to keep out of jail: claim self-defense. Or defense of others, as the case would be here.

The man sized him up, but evidently didn't like what he saw. "Yeah, whatever. She probably has herpes."

"Walk away," Everett repeated, and this time, the man spat on the floor and sauntered off, possibly to search for another victim. Everett was tempted to follow and issue a parking lot invitation, but caution overruled his annoyance. He didn't mind getting into fights, but he didn't want to get banned from this particular bar. There weren't many places for his band to perform. Ferry's Landing was a small town—not as small as Whispering Pines, where Everett lived, but small, nonetheless. There were limited venues for a mediocre cover band.

He half-walked, half-carried the barely conscious Amanda down the street to the motel. Thankfully, he knew the desk clerk, since Amanda couldn't remember her room number and her key was missing from her purse.

"You sure you know her?" Frances raised her eyebrow at him suspiciously, as if there'd be a more nefarious reason for his presence.

"Yeah. Sort of. So do you. This is Cara Vervaine's cousin. She's going to be working at the inn this summer. I just want to get her safely into bed and then I'll leave, I promise. Some guy at Shore Leave was trying to put the moves on her, and as you can see, she's not in great shape."

The mention of Cara's name sealed it. Cara managed the Inn at Whispering Pines, one of the businesses that anchored the island and kept the Ryan family's ferry afloat. Of course Frances knew her, they'd refer guests back and forth. Lodging options were scarce along this part of Lake Superior.

"Fine, you can take her, but I better see you leaving soon," Frances warned as she handed them the key. Everett wanted to argue with her and defend himself—what did she think he would do? He wasn't the type of guy who would take advantage of this situation, and he found the implication offensive. But then again, women needed to look out for each other.

He slowly guided Amanda as she staggered down the hall, glad of the first-floor room in a building without elevators. His initial plan was to tuck her into bed, but then he thought the better of it. At her level of intoxication, the bathtub might be safer. He could prop her up so she wouldn't choke on her own vomit, and he'd save her the cleaning fee from throwing up all over the mattress. Win-win.

As he settled her in, both of her hands flew up and grabbed him around the neck, pulling him off balance and forcing their faces close together. She was surprisingly strong for someone hardly able to move. "Thanks for getting me home, big boy." He could have gotten drunk off her breath.

"No problem." He tried to pull away without hurting her, but before he could, she pressed her lips to his. That was so not what he wanted. "Damnit, let go." He jerked back and her hands fell away. And he left her there, hoping she'd be alright. He'd wait until the morning to call her cousin—no need to wake her up and ruin somebody else's night.

Chapter Three

Housekeeping woke Amanda up. They came into the room far too early in the morning. She was still in the bathtub. Wait, why was she in the bathtub? At least she'd had the foresight to bring a blanket and pillow with her. And a towel. The towel had collected most of the vomit too. See? Her family said she wasn't 'responsible' but clearly she was. She knew how to take care of herself. Even without Nicole.

"Y'all are too early. *Temprano. Quiero dormir*," she told the surprised woman in the bathroom doorway.

"I speak English," the housekeeper replied testily. "And you are late. Check out was a half hour ago. You're going to have to pay for another night."

Fortunately, quick negotiations with the desk clerk got her out without having to pay more, though she wasn't given time to shower. She managed to wrangle just enough time to change her shirt and brush her teeth, before being unceremoniously pointed towards the docks.

"Next ferry to the island leaves in twenty," the desk clerk told her. "You had best be on it."

Was everyone so rude here? She thought Minnesota was advertised as a friendly state. Where was that rumored Midwestern charm? That's why she moved here. Well, no. That wasn't why. She moved here because Texas was stupid, and her family didn't care, and her awful terrible twin had abandoned her. Like a man was more important than a sister. Than a twin!

Stepping out into the sun made her squint and immediately reminded her of her pounding headache. It was far brighter than any northern sun had the right to be. Worse, she'd somehow misplaced her sunglasses in the motel, if she'd even remembered to pack them. Her last day in Texas had been nothing but tears and arguments. Her mother kept spouting nonsense phrases like 'you need to get away from your triggers' and 'you have a problem.' Yeah, she did have a problem. Her twin sister had left the city, moved out, and didn't invite her to come along, and, as a result, Amanda lost everything. It was Nikki's fault, not hers. But nobody seemed to see that. They just kept pointing out that Amanda kept 'cheating on her probation,' as though a couple of beers in the evening ever hurt anybody. She didn't own a car anymore, so it wasn't like she was out drinking and driving and taking out any more stop signs.

Amanda still wasn't sure why she'd accepted this whole arrangement, moving even farther away. Part of her thought maybe the distance would make Nikki miss her more, even though the twins hadn't spoken in months, and she didn't know if her sister cared. Perhaps she was unjustly punishing herself, accepting this temporary exile in the middle of nowhere. Or perhaps she finally understood she had run out of other options.

Despite her headache and desperate need for caffeine, she made it to the docks on time, and bought a ferry pass. A month pass, so she could come back to the mainland frequently. Sure, she'd agreed to live with her cousin and work on Whispering Pines Island, but she'd visited before. It was a tiny boring town with nothing to do. There was no way she would hang out there in her free time, and she assumed there'd be lots of that. Ferry's Landing wasn't much better, but at least there was more than one bar. And no nosy cousin trying to supervise everything either.

The view from the ferry office was nicer than she expected, especially the tall dockworker with broad shoulders and a shade of light brown stubble on his chiseled cheeks. Yum. She could watch that man all day. He wore coveralls unbuttoned to the waist over a tight undershirt, and his sleeves were rolled up, revealing powerful forearms. Just her type. If he had any tattoos, it'd be all over for her. She could almost hear her sister's voice in her head: *Me-me, stop drooling.* The man glanced over at her just then, and for a panicked second she was afraid she had said it out loud.

"You made it!" he called out in a lovely deep voice. Had they met before? Something about him seemed familiar.

"Do I know you?" She struck a flirtatious pose, head tilted and one hip thrust out. It probably wasn't effective, with her greasy ponytail and lingering odor of vomit, but it was worth a try. He sauntered over and looked her up and down.

"I take it you don't remember meeting me last night?"

"Refresh my memory."

"You kissed me."

"I did?" Wouldn't she have remembered that? She licked her lips. Not sore, so they couldn't have done too much—his stubble would have left a mark.

"You did. You kissed me in your motel room."

"Did we . . . did we do anything else?"

He took a step back and his smile faded. "Seriously? Like what? Are you asking if I raped you? No, we didn't do anything else. For the record, I didn't want to kiss you either."

"I didn't mean that . . ."

"I'm sure you didn't. I'm sure it's normal to ask men if they took advantage of an intoxicated woman. Don't worry, I didn't willingly touch you. In fact, I rescued you. You got drunk at a dive bar, almost went home with a creepy stranger, and I ended up carrying you back to your motel, where you assaulted me. Despite your unwanted attentions, I still made sure that you were okay. And then a couple of hours ago, I called Cara and let her know what was going on."

"You told on me! You asshole!"

"Yeah, clearly I'm the asshole here. Welcome to Whispering Pines." He walked off, grabbed a loaded dolly, and pushed it toward the waiting boat. She wanted to follow and yell at him, but fortunately the saner part of her prevailed. No need to alienate people already. And whoever he was, he obviously knew her cousin well enough to turn her in. Sure, technically she wasn't allowed to drink, but last night didn't count. She wasn't actually at her new job yet.

🌲 🌲 🌲 🌲 🌲

The smell of diesel fumes and the movement of the ferry over the water made Amanda ill. She had to lock herself in the minuscule bathroom and vomit until nothing but bile remained. Stupid motion sickness. She never had problems with it before, but she didn't have much experience with big slow boats like this one. She was used to the speedboats her friends took out on lakes back home—warm lakes, ones you could enjoy swimming in. Lake Superior was far too chilly for that, even in the height of summer—or so she assumed. She wasn't planning on jumping in and finding out.

When she emerged, wiping her mouth and hoping she was finished, she came across that man again. The attractive but rude one who claimed to have kissed her. Well, he said she initiated, but she doubted that. Though when drunk, Amanda did tend to make loads of bad decisions.

"You feeling okay?" he asked, but his voice lacked any concern. Instead, he appeared amused.

"I'm fine. Everything's great. I'm really excited to be here." She was lying through her teeth. She couldn't think of much worse, but then again, she didn't have a choice. Thanks to being featured as the Midland mugshot of the week, her boss had found out about her arrest and not only fired her, but also refused to give her a reference so she couldn't find another job. If her probation officer hadn't allowed the transfer—or if Minnesota hadn't approved it—she'd still be staying at her parents' house pitying herself. She'd lost her apartment when she lost her job. Nikki was the saver, she was the spender, and her fines and legal bills depleted her meager emergency fund rather quickly. And she couldn't keep up the rent payments without a roommate.

"Yeah, I can tell. You seem thrilled," the man said. "Aren't you working at the inn this summer? Tourist season starts in two weeks, you'll like the place better then."

"Sugar Pie, it sounds like you know everything about me already." Her words triggered a faint blush on his cheeks and the tips of his ears turned red. It gave her a rush of power. Was it her use of the endearment? Or because she punctuated it by placing her hand on his forearm? Probably the latter, given the way he edged his arm out of her reach.

"Small town," he muttered.

"Do you live here year-round?" she asked, mostly to change the conversation. She didn't want him to ask why she'd taken the job, or the reasons for her exile.

"I do. My family has run the ferry service for four generations. Name's Everett, by the way." He offered a handshake. She could feel the strength in his hands. It made her imagine what else he could do with them. But she wasn't supposed to be sleeping around either. Apparently, she was doing too much of that, in some people's opinions.

"Amanda. Or Mandi, if you prefer. So, I guess we met last night?"

"My band was playing, and you were drinking. A bit too much, it seems." That generated a flash of memory.

"You're the drummer!" She had a vague recollection of watching him play, fascinated by the rhythm in his hands, the muscles glinting under the lights. He'd been wearing a form fitting T-shirt with the sleeves ripped off, showing off the black tattoos on his upper arms. Oh, be still her heart, she remembered him now. "How did . . . how did you end up taking me back to my room?" It wasn't that she didn't believe his reassurance that nothing happened—her clothes were all on correctly this morning—but she wanted to fill in the gaps.

"You hit on me, I recognized you. You look like your sister."

"Of course I do, we're identical twins." Damn it, he must have encountered Nikki when they came up for Cara's wedding last year. How had Amanda missed seeing a guy like him? And why hadn't Nikki said anything? Nikki should be able to recognize Mandi's type from a mile away.

Everett wrinkled his forehead in confusion. "You don't look like it. You're a lot taller, and blonder."

"Oh, you're thinking of Amy." Her older sister, three inches shorter and definitely a brunette. Amy had worked at the inn here for years, until she too ran off and got married. Why did everyone keep doing that?

"Didn't realize you had more than one sister."

"I'm sibling number four of five. Two sisters, two brothers."

"I'm four of four, but we were all boys."

"High five, fellow four." She held up her hand in the universal gesture, and he laughed and slapped her palm.

"Well, Amanda, it was nice meeting the sober version of you. I need to get back to work."

"Do you want to hang out sometime? I'm here for the summer, maybe we can grab a . . . coffee or something?" She was used to going out for drinks. This new lifestyle was not going to be pleasant. How did a girl date without a cocktail to relax her?

"No offense, but I'm not into the party scene. And from what I saw last night . . ."

"Are you kidding me? You're in a band, and you were at a bar. Don't lie to me. Just say you aren't interested."

"I don't drink."

"Neither do I." Of course he laughed, and she stomped her foot in frustration. "I don't drink *anymore*. Last night was kind of my last hurrah. But never mind. Invitation revoked." She strode over to join the other passengers leaning against the rail and watching the island come into sight. She wasn't used to being rejected.

Chapter Four

When the ferry made its lurching stop at the Whispering Pines docks, she scanned the meager crowd looking for her cousin's face. And she wasn't there. Instead, Cara's husband Sam stood waiting. Great, that bought Amanda a little more time before the inevitable lecture about drinking. Plus, a few minutes alone with Sam might give her time to convert him into an ally. He wasn't the brightest crayon in the box; she should be able to win him over easily.

Sam had an easy grin, but it was less enthusiastic than last time she'd seen him. And he didn't offer to take her bags. And worse yet, he didn't bring one of the electric carts.

"Cara thought you might need the walk," he said, without apology.

"I don't mind walking," she replied, though she was annoyed. Cara knew she was moving here for months, so of course she would have lots of luggage. She brought two rolling suitcases, an overflowing backpack, and her large tote bag. "But could you at least help me with these?" She'd made it from her motel to the docks, barely. But the inn was a half mile away.

"Sorry. I was told not to. And I'm going to listen to my wife."

"She just wants to make things hard on me. It's not fair, Sam. I feel like everyone is against me." She managed to make a tear appear in the corner of her eye. But it didn't evoke the sympathy she expected.

"Nobody is against you. They all support you. They're . . . *we're* all your family. And family takes care of their own, right? But your parents believe there need to be consequences for what you did."

"This is abuse. I'm an adult, not a teenager."

Sam's face darkened. "You don't know what abuse is. Your parents—and the rest of your family—love you. Cara gave you this job as a chance to pull yourself together. Giving second chances isn't abuse. And forcing you to deal with your own actions isn't either. I'm going to walk on ahead. You remember the path to the staff house, right? Along the side of the inn's driveway? See you there." And then that sonofabitch deserted her, left her standing in the road, by herself. She wanted to scream. She wanted to throw things. And damn it, she wanted a drink. A nice refreshing beer.

She squashed that thought. That was the thought of an alcoholic, and she wasn't an alcoholic. Far from it. Last night was an anomaly. She had intended to go out for one drink, only one, but the bar had a two-for-one special. And then the band had a well-built sexy drummer, so she had to stay for the show, but she couldn't sit around without a glass in her hand. That would make her stand out. She always got enough attention anyway; she didn't want extra. A blonde woman without a drink meant strangers would walk up and hand her something she didn't order, and who knew what they might have slipped in it? No, it was far safer to keep her own self-purchased beverage on her at all times.

But apparently nobody understood that, and she was being punished again. She felt an urge, stronger than the urge to drink, to call her sister. Nikki would understand. Nikki would cajole her back into a better mood. Nikki would support her.

Or the old Nikki would have. This new married Nikki who had a no-contact order against her sure wouldn't. This selfish awful version of Nikki didn't invite her own twin to come live with her when Amanda's life collapsed. Amanda could have easily moved in with her sister and her stupid husband Griffin. It wasn't an invasion on their marriage to have a roommate. And why had Nikki even wanted to get married anyway? That had never been on either twin's radar, ever. Well, it sort of had, but in the abstract. When they were little, they talked about growing up and marrying twin brothers in a double wedding and sharing a house forever. But Griffin didn't have a twin, and even if he did, Amanda wouldn't have been interested.

She sighed deeply, gripped the handles on her suitcases more tightly, and began the long walk after Sam's retreating figure. She wasn't going to let them see that this bothered her. Kill them with kindness, that'd be better. And someday they'd all be sorry for how they'd treated her.

🌲 🌲 🌲 🌲 🌲

Her cousin was waiting with Sam on the porch swing when Amanda finally made her long slow way up the path. Neither of them got up until Amanda dropped her bags loudly on the ground in front of them.

"Well, I made it," she announced unnecessarily.

"I'm glad you're here." Cara hugged Amanda, but she felt the reproach in her cousin's arms. Or perhaps the hug was awkward because Cara was trying to avoid the smell of unwashed sweat and vomit. Pregnant women tended to have overly sensitive noses, or so Amanda had heard from her sisters-in-law.

"Awww, look at you, you're glowing, and you have the cutest little bump!" Amanda tried to worm her way back into Cara's good graces with compliments.

"I'm not glowing, I'm sweaty. This baby has raised my core temperature. Anyway, don't deflect. I heard you were drinking last night."

"It's no big deal, I just stopped in for a drink or two at a bar. I was stuck on the mainland. What was I supposed to do?"

"Watch TV in your motel room, maybe? You understand your probation can be revoked, right? You get that?" Cara's frown made Amanda feel a tiny twinge of guilt. But she wouldn't show it.

"Don't talk to me like I'm a child. I already took a pee test, by the time they schedule another all the EtG will be out of my system." The fancy expensive tests she was being forced to take checked the level of Ethyl Glucuronide remaining, which, she had been warned could stick around for four days. But she'd met with her probation officer yesterday afternoon, and she didn't expect him to call her in for a surprise test anytime soon.

"Mandi! I'm not talking down to you, I'm trying to keep you out of jail. Don't you see that? I love you, and I want to help stop you from destroying your life."

"Yeah, whatever. I need a shower. Where's my room?"

"Through here. Sam, could you please grab her luggage?" Cara opened the door and led Amanda through the living room to a bedroom. "This is all yours this summer. Usually, we have two or three people to a room, but our other full-time staff live in town."

"Lucky me." The room was smaller than the one back home, and there were two beds in it. She considered pushing them together so she wouldn't have to stare across the room at an empty bed and be reminded of Nikki. Up until they moved into a two-bedroom apartment at age twenty-one, they'd always shared a room. They shared everything; that's what twins were supposed to do. Not run off with some guy they barely know and ditch their other half.

She unpacked and showered, and felt a thousand times better. Well, maybe just a hundred times better. No, not even that much. She couldn't force false optimistic cheer.

But the smell of onions and peppers wafting into her room helped. She followed the scent to the kitchen, where Sam stood at the stove frying up some sort of egg concoction.

"Whatcha making?" she asked hopefully. As the executive chef at the inn's restaurant, she knew anything he cooked was sure to be delicious. She just didn't know if he was willing to share.

"Eggs are a good hangover cure," he replied, dumping the contents of the pan onto a plate. "Eat up."

"Aw, Samuel, you're a sweetheart after all." She took the food before he could change his mind.

"Well, it's your last hangover, so . . ." he shrugged, "enjoy."

"Do you happen to have coffee, too?"

"Cara can't have caffeine right now, so no. I don't keep any in the house. You need water anyway."

"That's fine." Amanda accepted the glass he offered, and settled down at the table to eat. "Yum! These eggs are fantastic!" This might turn into the summer she gained thirty pounds, if she wasn't careful. Did they always eat this well? Nikki's husband was also a chef, maybe that factored into her twin's willingness to abandon her. Amanda sure couldn't cook like this.

"I'm glad you like them." Sam took the seat across from her. "But do you know what would make that dish better?"

"Hot sauce?" she guessed. Honestly there wasn't much she could suggest that would improve upon his cooking—but best not to inflate his ego too much.

"No, not hot sauce." The annoyance on his face reminded her of her older sister's warning: don't criticize Sam's food or you'll end up listening to a very long speech about proper cooking techniques and flavor profiles and all kinds of things only he cared about. "Mandi, you need to think bigger. Imagine how fantastic that would taste with fresh eggs, with extra dark yolks from well-fed local chickens."

"I don't know if I'd notice . . ." Amanda began.

"We're not getting chickens!" Cara emerged from her own bedroom. "I try and take a short nap and you go behind my back to involve my cousin in your campaign? No, Sam, I've told you a million times. No chickens. No ducks. No quails. No flocks of anything."

"Chickens are the perfect pets for kids. They get to learn how to take care of animals, and where their food comes from. Didn't you read that article I showed you? Think of the children!"

"Children? You're having twins?" Amanda was so startled by his comment that she couldn't help interrupting their argument. Poor Cara. They did run in the family though. Four sets over three generations so far, and given the fecundity of her siblings, she wouldn't be surprised if there were more to come. God, what a horrifying thought—what if Nikki decided to reproduce soon? Her body would change completely and then they wouldn't be a matching set anymore.

Cara sank down into a chair, hand on her belly. "Thankfully, no. I don't know how I'd handle that. Just one baby, who will definitely be far too young to look after a flock of chickens."

"But Cara . . ." Sam protested.

"No. Final answer."

"I'm the chef. I should be in charge of how we source our food supply," Sam muttered under his breath. "Enjoy your slightly inferior meal, Mandi."

"Don't worry, Samuel, it's delightful. I can't even detect the lack of sufficient Omega-3s." She smiled, proud of herself for remembering an advertisement she read on a carton of eggs once. "Besides, do you really want birds running around outside? I've heard rumors that you're a terrible neat freak." Amanda would describe herself as an overall clean and organized person, but she'd been informed that Sam took everything to a whole different level.

"I'm not a neat freak. I believe in not living in a pigsty. There's a difference."

"Poor little Sam. What are you going to do when the baby arrives?"

"Why do people keep asking me that? Babies are small, and they can't even move on their own for a couple of months. They can't make that much of a mess."

Amanda looked at Cara and raised her eyebrows. Cara shrugged. "He'll find out in September."

Chapter Five

O'Connell Family Chatroom

Kenny: Check-in. You all here?

Nicole: Everyone but Mandi.

Kenny: Duh.

Nicole: Be nice to me.

Danny: You know she's banished from these chats until the protective order is up.

Nicole: Whatever.

Amy: What's going on?

Kenny: Just wanted to update anyone who cares—Mandi made it to Cara's place.

Amy: Was there any doubt?

Kenny: Yes!

Danny: Yes!

Nicole: Yes!

Amy: Ummm . . . wow.

Nicole: I thought she'd refuse to go at all. I was expecting her to show up at my door with a suitcase and pretend nothing had happened.

Kenny: Same here!

Danny: I thought she'd flee when she had to change planes in Denver.

Amy: What would she do there?

Danny: Shack up with some guy? Use Nikki's identity to get a job? I don't know, I didn't think it through. I'm not the one who was trying to escape.

Kenny: She's not doing great. Her first night there she got drunk.

Amy: Already? Damn it! Are you sure?

Danny: Ha, pay up, Amy. I told you! You owe me 100 euros.

Amy: Nice try. 100 dollars.

Danny: You made the bet; I assumed you meant in your local currency.

Amy: Don't use the exchange rate to extract more money from me. We always bet in dollars.

Nicole: STOP! Are you assholes betting on my sister's recovery?

Danny: *Our* sister. And yes. Amy thought she'd make it a whole month.

Kenny: My money was on Memorial Day. Beer and barbeque are inextricably linked.

Amy: Oooh, look at Mr. Fancy Vocabulary. Is that from your word-of-the-day calendar?

Kenny: Shut up.

Nicole: At least she made it to the island, right? That's a positive sign.

Danny: Yes, she did the bare minimum to act like a grown-up instead of a baby.

Amy: Speaking of babies, want new pics of Violetta? She can hold her head up now!

Kenny: Ummm . . . I saw all six hundred that you put online yesterday. Gotta go. Email me the cutest one. But only one. You keep crashing my inbox.

Danny: I think Mel is calling me. Later!

<KENNY has left the chat>

<DANNY has left the chat>

Amy: Told you that was the way to get rid of the boys.

Nicole: You were right. So? Have you called your island source yet? You promised.

Amy: I'll call him tonight. Well, tonight for y'all. It'll be early tomorrow morning for me.

Nicole: Find out how she's really doing, without Cara's spin on it. But don't tell your source that I'm the one asking. Ask him if she's found a meeting yet. And if she's okay.

Amy: I will. But I promise, she's fine. Everyone on the island will take good care of her. A few months of peace and quiet will be beneficial for Mandi. She'll have plenty of time to think and figure out how to fix her life.

Nicole: I hope so. This is killing me!

Amy: I know. But it's just for a few months and then you'll have your twin back, happier and healthier than ever. And sober too.

Nicole: You're probably right. Love ya, sis!

<NICOLE has left the chat>

Chapter Six

Nine at night, and she was already getting ready for bed. There was literally nothing else to do here. Whispering Pines shut down completely at night. Except for the single solitary bar in town, but she needed to avoid the temptations there. Not because she was concerned she might drink—she could stop herself if she wanted to—, but because it would be annoying to watch a bunch of strangers consuming alcohol without her. She still couldn't figure out why her cousin moved here in the first place, and why her older sister worked here for so many summers. No movie theater, no late-night restaurants, no clubs, not even a bowling alley.

A knock on the door jolted her out of her self-pitying reverie. As always, her heart cried for Nikki, but obviously it couldn't be her.

"Can I come in?" Cara asked, opening the door and peeking around. Her reddish-brown hair was in a messy bun and she wore pajamas that stretched tightly over her midsection. See? Cara was going to bed too. Nobody had anything to do around here.

"Not if you're here to lecture me."

"I promise I'm not." Cara seated herself on the bare mattress of the other bed and rested her hands on her cute little bump. Her belly button was starting to poke out, and Amanda had to force herself not to stare in gross fascination. "It's weird having you here."

"Thanks, you're so friendly and welcoming." She didn't bother to hide the sarcasm in her voice.

"I don't mean it like that. I used to share this room with Amy. The bed you claimed was the same one she slept in for seven summers. When she and Fabio got engaged, I had hoped they'd both come here for the following tourist season, but instead she decided to stay in Europe, and it broke my heart. I missed her so much. I still do. Having you here in her place . . . it's weird, but in a good way, in a nice-to-have-family-around way."

"Oh." Amanda sat down on her own bed. "I never understood why you and Amy spent every summer here." She had been envious of some of her sister's travels, especially when she worked in beach resorts in Thailand—Mandi and Nikki willingly visited her there, multiple times. But she didn't get why Amy would choose to give up exotic locations to spend months in the dreary Midwestern United States. Especially here, on a rural island. No cars, no cell service, in a village scarcely large enough to show up on a map.

"Out of all the seasonal jobs, this was the best. Whispering Pines always felt like a break from the real world, like taking a step back and relaxing and having time to breathe. Life is slower here, the work pays well, having room and board included helped us save for other trips, and of course I love the people on this island."

"You say that like you lucked into it. You inherited a share of this place; you could pay yourself whatever you wanted." Cara's late mother had owned part of the inn with her brother, Paddy. It had been held in trust until Cara turned twenty-five.

"Yes, but I didn't have to work here too. My degree is in accounting, I could have gotten a job doing that somewhere else and made more money, and still received my inn profits."

"But that would have been boring." She couldn't imagine her cousin sitting around in an office somewhere, wearing a suit and crunching numbers.

Cara laughed. "I know, it would have been terrible. I'd have missed out on a ton of adventures, and I never would have met Sam. I love the life I've led. There have been some lows, but the highs outweigh them." Amanda knew the lows—Cara had once been engaged to someone else, a manipulative and cruel man who killed himself in a dramatic and misguided attempt to punish Cara for leaving him. The highs? Well, possibly marrying a gorgeous man with a ripped physique who absolutely worshiped her. He didn't have a brain in his head, but his combination of body, devotion, and cooking skills probably made him a worthwhile choice for a life partner.

"Must be nice to have lived a life like that. I guess that's why you're willing to give up all the fun and settle down into mediocrity and boredom."

"It's really not that bad here. Quit acting like a victim."

"I am a victim. My life is in shambles." Amanda sighed dramatically and wiped an invisible tear, a move all the O'Connell women had perfected. It was meant to invoke sympathy.

"No, it isn't, and it never has been." Cara shook her head, immune to the familiar manipulations. "You don't get it, do you? You know what you and Nikki always have going for you? Sheer luck. You both float through life like nothing can go wrong, and it doesn't."

"You're saying that to the woman on probation."

"I'm saying that to the woman who smashed her car into a stop sign while completely wasted and got the charges reduced to something that won't stay on her record if she completes an easy six-month probation. You walked away without a scratch from that accident, you didn't hurt anybody else, and sure, it's cost you a lot of money, but you still have family support. Your father paid for an expensive attorney, your sister-in-law helped negotiate a hell of a deal with the prosecutor, and when your landlord evicted you, your parents let you live in their big beautiful home rent free while you got your shit sorted out."

"And now I'm here, so my luck sort of ran out."

"Don't be so dramatic. You lost your job, and it's hard to find another one while on probation, but again, due to your luck, the new hire I had set for this summer backed out. So you got a rather cushy job and a free place to stay for the duration of your probation, and after you complete it, you won't have a record or an empty spot on your résumé. Plus, should we talk about last night?"

"Last night was terrible. Are you seriously going to make me relive it?" It was embarrassing, that's what it was. Especially if it ended the way she'd been told, with her forcibly kissing an unwilling man in a hotel bathtub.

"Last night you got sloshed at a notorious dive bar and managed to run into not only the one sober person in the entire place, but the only one who would recognize you—by your eyes and accent, he said—and was trustworthy enough to rescue you so you didn't wake up naked in some stranger's bed. That's more luck than most women have. You—your twin too, but you in particular—just get away with everything."

Amanda wanted to protest, but Cara made a good point. Nothing truly terrible had ever happened to her, and even this summer wouldn't be as awful as she tried to make it sound. She'd take time to reset her life. Sure, she was trapped in a boring, cold place, but she could make the most of her time. Her mind wandered briefly to the muscles on that ferryman—Everett, right? A closer examination of what he kept under his shirt could help the summer pass.

"Maybe life won't entirely suck here," she conceded reluctantly.

"I hope it's somewhat better than just not sucking. I've kind of been looking forward to having you here. You and I haven't gotten to spend much time together over the years, with all my traveling. It'll be nice to get to know you again. Team Red for life, remember?" She held out a fist for Amanda to bump.

"Team Red! You, me, and Kenny. It's been a long time, hasn't it? Whenever I shop for a new jacket, I'm always drawn to the red ones." She smiled at the memories. When she and Nikki were babies, her parents had lost Kenny at the zoo. It wasn't entirely their fault. They were babysitting Cara too, so they had six kids to keep an eye on, and Danny was so hyperactive they kept counting him twice. Their solution, after tearfully reuniting with their missing son, was to buy all outerwear in two colors: blue and red. Amy, Danny, and Nikki were always dressed in blue, the others were Team Red. It made it easier to keep track without wondering if identical twins were getting counted twice.

"I usually go for black. Red never quite looked right with my coloring," Cara admitted. While she was an O'Connell in so many ways, her reddish hair and light golden eyes came from her mother's side.

"We won't kick you off the team for that. We used to have good times, didn't we? What happened, Cara? Why does life have to get so much harder when we grow up?"

"My mom died, that's what happened to me. You, I don't know. You've always had everything, Mandi. Maybe your life was too easy. Think about it. When have you had to struggle for anything?"

Amanda closed her eyes and pondered the question. She hadn't always done well in school, but that was due to paying more attention to the boys in her class than her teacher. Not a struggle at all. When she and Nikki graduated from high school, they spent the trust funds they'd received from their late grandfather to take a gap year and travel around Europe. There were food poisoning incidents and drunken mishaps and one particularly scary mugging, but that was it. When she really thought about it, the only struggle she'd ever faced was the one she was currently dealing with: the temporary loss of her twin. It was temporary, right? Once this probation was over, they could go back to the way things were, no problem.

But she had a nagging sense that the changes were permanent.

"Right now," she finally admitted. "This is my biggest struggle. How I'm going to get through life without Nikki. How I'm going to face every day alone."

Cara crossed the gap between the beds to wrap Amanda in a warm embrace. "You aren't alone. You've got me. Sam too, no matter how gruff he acts with you."

"Sam still hates me. A couple of little pranks and he thinks he has the right to cast judgment."

"The first time you met him, you tried to sleep with him."

"Kiss, not bang. And so did Kenny. It was for a bet! Not for real! And you know I never would have gone further. We were testing his loyalty to you." They did similar pranks to every new significant other that someone brought home. Sam should have felt included, not harassed by it. But he apparently was a little sensitive.

"Yes, and his loyalty to me means that even though he doesn't trust you, he'll still do whatever it takes to help you. Family is family. My last name may have changed, but I'm still an O'Connell. And I'm still Team Red."

That touched something at the very core of Amanda's being. *No matter what happens here, I am not alone. I have family. I have support.* Sometimes it didn't feel like it, especially with the way her siblings had been avoiding her lately, but she knew the love was still there.

She wiped away the real tears that started to leak from her eyes. "Thanks, Cara. That means a lot to me."

Chapter Seven

Amanda woke up to the sound of someone knocking on her bedroom door. She squinted at the clock, groaned in disgust and covered her head with her pillow. Let Nikki handle whatever it was. Amanda did not get up in the pre-dawn hours for anything.

A few more annoying minutes of the methodical knocking woke her up enough to remember that she was on Whispering Pines Island, and Nikki wasn't here. Nikki was long gone. And whatever maniac stood on the other side of the door was obviously not going away.

"What do you want?" she snapped as she yanked the door open to find her least favorite roommate. Sam's broad back took up all of the space in the doorway, where he was frozen in an awkward over the shoulder knock. "Sam, what the hell are you doing?"

"Cara told me to get you up early," he said, still not turning around. "Are you dressed?"

"I'm decent, if that's what you're asking," she replied. "Are you afraid of seeing a woman other than your wife? I never took you for one of those types of men. You can't handle a little temptation?"

"I don't trust you not to answer the door naked, but believe me, I wouldn't be tempted," he said, rather cruelly, finally turning to face her. "Get ready. We're going for a run in five minutes." He looked ready to go in a T-shirt, shorts, and a pair of those obnoxious toe shoes that runners seemed to think made them faster.

"Who's this 'we' you're talking about? Isn't Cara a bit far too along in her pregnancy for running?" It was too early for any kind of physical activity.

"We is you and me. Running is good for you. People who have drinking problems need to replace their addictions with something else, so you're going for a run. The endorphins are a healthy alternative to alcohol."

"All of those words have too many syllables for you. You memorized that from somewhere," Amanda said, somewhat crossly.

"That's what Cara told me to say. Four minutes left."

"Sam, you can't force me to go running with you." She fought the urge to stomp her foot. If she did, he'd call it a temper tantrum, and he'd still not shut up about his stupid running plan.

"Three minutes. And I know you used to be a runner, we're just going to go on the road around the island, it's not that far. This is easy for you."

"None of this is easy for me." She took a step backwards and slammed the door. For a moment, she thought about going back to bed, but then she realized Sam would start knocking again. He was implacable, a trait Cara probably appreciated, but Amanda sure didn't. That asshole was never going to let her sleep.

Fortunately, she had brought her running shoes. It'd been a couple of months since she'd worn them. She and Nikki used to run together. They competed in races too, and did pretty well at them. But Nikki had decided to move away and then all this legal nonsense kept them apart, so what was the point of running? Why bother, if it was just her, on her own? Where was the fun in that?

The knocking started again. "Time's up. Let's go."

"Why are you such a bully?" Amanda asked as she opened the door again. She had deigned to dress in exercise clothing, but still had to make him wait while she tied her shoes.

"Because it's my cardio day, and Cara is making me take you with me," Sam said. He looked as annoyed as she felt.

"And you always jump to obey your wife? If you tell her I went with you, I won't deny it."

"I'm not going to let you trick me into lying to her. Let's go."

Amanda was tired of arguing—tired of everything, really— so she followed him out the front door. Maybe this would be fun. Maybe it would feel good to run again. It had been months, but she was still in decent shape. She could do this, if only to rub it in Sam's stupid face. He clearly expected her to falter, but she'd prove him wrong.

Outside, the air was fresh and crisp. And too damn chilly. She briefly regretted choosing a T-shirt, but before she could go back inside to grab something warmer, Sam had already taken off down the path leading around the main building to the paved road that encircled the island. The competitive O'Connell spirit surged through Amanda and she took off after him.

She made it to the road, and even down a little way past the inn, before a stitch in her side made her call a halt. Sam rather annoyingly jogged in place next to her, his dark curls bobbing up and down on his head. She wanted to reach out and yank them.

"Keep going through the pain," he said. "You're a runner. You can do this."

"I'm dehydrated and running on an empty stomach," she protested.

"Sounds like you weren't very prepared."

"You didn't give me time! This is your fault!" She pressed her hand to her side and took deep breaths. "Maybe I'll go back to the house."

"Nope. We're going all the way around. Five miles. So you better get moving."

She had never thought of Sam as a cruel man. A slightly stupid one, yes, but never cruel. Guess he was showing his true colors today.

Sam kept jogging in place as he waited for her. God, he was so exasperating. "Go on ahead without me."

"Cara said I have to wait for you. Believe me this is a lot harder for me than it is for you."

"You're just saying that to make me feel better. This is much more difficult for me. Everything is. I'm the one starting over in a new place. And I'm the one who was dragged out of bed unwillingly by a monster this morning."

"I'm not just saying that. I don't care about sparing your feelings. This is harder on me because I'm the one who didn't want you here in the first place. You're too disruptive and immature. I only brought you along on my run because my wife made me."

"She certainly has you whipped, doesn't she? I guess I know who wears the pants in your relationship." She hoped he would take the attack on his manhood as an insult, but he laughed.

"Nice try, Mandi. Let's go." Then Sam took off again not even bothering to see if she followed. Her side still ached but now she was propelled by frustration and annoyance.

When she caught up, she grabbed his arm and forced him to stop. "What's your problem with me?"

"My problem? My problem is that you're a spoiled little brat." The words came as harsh as a slap to the face. "You've had everything handed to your whole life and you're ungrateful. You have a family that will do anything for you, and you just throw it back in their faces. You've never once taken responsibility for any of your mistakes. Now you're here, stressing out my wife when she's pregnant and really needs a break. Should I continue?"

"How do you think Cara will react when I tell her what you said to me? She's part of my family, and she won't appreciate your terrible treatment of her poor cousin."

Sam's laugh came out harsh and angry, a far cry from his usually contagious chortle. "You're not going to tell her what I said, because you don't want to open up that can of worms. Do you honestly think she's happy to host you while you go through whatever this is? She manages the inn, she has her cabin rental business, she's helping Tim and I start our microbrewery, and she's literally gesticulating . . . no . . . gesturing . . ." He paused in his tirade and ran his hands through his hair.

"Gestating, you moron."

"Yeah, that. She's *gestating* a child. My child. Do you have any idea how much energy it takes out of her? She doesn't need to deal with all your nonsense on top of everything else. She needs to be surrounded with people she can rely on, rather than babysitting you. But for some unknown reason she seems to think she is obligated to help you, so I'm stuck putting up with you all summer. But I'm not going to let you coast by. I'm keeping an eye on you and making sure you do nothing to upset my wife, do you understand me?"

"You're an ass, that's what I understand!" Screw him. Amanda turned around and jogged the other way, back to the staff house. It was far too early to put up with his ridiculousness. Who was he to judge her? And he was wrong anyway, wrong about everything. She did take responsibility for her actions, at least the ones that were truly her fault. And Cara was happy to have her. She'd said so, hadn't she?

Chapter Eight

The real tourist season hadn't started yet, which gave Amanda plenty of time to ease into her new job. There were only a smattering of guests and no events scheduled until the official kickoff of the island summer—though why they pretended there was anything summer-like about the fifty-degree days was beyond Amanda's understanding.

While she wasn't a big fan of the uniform—polo shirts, really?—she didn't mind the hours. She worked the later shift, 2:00 p.m. to 11:00 p.m., with an hour for dinner. And she couldn't complain about the workload at this point. Cara had spent two days teaching her how to use the computerized reservation system. That was so easy Sam could probably do it.

Her third day promised to be much more interesting: learning the island.

Apparently, her job as Guest Services Coordinator included everything in the inn's lobby, from front desk to concierge. The guests that came out to Whispering Pines would be full of questions about things to do and places to go, so instead of handing Amanda a stack of brochures to flip through, Cara told her to spend the day meandering around. She was supposed to check out all the local businesses, introduce herself to the owners, learn what they sold or what services they offered and become familiar enough to give advice. Great, the assignment got her out in the fresh air, a respite from sitting around on her ass. She wasn't even going to object to having to wander around in the cold, since at least she wasn't forced to go out in public wearing that boring uniform shirt.

Her first stop was Gallery Row, the collection of artist galleries, studios, and workshops that lined a small plaza immediately north of the village's main square. She went in all of them, as ordered. Well, that was an exaggeration. She went *past* all of them. Some weren't worth checking out. Piney Island Yarnworks, boring. Soapistry Hand Made Soaps, smelly and gross. She did visit the blacksmith, because she spotted him outside at his forge and he had glorious muscles, and she peeked in the glassblower collective to investigate their muscles, but found mostly women. She spent a few minutes in some of the various galleries, but she could have learned everything she needed to know just by reading the store names. Great Lakes-themed art, everywhere. Boring.

After that, she headed to the main part of the village. There was a gear rental shop, but the kayaks and bikes out front showed her everything that mattered. Down the street was a diner, but she'd been there before, when she came out for Cara's wedding. A pizza shop, where they'd eaten last night at a table waited on by the owner. A bakery, already closed this time of day.

And finally, there was one last business, one more interesting than the rest. Cara did give strict instructions, didn't she? Learn the town? So really, Amanda was obligated to do so. Obeying the boss was crucial to keeping her job.

Even though she wasn't doing anything wrong, even though as an adult over twenty-one years of age she was able to perfectly legally walk into a bar, Amanda still looked around and made sure nobody was watching before opening the door to The Digs and going in.

The atmosphere closed around her like a welcoming embrace. The dark wood, the smell of spilled beer, the people smiling and chugging their drinks, this was where she belonged. This was the kind of place sociable people went, people who didn't sit around in their quiet little houses and stare at the clock on the wall and count the minutes and wonder why they were wasting their youth.

She took a seat at the bar and leaned on the counter until the bartender spied her and came over. This was the one flaw in her plan. She recognized him right away: Tim Diggins, Sam's groomsman. She'd had a drink with him at the wedding. Also, he happened to be married to her new co-worker Tyrell, but she doubted Tyrell wasted much time talking about her outside of work. She'd barely encountered him anyway, since he spent his time doing guest relations with their few off-season visitors while Cara showed her the computers.

"What can I get for you?" Tim asked, without betraying any recognition. Good. This might work.

"You got any happy hour specials?"

"Certainly do. Let me make you something fun." He turned to grab bottles, and she grinned. One drink. That wasn't a big deal. She could have one drink.

He set a glass down in front of her, and she picked it up to study the contents. Something with cranberry juice. He probably thought all women liked sweet girly drinks. Amanda could throw down with the best of them—you name it, she could drink it. But she wasn't going to argue here. She took a sip. Yes, cranberry, and lime, and . . . soda? That was all?

"What is this?" she asked politely.

"A Virgin Cape Codder."

"I didn't order a virgin drink. I thought you were mixing me a cocktail!"

"And I thought Sam told me not to serve you alcohol."

"Sam was down here gossiping about me?"

"Sure was. We brew beer together; you may have seen some of them. Or maybe not, since he said he had to install a locking refrigerator for your stay."

"He didn't need that. I'm not an alcoholic." Rage boiled up inside her. Everyone kept acting like she had a problem. She didn't. There was nothing wrong with occasional binge drinking; everybody did it. Was everybody an alcoholic? No, of course not. She was being unfairly judged, her character maligned, because of one teeny tiny mistake that could happen to anybody.

"I didn't say you were, and neither did he."

"Since we've established that I'm not an alcoholic, can you splash some vodka in this?" She held the glass out to him.

"Is your probation over? I thought it went through to September."

"You know about that too?" How infuriating! Who else knew all her business? The year-round population was under two hundred, though Cara said it more than tripled in the summer. Should she assume that every single one of them had been informed? Perhaps Sam posted a notice in the community center with her picture on it. *Warning: On probation. Do not approach.*

"Small town." Tim crossed his arms. "I have the right to refuse service to anyone, and believe me, I'm more scared of Cara than I am of you. You can stay in here as long as you don't touch any alcohol. You try and drink in my bar, I'll throw you out on your ass. And I'll call your cousin."

"Is every man here a tattletale? What kind of place is this?" Her shoulders slumped. He was right. She shouldn't be drinking. Not because she had an alcohol problem—which she most certainly did not!—but because it technically violated her probation. And though she wasn't likely to be called in for a test before her next scheduled one, maybe she was better safe than sorry.

"This is a place where we take care of each other. And one aspect of that is keeping our loved ones out of jail."

"Now I'm one of your loved ones?" Despite the fact that he was married and decidedly not straight, she couldn't help but toss her hair flirtatiously. Even sober, she couldn't control that instinctive behavior.

"No. But Sam and I are business partners, and you're his family. Besides, Cara and I have been friends for years, and it was your uncle that hired my husband and brought him here, so I owe him big time."

"Paddy's not my uncle." Cara's uncle was her late mother's brother, so no familial connection to Amanda at all. Though he had spent many Christmases with their family. And the occasional Thanksgiving. And once, when they were younger, the entire O'Connell clan stayed at Paddy's inn for a week.

"Paddy is everybody's uncle. He's part of the fabric that holds this island together. Family is family." Tim was clearly not going to budge on any of this. And maybe he was right. Maybe the whole family was right. Not about her so-called addiction, but about her need to temporarily quit drinking and get this whole mess of trouble off of her back.

"Fine. I won't ask for any alcohol, you've convinced me. But this is too sweet. For my next round, can you make something that tastes like whiskey?"

"I'll see what I can do." Tim's wide smile grew friendlier now, and Amanda felt just good enough to return it.

She sat there, nursing her drink and wishing she were elsewhere. But if she were in Texas, she'd be sitting around her parents' house, unemployed and broke. No, no she wouldn't. Surely she'd have found a job by now, even if it was something mundane like retail sales. She'd be working and paying back her dad for all the legal bills she hadn't been able to cover herself, and planning a new life, one that wasn't dependent on Nikki. She could live without her sister, really. It might be empty and hard and lonely, but she could do it.

"Is this seat taken?" A man gestured at the stool next to hers. He was about her height, with thick brown hair and a devil-may-care smile.

"Go right ahead." She smiled automatically. It was reflex, man sits next to you at a bar, you smile at him.

"Do I detect an accent?"

"You have excellent ears to pick that up. I'm from Texas." She added a little bit of an extra drawl for emphasis.

"One of my favorite states. I'm Logan, I've got a summer home here. You?"

"Amanda. Just a seasonal worker taking a break."

"Let me buy you a drink." Logan waved Tim over and ordered a whiskey on the rocks and, "whatever the lady's having."

The lady, it turned out, was having a surprisingly tasty virgin blueberry Moscow mule. She especially liked the copper cup. The lady was also accosted by someone taking the seat on the other side of her.

"Seems like I keep running into you in bars. So much for the last hurrah, you're drinking again, I see?"

She turned at the sound of Everett's disapproving voice.

"Tim made something special for me. You should try it."

"I told you I don't . . . oh. Special, I get it." Everett looked past her at the man and gave him a nod.

"What's so special about it?" Logan asked.

"It's non-alcoholic," Everett said. "Or at least that's what I assume she meant."

"I would have said virgin," Amanda smiled coyly at both of them.

"You don't drink alcohol?" Logan raised his eyebrows in either surprise or disappointment, she couldn't tell which. Was he going to stop flirting if she admitted the truth?

"The bartender won't serve me. I guess he thinks I get a little out of control." She twirled a long lock of hair around her finger and shrugged innocently.

"That's something I'd like to see. Let me order you something else." Logan waved at Tim again.

"Amanda . . ." Everett's voice took on a warning note.

"Oh, my goodness! I'm in one of those cartoons where I have a tiny little devil on one shoulder and an angel on the other. Drink, don't drink, whatever do I choose?" She fluttered her eyelashes at both men. Flirting was fun—she finally found something to enjoy here. Logan was cute and Everett . . . well, he was something. When he looked at her, she could feel it through her entire body. And when she touched him—even the lightest skimming of her fingertips across his biceps—she felt a sense of connection, like she'd found a missing part of herself. And that was strange, because there was a part of herself missing, but that part was in Austin, probably having a grand old time without her.

"I don't mind being your devil," Logan said. He had a wicked air about him. He'd be fun to take home—if she were drinking. Sober, she wasn't as interested in the whole casual sex thing. Flirting was easy, but she always felt too self-conscious naked to move beyond that without the blur of alcohol to relax her.

"This is absurd," Everett muttered, tapping his fingers on the bar. He was looking everywhere but at her.

"Why are you here, Mr. I-don't-drink? You do know this establishment was created almost exclusively for the purpose of serving intoxicants to the public, don't you?"

"I'm dropping off some paperwork." Everett indicated the clipboard in front of him. "Some of us work for a living."

"All of us work for a living, including us devils." Logan winked at Amanda before calling out to Tim, "How about a round of shots?"

"For all three of you?" Tim frowned.

"Yeah, why not?"

"Because I won't serve one of you, and I'm pretty sure Everett over here isn't doing shots."

"No? That's alright. I've got plenty of beer back at my place. Amanda, you want to get out of here?"

Old Amanda would have. Old Amanda would have taken him by the hand and led him out, casting a triumphant look back at Everett on the way. But she was trying something new this summer. Also, she suspected that if she left with another man, any interest Everett might be developing would evaporate rather quickly, and she wasn't ready to let him slip away. So, she decided to make the mature and sober choice here, and shook her head.

"Sorry, I think I'm going to stick around and sample some more mocktails." Clearly, she made the right decision, as evidenced by the ease in which Logan merely shrugged and moved to the other end of the bar near a trio of pretty brunettes.

"You don't want to take up with any summer people anyway," Everett said.

"Why not?"

"It's embarrassing to have a one-night stand with someone you'll keep running into all season. If you want a fling, do it with a tourist. They only stay here for a couple of days."

"Or a local?" she arched an eyebrow at him and laughed when the tips of his ears turned dark red. "You sound like a man who speaks from experience."

"Wisdom doesn't always require experience." He picked up his clipboard and turned to go. "See you around, Amanda."

Chapter Nine

After another long hard morning, Everett took his lunch to his favorite park in Ferry's Landing. It was a tiny pocket-park a quarter mile from the docks, boasting a pleasant view of Lake Superior. The real selling point, though, was the lack of a playground. Every other park in the area was filled with screaming children from dawn to dusk. There was no escaping the noise. This was the only outdoor space where he could find a moment of peace and quiet.

He sat down on one of the benches, unwrapped the first of his sandwiches and then noticed the tall blonde woman approaching. Amanda. Damn it.

She waved with a luminous smile on her face. He waved back, half-heartedly. She was pretty and bright and so goddamn sexy, but he avoided the party scene, and she quite clearly did not. She was also in the wrong place for that. She stuck out like a sore thumb in this part of the world.

"Hello again, Everett, mind if I join you?" Her accent always jarred him. It catapulted him out of place, turning him into the outsider somehow, even though he was the one who was born here.

"I suspect you'll join me anyway, no matter what I say."

She plopped herself down on the bench right next to him, so close he imagined he could feel the heat from her leg through his coveralls. "True. It is a public bench. If you choose not to dine with me, you are welcome to move."

"Even though I was here first?"

"I notice you aren't moving." She opened her large leather tote bag and pulled out an insulated mug and a fork. "I'd offer to share, but you look like you've got a lot of food already. How many sandwiches are you planning to eat?"

"Four." He took an enormous bite. When he finished chewing, he pointed out, "I work twelve-hour days hauling crates around a dock. I need the calories."

"You are a big man. What are you, six-five?"

"Six-four."

"Mmmmm . . . I like tall men." Here came that damn electric hand again, on his thigh this time. He pushed it off, but the tingling sensation remained.

"Everybody does. Stop flirting with me."

"Why are you always so serious, Everett? You're just about the only person I know for a thousand miles, and you aren't being very nice to me."

"I am being nice. I haven't walked away, have I?"

"Not yet. But I don't think you want to anyway. I think you like when I flirt with you, don't you, Sugar Pie?"

He almost choked on the bite in his mouth. "Don't call me Sugar Pie." That accent combined with that endearment made him nervous. There was something dangerous about Amanda, something that threatened his carefully controlled life. She was too much for him. She made him feel things he shouldn't be feeling.

"Why are you acting like you're immune to my charms?"

"Oh, believe me, I'm not immune. But you need to stop."

"Fine. I shall sit here in complete silence."

He didn't believe her, but she did manage to keep quiet and focus on her food for almost a full minute before she spoke again.

"Why do you hate me, Everett? Is it because I was mildly intoxicated when we first met?"

"Mildly?" he snorted. "Amanda, if I hated you, I wouldn't still be here. What are you doing on the mainland anyway?"

"I had a meeting to attend. I'm having a hard time with this scheduling. I had to get here almost an hour before it started and stick around for another two hours after. I ought to complain to the ferry service about their timing."

"Good idea. We'll definitely add some runs, just for you. You can afford to pay a couple hundred dollars each way, right?"

"Don't I wish. I'm so broke, I'm better off swimming."

She didn't carry herself like someone who was broke or even close to poor. He didn't know much about fashion, but he could recognize quality, and he suspected her clothing and the purse she carried were worth more than everything in his closet. Plus, that blonde hair had to be expensive to maintain. Her roots didn't show at all. Not that he had been staring. He merely happened to notice. That was all.

"What was your meeting?"

"Nothing special. Just . . ." She stared out over the lake for a second, and he caught on.

"Just twelve steps?"

"Sort of. Look, I'm not actually an alcoholic. I go to the meetings as part of an agreement I unwillingly made."

"With Cara?"

"And with my parents. And my probation officer."

"Probation? Really?"

"It was all a misunderstanding. I drank a little too much on an empty stomach and I hit a stop sign. Nobody got hurt or anything, but everyone acts like it was such a huge deal. The judge reduced the charge to obstruction of a highway, but I'm still not allowed to drink, and I have to do all sorts of check-ins."

"That sounds fun for you." That also explained why Tim refused to serve her at The Digs the other night. She had called her night at Shore Leave a last hurrah, but obviously she wasn't finished. She just needed to find someone unaware of her problem who would be willing to sell to her.

"It's only six months, thanks to an extraordinarily expensive attorney. That's why I'm broke. My daddy paid for everything, but he's making me pay him back."

"That's fair."

"Yeah, I know. But it's painful knowing my paychecks don't go to me. At least they give me room and board here."

"And six months' probation doesn't sound so bad, especially compared to jail time."

"True. But there are other requirements too. Like I had to do 120 hours of community service and I have to suffer through two meetings a week."

"How are you going to manage all those service hours?"

She laughed and waved a hand dismissively. "Are you kidding, Sugar Pie? That's all done. I signed the plea agreement in mid-March and got all my hours in by the end of April. It was the easiest part of this whole mess."

"What'd you do?" She certainly didn't seem like the kind of person who would pick up trash along the highway, or any of the other usual things he would expect community service to entail.

"I volunteered at a retirement home. I planned events and met with all kinds of people. Do you realize how many old folks there are that get shoved in a home and ignored by their families? They're lonely and need someone to talk to, someone willing to show them a bit of compassion."

"You sound like you enjoyed it." That was a whole different spin on her. He waited for her to start complaining.

"Of course I did! I love listening to people's stories. They remind me of my great-grandmother." Her eyes grew misty as she spoke, and Everett watched her face in fascination. She was being honest. A real person lurked beneath the superficial party girl veneer. "Do you know the first thing I did when I got up here?"

"Yeah, you got wasted at Shore Leave."

"Oh, pooh. You would have to rain on my parade. I meant the first significant thing—and don't you dare say it was kissing you, if that indeed happened. No, I sent a whole mess of post-cards to the residents that I loved. I already miss working there."

"There are retirement homes here." His own grandmother had resided in one, actually rather close to this park, when her Alzheimer's started to require more care than his grandfather could provide. He'd always hated visiting her. He didn't want to admit it, but as a child he found old people creepy, something about their toothless gums and vacant eyes. But that may have been his childish exaggeration coupled with the type of people found in his grandmother's locked ward. Whatever experiences Amanda had with nursing homes sounded vastly different.

"Maybe I'll look into that. I need to find something to do in my free time. There's not much else going on. I swear, I don't understand how people can stand to live in a place like this."

"Some of us grew up here and like it," he informed her rather stiffly. Whispering Pines Island may be small and quiet, but that didn't mean it was bad. "Sorry our island isn't fancy and metropolitan enough for someone like you."

"You make me sound like a snob. Maybe my view is skewed because I'm not here by choice. This is part of my punishment, you know. Instead of jail, I got banishment. Even though I only made one teeny tiny mistake, and nobody got hurt."

"Typical alcoholic," he muttered, then realized he'd said it out loud. Still, he was right. "Amanda, you're making excuses and justifications. That's what alcoholics do. The first step to re-covery is admitting you have a problem."

"Let's see. You told me you don't drink and yet you seem to know an awful lot about recovery. I'm starting to suspect you're an alcoholic yourself."

"Nope. I've never touched a drop. But my father was." Everett tried to sound calm and stoic, but talking about his father always stabbed a needle of pain into his heart.

"Was? But he isn't anymore? Did the meetings help him?" Amanda asked the question innocently. Of course she wouldn't know; as a newcomer to the island she wasn't familiar with the Ryan family history yet.

"He stopped drinking when I was ten. He went boating out on the lake with friends, and, as usual, he had too much to drink. Only this time he decided he needed to . . . umm . . . relieve himself off the back of the boat while it was in motion. He fell in."

"And his friends pulled him out and he realized he had a serious problem and vowed never to touch alcohol again?" Amanda guessed, with naïve optimism.

"I wish. But no. The propeller is in the back, Amanda." She didn't look like she understood, so he elaborated. "His friends were only able to pull part of him out. Death was the only thing that could stop him." The image—even though he did not witness it himself—had never left his mind. Blood on the water, and his father, that larger-than-life jokester, floating in pieces. He closed his eyes to try and shift it away.

"Oh. Oh! My goodness, I am so sorry." She placed her hand on his arm, just above his elbow, and again he felt electricity under his skin, pulsing and sending a shockwave all the way to his heart. Her fingers tightened for a second, then pulled away.

"It happened a long time ago," he replied, as though time had created enough distance to mute the pain.

"You never get over losing someone you love," she told him, with tears in her eyes. He had the urge to hug her, even though they were talking about his own father, and if anyone needed comfort it should have been him.

"Have you? Lost someone you loved, I mean." Probably a stupid question, everybody lost someone sometime.

Rather than answering directly, she lifted the pendant on her necklace and held it up to him. "Look at this."

"It's very pretty," he said, as that was the answer she likely expected. The piece looked like an antique, but he wasn't a jewelry person, so he couldn't say too much about it. Oval shaped, with a kind of weird spirally metal thing around the edges. Filigree? Was that what they called it? He should ask his sister-in-law, she would know. Amanda still held the necklace out for his inspection, and he struggled to keep his eyes from straying down the neckline of her shirt. He tried to force himself to think gentlemanly thoughts, but the view made it difficult.

"It's camphor glass, surrounded by white gold. The etched chain is original, but I've had to have the clasp repaired a couple of times. My great-grandfather gave this to my great-grandmother when they were courting, way back in the late 1920's. It is my most prized possession."

"You must have been very close." He drew back, so his eyes wouldn't keep betraying him.

She smiled. "We were. I was her primary caretaker in the evenings. I used to spend hours reading to her, and talking with her, and hearing her stories. I loved her so much. She was almost a hundred years old when we lost her, and even though I knew it was inevitable, I cried for weeks. She passed away two years ago, and I'm still not over it. Other than my twin, she was my favorite person in the whole world. I never take this necklace off, it keeps me connected to her."

"Never?" A sudden extremely inappropriate fantasy of Amanda wearing nothing but her necklace popped into his mind, making his cheeks turn red and his pants become uncomfortably tight. He wished she hadn't revealed her humanity—it stripped away her frightening otherness and made her more approachable, more accessible. More attractive, if that were possible.

"Why the sudden blush, Sugar Pie?" she asked with that goddamn sexy accent, making the situation even harder for him.

"I just realized my lunch break is over. I need to head back to the docks." He stood, holding his lunch box awkwardly at waist level.

"Well, it was lovely dining with you." Amanda rose to her feet as well. "I have a couple of errands to run before heading back to the island. I'll see you on the boat? Oh, and tomorrow night too, right? You're coming to the party?"

He chewed on his lower lip in hesitation. He'd been invited to a small gathering to celebrate the start of tourist season at Cara's house—Amanda's house now, too—but hadn't planned on attending. He'd have to ask if he could trade shifts with Duncan. His brother wouldn't mind, he was antisocial anyway. "Yeah, I guess I'll probably see you there."

No, wait, what was he thinking? He couldn't go to the party. It would put him into Amanda's orbit again, and he could already feel himself being sucked in.

Chapter Ten

Amanda drifted around the room, introducing herself to people and trying not to let the smell of beer get to her. This was a test, a severe test, and she planned to pass. Cara watched like a hawk, and more than once she'd caught Sam monitoring her as well, eyes on the cup in her hand. That was unnecessary; she was sticking with soda. Obviously, she didn't need to drink alcohol. She wasn't an alcoholic. She would *like* to sample some of the beers—Sam brewed them himself and everybody raved about them—but she didn't *need* to.

A sudden prickling on the back of her neck made her turn, and she saw Everett walking through the door. He was all cleaned up, tight jeans, an unzipped hoodie showing off the well-fitting T-shirt stretched tight across his abs and . . . oh. He also brought a date, a petite woman with long black hair. She was cute, and they clearly knew each other well. Figures. All her flirting, but she never bothered to ask if he had a girlfriend. No wonder he turned down her invitation to coffee.

Her hand automatically brought her cup to her mouth. She downed her beverage, then immediately started choking and spluttering. What worked with vodka did not work with carbonated soda. Some of it went up the back of her nose, leaving uncomfortable tingles.

"You okay?" Cara appeared at her side instantaneously, with a concerned look on her face.

"I'm fine, it just went down the wrong pipe."

"Because you took it like a shot. That is pop, isn't it?" Cara took the cup out of her hand to examine the remaining dregs.

"Yes, mom." She rolled her eyes.

"Mandi, I'm trying to help you." Cara grabbed a napkin off the nearest table and handed it to her. "You've got spit on your chin. And you need to relax. This is supposed to be fun. I know you're on edge because other people are drinking, but you'll make it through."

"It's got nothing to do with that. I'm fine. I was surprised to see Everett here, that's all." Minor lie—she did expect to see him, just not with a pretty little girlfriend by his side. Her cousin gave her a knowing smile.

"I should have guessed there was a man involved. Have you talked with him since he rescued you at the bar?"

"We had lunch the other day. He's . . . nice." Or at least he seemed nice. Funny how he'd been so willing to have a morbid conversation about his dad's tragic death, but had completely neglected to mention important details as to his current life. Specifically, the existence of the dark-haired girl that he was handing a drink to at this very moment. A beer. So apparently, he didn't have a problem with women who drank after all.

"He'd be good for you. He doesn't drink."

"Oh, is that the standard now? I should only pursue sober men? I'm not . . ."

"Not an alcoholic. Yeah, I heard you the first fifty times you said that."

It was so unfair, how one mistake had tainted everyone's perceptions of her. She wanted to call Nikki and cry, but Nikki would probably agree with Cara. But she and Nikki were identical. If Mandi was an alcoholic, her twin was too. That's how genetics worked.

"It doesn't matter. I'm not interested in him. And don't try to fix me up with anyone else Cara, your taste is suspect."

"You don't like my husband?"

"I prefer my men with brains, but you do you." With that, she walked away. It was petty, but she didn't need Cara mothering her. Plus, she felt a bit discombobulated at discovering the one interesting person was taken. She thought they had a connection. Maybe he didn't feel anything, but she sure did.

Eventually, after sampling some of the hors d'oeuvres and making small talk with her new coworkers, she made her way over to Everett. She'd waited until he was alone, of course. Meeting his girlfriend was sure to be an awkward encounter.

"Hey, Sugar Pie, whatcha drinking?"

He held up a glass of pink liquid with a sprig of green garnish. Sam had recently acquired a soda machine and the table was lined with many of his recent 'experiments.' He was almost as annoying about those as he was with his craft beer. "This is strawberry with mint. It's delicious."

"Not very manly, is it?" she teased.

He laughed. "Amanda, I'm a two-hundred-and-thirty-pound dockworker with biceps the size of your thighs. Everything I do is manly. I could prance around here in a fluffy pink tutu and still be the manliest man in the room. Cheers." He pursed his lips and extended his pinkie finger out as he lifted the glass and took what was perhaps the world's most delicate sip.

"Mmmmm. I sure would like to see you in that tutu. But I have a sneaking suspicion your girlfriend would not approve." She resisted the urge to touch him. Now that she knew she was taken, she'd keep her hands to herself.

"Girlfriend?" His eyebrows knit in confusion.

"Don't play games with me. I saw you come in with her. She's adorable. Wish you'd mentioned her to me before, I wouldn't have wasted my flirting skills on you."

"You think you have flirting skills? Hopefully, they're better than your observation skills. Nessie is my sister-in-law. Not my girlfriend, not ever."

"Duncan is married?" She never would have guessed that. From her brief encounters on the ferry, she'd discovered him to be a man of sullen silences, not the sort anyone would go for, especially someone as adorably petite and smiley as Nessie.

"Wrong brother. I meant my oldest brother, Conner. And not anymore, they split a few years ago. But still, Nessie's practically my sister. I like to think she's the one we kept in the divorce."

"Ahh, that's right, my fellow fourth born. I had forgotten there were more than just the two of you. Everybody always talks about the ferry brothers as a singular entity." She'd picked up on it, because as a twin, she was treated the same. In her family, there were the boy twins and the girl twins, that's how they'd been referred to her whole life. Never as individuals. But she wasn't the one that minded that. She'd liked being part of a matching set.

"My poor mom had four sons in five years, of course everyone thinks of us as a group. But Conner is long gone, and Malcolm is off serving in the Coast Guard. He's stationed on a cutter in the Pacific and has all sorts of adventures." He smiled as he spoke, but Amanda thought she detected a bit of wistful sadness in his voice. He must miss his brother. Or perhaps, like her, he felt constrained by this tiny island. No, that couldn't be it. He clearly stayed here by choice.

"One of my brothers is a stay-at-home dad, and the other is a tax guy. Your Malcolm sounds much cooler than my Kenny and Danny."

He shrugged. "Everybody likes to do different things."

"What kind of different things do you like to do?" Now that she knew he was single, she couldn't help touching him while she spoke, a light grazing of her hand on his arm, nothing more. Something drew her to him, made her want to get closer, but he backed away.

"I don't know. Nothing. Hey, there's Matteo and Cherry, I better go say hello." And he abandoned her there, standing by the drinks table alone. His lack of interest in her made him more attractive in her eyes. She always did like a challenge.

🌲 🌲 🌲 🌲 🌲

When being around so many people drinking got to be too much for her, she went out to the porch swing. She wanted to cry. Not being able to drink kept her isolated from a major social activity. Maybe people didn't care, but maybe they were whispering behind her back. *There's Cara's cousin, the fuck-up. She's such a drunk. Can't wait to see how she makes a fool of herself next.*

She didn't belong here, trapped with those strangers inside, the ones with their happy laughter and craft beers and contentment in rural life. She shouldn't have taken Cara up on her offer; she should have gone somewhere else to start over, somewhere nobody knew her at all.

But if she did that, she'd pick someplace warmer. It was May. Why was it still so cold?

The porch light dimmed for a moment, and she looked up to see someone tall silhouetted against it. Everett.

"Mind if I join you?"

"Go ahead." She hadn't expected him, not when he'd so quickly backed away from her earlier.

He offered her one of the cups in his hand. "I brought you blood orange. I've got licorice. Is that manly enough?"

"Sam makes some odd concoctions. Licorice sounds gross. You don't have to prove your manhood by drinking that."

"Good. It smells awful. I respect Sam, but I'm not always open to trying his experimentation. I'm a man of simple tastes." He set the soda down on the porch rail and joined her on the swing, wincing as the wood creaked under his weight. "Having fun tonight?"

"Not really."

"It seems cruel to serve beer at a recovering alcoholic's house."

"Stop calling me that. I'm just someone who occasionally binge drinks. I'm in my twenties. That's what I'm supposed to be doing. And it's not cruel, it's a challenge. Cara offered to make it be alcohol-free, but if I agreed to that, then I'd be admitting to a problem I don't have."

"So instead you're suffering?"

"I'm not suffering at all. I'm actually having a lovely time, thank you very much."

"A lovely time alone on a porch instead of inside a party full of people? You don't seem like the type to enjoy sitting around by yourself."

"I guess that means you don't know me terribly well, do you? And I object to your characterization. I'm not just sitting around, I'm watching for UFOs." She gestured toward the pines that lined the path to the house. "If one comes, it will likely touch down in those woods over there."

Everett gave her a strange look, probably wondering if she needed to be carted off to a mental institution. "You're waiting for aliens? For real?"

"I suppose not. But if we were in a sci fi novel, this is about the time they would show up."

"But we're not . . . Amanda, have you been drinking?"

"Of course not! Okay, I realize I sound like a weirdo. But I always wonder what my genre is. Everyone's life is a story, so where does mine fit? And wouldn't it be a hell of a lot more interesting if it weren't some generic memoir? Like if this were science fiction, yes, we'd be meeting aliens. And if we were in a romance . . ." She put her hand on his knee and squeezed, laughing when his leg spasmed. Everett, this big tough man, was ticklish. File that away for later.

"Too bad we're in a . . . what are those boring ones they make you read in school? A nonfiction."

"There are tons of fascinating nonfiction books too, Everett. What would your life be? An adventure? Humor? A sexy mystery? A rock 'n' roll saga?"

"Hmm." He scratched his chin and stared off into the distance, either waiting for a UFO or actually considering his answer. It was perhaps the sexiest thing she'd ever seen, a man taking her seriously. "I don't know. Nothing too exciting, but maybe a drama about betrayal. A hard-working family struggling to pick up the broken pieces."

That wasn't what she expected at all. "Is this about your daddy?"

"Please don't say daddy. But no, I was thinking about my brother, Conner. He betrayed all of us, and I've spent the past seven years trying to make things right again."

"Believe me, I understand sibling betrayal. It's the worst kind, because you grew up with what you thought was an unbreakable bond, and they just . . . sever it. And they don't even care." She leaned over so she could rest her head on his shoulder. "Tell me your story, Sugar Pie. Fill me in on your sordid tale of heartbreak and betrayal."

"I didn't say heartbreak. And if I tell you, you have to promise to listen and not keep interrupting."

"Oh, bossy! I like it!" At his frown, she drew her fingers across her lips in a zipping motion and mimed locking them and tossing away the key.

"I don't believe that lock is powerful enough." He raised an eyebrow and waited. Amanda kept her mouth tightly closed, even though she desperately wanted to inform him that despite the way she tended to ramble, she was an excellent listener as well. Just when she was about to burst, he continued.

"So . . . Conner. He was the oldest of us. He kind of took on a father figure role when our dad died, so I always looked up to him. One day, soon after I turned eighteen, he handed me some papers and told me I had to sign them. He said he was helping mom change the banks we used for the ferry business—all five of us owned equal shares, passed down from Grandpa. I signed, no questions asked, because I trusted him."

Everett paused and ran a hand through his hair. He looked away, and Amanda had to physically bite her tongue to keep from saying anything. He sighed and started again, but the bitterness in his voice broke her heart. "He lied. He tricked me and Malcolm, and with our signatures he was able to take out a loan for 60% of the ferry's value. Would it surprise you that he never made a payment? We didn't even find out until we got the foreclosure notice, around the same time Conner disappeared."

Everett's voice cracked at the end of his story, and Amanda wanted nothing more than to wrap her arms around that massive torso and comfort him.

She mimed unzipping her mouth. "That's awful. Why would he do such a thing?"

"Gambling. It's funny, he started out going to meat raffles, and I guess got addicted to winning. Then it was casinos, and poker games, and who knows what else. He spiraled out of control, and none of us knew. We had to use every dollar we had and borrow from friends—including your Uncle Paddy—to rescue the business. The last time I ever talked to Conner was about a year later. He showed up, claiming he wanted to talk to Nessie. Duncan and I let him on the ferry. When we got about a hundred yards from shore, we stopped the boat and asked him what happened. He didn't even apologize. He said it was a sure thing, and it wasn't his fault he lost. We tossed him overboard and watched him swim back to the Ferry's Landing dock. He never tried again."

Amanda stopped herself from getting into another 'not my uncle' explanation, and decided to ask Cara if she'd ever heard of meat raffles. It wasn't relevant now, in the middle of a conversation where a man was baring his soul.

"Oh, Sugar Pie, I'm so sorry." She rubbed his back with one hand. "Treachery always hurts more when done by someone you were close to."

"Families are the ones with the power to cause the most damage," he confirmed. "Didn't you say you suffered a betrayal too? What's your story?"

"Oh my goodness, I don't know if I want to tell you now, it sounds so trivial in comparison."

"I'm sure it's not trivial. It was enough to drive you a thousand miles from home."

"It was Nikki, my twin. She got married."

"That's all?"

"Isn't that enough?"

"To your ex-boyfriend?"

"No, yuck, don't be disgusting. We have extremely different . . . desires. He's a skinny ginger only an inch taller than us. We had to wear flats at their wedding. Personally, I like my men with some meat on their bones." She gave Everett a significant look, and he shifted uncomfortably. Everett and Griffin were as different as night and day. How had Nikki developed such terrible taste in men?

"Is he abusive or evil in some way?"

"No, Griffin's an okay guy. He worships her, and he'd never hurt her."

"I don't get it. Where's the betrayal?"

"She got married! Without me!"

"She didn't invite you to the wedding?"

"Of course I was there, I was the maid of honor. In flats, like I said."

"Amanda, I'm not following this at all. Your twin's great betrayal was simply . . . falling in love and getting married? And not letting you wear high heels? That's it?"

"It has nothing to do with the shoes! We were supposed to do those kinds of things together! She left me behind! I begged her not to do it. I told her she was choosing between me and him, and she chose him."

"That is the most selfish thing I've ever heard," he responded. He obviously wasn't getting it.

"How is that selfish? We came from the same egg. We started out as one single cell, together. We're two halves of a whole. We were made to spend our lives together, to have the same experiences together. Why couldn't she wait? Or not get married at all? They knew each other for less than a year. What's wrong with dating longer first? Why be in such a hurry? And when I told her not to, when I told her she was abandoning me she called me . . ." Amanda trailed off and put her head in her hands.

"Called you what?" he finally asked.

"Selfish. She called me selfish."

Everett laughed loudly, roaring and slapping his leg until Amanda started giggling too.

"Oh, fine, Sugar Pie, I see your point. And Nikki's point too, I guess. I would have gotten over it eventually, if I hadn't accidentally drank too much. But she's not speaking to me right now."

"Why not? Call her and apologize and tell her you realized the error of your ways. It seems to me like there's a very easy solution to this whole thing. Communication matters, that's one thing I learned from Conner."

"Well ..." Amanda ducked her head in slight embarrassment. "Not talking to her might be one of the conditions of my probation. I may have failed to mention that she has a restraining order against me."

"What? Why?"

"You see, it may be that on the night in question, when I was arrested, I may not have used my own legal name. The officer may have somehow gotten under the impression that I was Nicole O'Connell, not Amanda O'Connell. And that's fraud and identity theft, at least according to the law, even though it shouldn't count for identical twins. For all we know, we were switched at birth and I am Nicole."

"You really messed up, Mandi."

"Yeah. Yeah, I guess I did. I'm a horrible person, no wonder you don't want to talk to me."

"I wouldn't call you horrible. You just make bad choices."

"In my defense, I was pretty drunk at the time."

"That's not a good excuse."

"You're right. I'm sober now, but I can still make mistakes."

"Like what?"

She leaned closer and licked her lips. "I don't know, can you suggest any?"

He swallowed visibly, but didn't back away.

"Amanda ..."

"Everett." The last syllable hung in the air between them. What was it about him that drew her like this? Was she so desperate she'd throw herself at the first guy who showed any kindness? No, that wasn't it. Plenty of men were kind to her. Everett was something else entirely.

He was the one who moved first, bringing his hands to her face and drawing her closer. He hesitated briefly, staring into her eyes, then took a deep breath and plunged forward.

Amanda had had many first kisses over the years. Far more than she could remember, but that was because they usually came about after an evening of flirtations and alcohol, and only happened when she was drunk enough to feel relaxed. She always needed the melty confidence she got when her limbs were slack from intoxication and her mind was free enough to allow someone else to get close. She was none of those things right now, which made Everett's sudden move—and her reception of it—so surprising.

Everett's lips on hers brought with them an unexpected jolt followed by a sense of homecoming. *When it's right, it's right,* Nikki's voice whispered in her head, the same words she'd said when defending her choice to get married. For a second, Amanda wondered if the sheer rightness of this moment could possibly be what her twin had been talking about, but Everett's warm soft lips swiftly drove all thoughts of her sister away. He was good at this. Really good.

Chapter Eleven

Sometimes she dreamt about Nikki. She sat across from her twin in a bar—because Nikki had a part-time job as a bartender, not because Amanda was an alcoholic!—but no matter what Nikki served her, Mandi couldn't drink it. She'd lift the glass to her lips, and by the time the rim touched her mouth it would already be empty. She tried to complain, but Nikki couldn't hear her. In fact, her sister looked right through her as though she wasn't even there.

She would wake up from those dreams with the disquieting sensation that her sister was gone from her life entirely. The months since they'd last spoken felt like an eternity.

That last phone call echoed in her head sometimes. "I have a no-contact order against you. Stop calling me."

"Me-me, don't worry about the order. That's just a court formality. The only way I'd be in any trouble is if you turned me in." Sure, no-contact with her supposed 'identity-theft victim' was a condition of her probation, but she didn't expect her twin to actually take it seriously.

"I know." Nikki sighed loudly into the phone. "And I will. This separation is good for us. It's good for you. You're too enmeshed with me. You need to learn to stand on your own."

"I've always stood on my own. You're the shadow, not me," Mandi had snapped, even though she knew it wasn't true. She might be the louder twin, the more outgoing one, but she was also the most dependent. She needed her sister, relied on her for everything.

"Good-bye, Mandi. I'll talk to you in September." And Nikki, who'd abandoned her once to get married, had hung up on her, abandoning her again.

Screw Nikki. She didn't need her anyway. And she didn't need the empty ghost drink her stupid sister kept serving her in her dream either. There were still hours to kill before her opening day shift, so she rolled over to try to fall back asleep. If only Cara and Sam would shut up it would be easier. Their voices carried from the living room, and she realized they were talking about her.

Curiosity and irritation dragged her out of bed. She quietly crossed the room to the partially cracked door so she could eavesdrop better.

"I don't trust her," Sam was saying. "I'm sure she was drinking at the party. We just didn't catch her."

"She wasn't. I watched her the whole time." Wow, for once Cara was standing up for her.

"You spent half the party in the bathroom," Sam argued.

"Your baby is sitting on my bladder. You were the one who was supposed to keep an eye on her while I was gone. So if she did drink, it was on your watch. But I don't think she did."

"Does she always make out with strangers while sober?"

"Are you calling my cousin a slut?"

"That's not what I meant. I . . ."

"Sam, relax. She's met Everett a couple of times, it wasn't random. And he won't affect her recovery. If anything, he can help her."

"I don't care about your cousin." Sam was such asshole. "You know Everett. He's probably the nicest guy on this island. He'd give anyone the shirt off his back. Plus, he works ninety hours a week. Don't you think he deserves better? Shouldn't he spend his off hours with someone more, I don't know, stable?"

"What exactly are you trying to say? She's not stable? Are you calling her crazy?"

"No, of course not, she's not crazy, just difficult." Sam sounded like he was trying to placate her, but he wasn't doing a very good job of it.

"What do you mean difficult? You hardly know her!"

"I know her well enough. You're the only sane one in your entire family, Cara."

"Now you're insulting my family? You married into it."

"Yeah, so maybe I'm crazy too. Wait, no, no, sweetheart, are you crying again?"

"I'm hormonal. Leave me alone."

"Y'all know I'm awake, right?" Amanda finally yelled, putting a stop to their conversation. She opened her door the rest of the way and stuck her head through. "And I do believe Everett is old enough to make his own decisions without your input, Samuel."

"Own mistakes, you mean."

Had there been anything handy to throw at Sam's stupid face, she would have done it.

"That's what we all said about Cara too. Old enough to make her own mistakes." She slammed the door before he could reply and before Cara could correct her. Then she climbed back in bed and covered her head with her pillow. Better to try to go back to sleep. She could deal with them later.

🌲 🌲 🌲 🌲 🌲

Amanda's bad mood stayed with her as she started her shift in an empty lobby. So much for the busy season.

"Is it always this slow?" she complained to Tyrell. She had been promised that it would be busy and active, and that she wouldn't be sitting around bored anymore. And those promises, like the rest of her life, had all been broken.

Tyrell glanced up from the computer. "We let the guests check-in early on opening day, so most them arrived on Sato's shift. The others will probably be here on the next ferry. You should have figured out by now how time works on the island. We live and die by the ferry."

"Live and die by the ferry? And they say I'm the dramatic one."

"You'll get used to it." Tyrell went back to what he was doing, because at least he had some task to keep him busy. After a moment of her staring at the back of his head, he turned to her again. "Mandi, I promise, there will be plenty of work. When the ferry gets here, you can drive one of the electric carts down to pick up guests."

"Cara said I'm not allowed to drive the carts," Amanda pointed out. It was a stupid rule. Sure, her driver's license was suspended, but that didn't mean she couldn't drive an electric golf cart. Kids could handle those.

"Oh, yeah, insurance won't cover you. I guess you're stuck hanging out at the desk and practicing your best customer service smile instead."

"Like this one?" She widened her eyes as she pushed her lips into the biggest toothiest grin she could manage. Tyrell cringed.

"We have a no-scaring-our-guests policy. Is this seriously your first hospitality job?"

"I taught preschool for a few years. Before that, I worked in shop selling designer jeans." She hadn't minded either job. Actually, she'd rather enjoyed working in the preschool. Kids were fun, especially when she knew she could let them get as messy as they wanted and then send them home for their parents to clean up. Her favorite time of day was always story circle though. She loved reading to the kids, using theatrical voices, and watching as the little one became enraptured. That's what she missed about that job. She didn't miss the snarky moms or the leering dads, or the way her boss held her to a high moral standard even outside the workplace.

"We've had guests throw tantrums like toddlers, so you're pretty well trained."

"How long have you worked here?" Amanda asked, when Ty looked like he was going to resume his computer work. She needed conversation, damn it.

"A couple of years. I only meant to stay for one summer. I had finished my degree in hospitality management and I planned to gain experience here. Then, with a reference from Paddy, I was going to get a job at a five-star hotel in San Francisco and go live the good life."

"What stopped you?" Who would dream of a big liberal coastal city and settle for a cold Minnesota island? San Francisco promised adventure and interesting food and exciting events. Whispering Pines was dull and dreary and far too quiet.

"You know what stopped me. You've met him. Tim is a rural Midwesterner, through and through. He'd go crazy in a city, and I'd go crazy without him, so we compromised."

"Not much of a compromise," Amanda said. "More like you gave in. Aren't the winters terrible here?" Worse so for him, probably. He was a disabled vet with a prosthetic leg. She couldn't fathom trying to walk around outside in a blizzard herself and she had both legs.

"I grew up in Green Bay, so it's not that different. And yeah, I have to use a cane because of the ice, but Tim hand carved me a beautiful one with a sharp spike on the bottom. Honestly, I'd rather live here with him than live anywhere else without him." Tyrell's thumb unconsciously spun his wedding ring as he spoke, and Amanda felt a brief flash of envy that she quickly tamped down. Sometimes it seemed like everybody but her had someone. Good thing she was better off alone. She didn't need a man. Or a twin, for that matter. She didn't need anyone anymore.

"Tim seems great and all"—slight exaggeration, he was an ass who refused to serve her in his bar—"but I can't imagine giving up my dreams for some man. I wouldn't give up anything for a guy."

"Then you've never been in love." Ty checked his watch. "I'm heading down to the docks now. We've got three rooms arriving. When I return, you'll have plenty of things to do besides harass me."

Chapter Twelve

Living with a married couple was annoying. Sam followed Cara around like a lovesick puppy, always making her food and kissing her belly and doing everything for her. Ugh. It was sickening. And Cara, well, she did things for Sam too, or so Amanda overheard late at night when they thought she was sleeping. Gross.

So not only had she been exiled to a distant dreary place, she was forced to witness a deliriously happy couple, which only served to remind her of her own lonely solitary state. Any chance of changing her status had evaporated the night of the party, when Everett had delivered the most intense kiss of her life, then, after a few minutes of heart-pounding lust-inducing action, abruptly stopped, apologized, and practically fled. Was she not worthy of his attentions? Had he realized, as Sam seemed to imply, that she was a mistake?

Why should she stay here alone? What held her to this cold, miserable, isolated island?

Nothing. She had no boyfriend, no lover, and worst of all, no twin sister. Amanda wasn't cut out for this. She needed action and activity, and a better way to distract herself from the loss of her other half.

She needed to escape.

While she had promised to turn over a new leaf and develop a more mature decision-making process, she was going to have to do that some other time. Right now she was going to follow her instincts, instincts that told her she'd be better off elsewhere. So she ran away. Yes, like a teenager rebelling against being grounded, she decided that she wasn't going to put up with her punishment anymore.

She didn't want to arouse suspicion, so she left most of her things behind. A full closet would make Cara think Amanda would come back. She only took one backpack crammed with a couple of days' worth of clothes. That was all she would need anyway. Eventually, she'd find a job and replace her clothing. Or just borrow from Nikki, especially if her sister had jumped on the baby-making bandwagon and ballooned out like everyone else. Nikki would gratefully open up her closet to her twin so that someone could get a use out of her rather extensive wardrobe. And Sam would probably want Amanda's stuff out of the house as quickly as possible, so he'd box it all up neatly and ship it to her.

She didn't bother leaving a note. Cara would figure it out sooner or later. And besides, today was Amanda's day off. She didn't owe anyone an explanation of how she spent her free time. By the time her cousin noticed, she'd be long gone. Sure, there was a tiny twinge of guilt that her coworkers would have to cover her shifts, but they'd get over it. Tyrell always talked about wanting more hours anyway. And there were people they could call in—like whoever was expected to cover for Cara when she had her baby.

Fortunately, Everett wasn't around when she took the ferry across the lake. She didn't want the flush of guilt or desire to stay that the sight of him might induce. That kiss . . . she needed to erase it from her memory.

She held on to her confidence in her decision all the way to Duluth, but once she was sitting in the airport waiting for a standby flight, she started to have second thoughts. Even if she made it on a plane, by the time she got to Texas it would be late. That shouldn't matter too much, but Nikki worked as a bartender. She wouldn't be home, and she'd be furious if her sister showed up at the bar—Nikki had wholeheartedly bought into this whole 'alcoholic' thing. But obviously, she knew it couldn't be true. They were identical. If Mandi had an alcohol problem, so did Nikki. They were the same person. Same genetics. Same DNA. Same everything.

No, she was doing this. As soon as there was an available seat, it would be hers. There couldn't be that many people trying to get last minute tickets, and this wasn't a busy airport. There would be space for her today. She was optimistic enough in her chances that she was willing to sit at the gate for hours. Her eyes kept wandering toward the bar, but she was stronger than that. She didn't need a drink. If she didn't drink at the airport, that would prove to everybody that they were wrong about her.

But the first flight was full, and the second. And the last one of the day as well. Stupid small airport. She should have taken the bus to the Twin Cities instead. They probably had more flights.

She sighed deeply. Now what? Rent a hotel room and count on a seat tomorrow? Buy a full-price ticket that she couldn't afford? Or give up and go back to Whispering Pines in defeat?

The guilt set in. It wasn't so terrible there. Cara was a fair boss, and the job was pretty easy. She didn't particularly like sharing a home with a happy couple, but if she ran away to Austin, she'd be doing the same thing. Except it would be worse with her twin, because every day would be a reminder that her beloved sister chose a man over her.

Shame flooded her. Her family was trying to help, and she was throwing it back in their faces. Maybe she really was as terrible a person as everyone thought.

At least none of them knew what she had done. She left for the bus terminal, and snagged a seat on the last northbound bus heading towards Ferry's Landing. No problem, nobody would have to know what happened. She could sneak back to the island quietly and pretend she hadn't wasted her entire day off sitting around the airport hoping for an escape. But when the bus finally arrived, the last ferry had already departed, stranding her on the mainland.

It was enough to drive a woman to drink.

And would that really be a big deal? She wasn't an actual alcoholic. And she'd been called in for a surprise urine test a mere two days earlier. She didn't have another one scheduled for a couple of weeks, and she probably wasn't unlucky enough to get called in at random again. One drink never hurt anybody. She could have one drink, just one this time, and gather her thoughts. It would clear her head, so it was a good thing. A helpful thing. It was for her health.

Shore Leave was easy to find again, but it wasn't easy to get in. As soon as she started to pull the door open, a hand came out of nowhere above her and slammed it shut. She turned to yell at whomever was blocking her and found Everett glaring down at her.

"What are you doing, Amanda?" he asked, not removing his hand from the door.

"Just ... looking for somewhere to hang out," she replied. "They serve cokes too, you know."

"Oh, I know. But I don't think that's why you're here."

"What are you, my guardian? Look, I missed the last boat, I'm stuck. I have nowhere else to go. Wait, if you're here is there a later ferry run?" There might be a way back after all. That would be better than trying to find a place to crash here for the night. She was still a bit too broke to want to pay for a motel room.

"No, I had band practice, so I'm staying in Ferry's Landing. No ferries till morning. I'm heading to a late-night diner right now. Why don't you come with me?"

What choice did she have? She couldn't insist on going in the bar; he'd tell Cara, and Cara would tell Amanda's parents and then she'd be subjected to more lectures about fixing her life. Which didn't need fixing.

"Are you asking me on a date?" She used false confidence to try and take control of the situation, and she liked the way he sheepishly ducked his head.

"I'm asking you to keep me company while I eat. That's all."

"Sure sounds like a date to me, Sugar Pie." She linked her arm in his. "I accept your invitation."

Chapter Thirteen

Everett watched Amanda as she munched on a big plate of French fries, chewing blankly. Something deeply unhappy emanated from her. He could sense it. Part of him wanted to hug her, to try and make her laugh, to do something to chase away the darkness.

"Spill it. What's really going on with you? Why are you trapped on the mainland? What were you doing in the first place?"

She took a deep breath. "Honestly? You're going to mock me. I might look like a grown-up, but on the inside I'm still a petulant teenager. I was running away."

"Yeah? My brother and I did that once, when I was eight and he was nine. We headed north. We were going to live off the land in the woods. You know, build a shelter, lay traps for animals, drink from streams, the whole mountain man thing."

"And what happened?"

Truthfully, Everett had been terrified and begged Malcolm to let him go home, but Malcolm had broken a vase that had been handed down in the family for generations, and he was far more afraid of their parents than the dark forest. They spent one night sharing a sleeping bag, wide awake and fearful, and returned the next morning, lying to their older brothers about what a grand adventure it had been. "We didn't make it very far, and my dad spanked us both," he admitted. "But Duncan and Conner were impressed, so it was worth it."

"I spent the whole day sitting in the airport hoping for a flight. Slightly less impressive." Amanda gave him a weak smile. "But I didn't have a drink, so I'll call it a victory."

"I'm proud of you," he said, hoping that was the right thing to say. Amanda was too pretty to talk to. She made him uneasy. Her accent and her rare laugh made his heart beat faster, and that worried him. He couldn't get involved with a drunk. Her life was a mess, and he didn't need it to spill over into his. Even if he did kiss her the other night. Even if he had dreamed about her every night since, waking up with images of her imprinted on his mind and body.

"I'm not an alcoholic," she replied testily. So that had been the wrong thing. "Where are you staying tonight?"

"I have a place here . . ." He trailed off. Amanda needed somewhere to stay, didn't she? "It's tiny. Like super small. But if you need somewhere to go . . ."

"Thank you kindly, I do. I don't have the money for a motel, and I don't think sleeping in the park is very safe for me. I thought you lived on the island though."

"Yeah, but we have a room behind the ferry office to crash in. I have band practice twice a week, so that's where I stay. But I'm warning you, there's not much room."

"You keep saying that, but I don't mind cramming into a tiny space with you," she smiled, and a rush of heat and desire traveled all through his body. This was probably a terrible mistake.

"Are you flirting with me again?"

"Maybe. Is it working?"

"No. Eat your fries." She stuck her lower lip out in a pout, and it took every ounce of self-control he'd ever developed not to lean across the table and kiss her. "So tell me, why were you running away? Is life really so bad here?"

"No, it's not. It's just, I got to thinking . . . oh, you wouldn't understand."

"Try me."

"Yesterday during my shift I was staring into the lobby, and I realized this was where it all started. Where my life started to go wrong, I mean. You see, we visited up here last year for Cara's wedding. Why weren't you invited, by the way?"

"I was, but I got hit with the flu that week. I didn't think Cara and Sam needed a virus for their honeymoon." He'd heard the stories though. The O'Connells knew how to throw a party. What if he had been there? He probably would have watched Mandi drinking and dismissed her entirely, that's what.

"What a shame. Anyway, I was standing in the lobby of the inn a couple of days before the big event, and this guy Griffin came strolling in. He was Sam's roommate in culinary school, and he had volunteered to do the catering. Do you know what I felt when I saw him?"

"What?" he asked, though he had a good guess. He recognized the name as Nikki's husband. That explained everything. Love at first sight, so Amanda's issues all boiled down to jealousy. She'd lied when she said she had no interest in her brother-in-law. She wanted what her sister had.

"Nothing. I felt absolutely nothing at all. When you meet someone who's going to change your life, one of two things is supposed to happen. If they're going to change everything in a good way, electricity strikes you, right to your core. And if it's in a bad way, an impending sense of doom descends upon you like a heavy cloud of darkness. But when I saw Griffin, I felt nothing. And yet, he's the one who swept in and took my sister away. And without Nikki, I ended up getting arrested and losing my job, and our apartment . . . I lost everything. And I never saw it coming. My life's utter destruction started on the island, right where I now work. And I have to look at that spot every day and ask myself how I could have been so blind, how I could have missed the warning signs." She put her head in her hands at the conclusion of her rather over-dramatic speech, and Everett used the opportunity to stifle his smile. She wouldn't appreciate the humor he found in it.

"Maybe you didn't feel anything because he didn't ruin your life," Everett suggested gently. "Maybe your sister got the electricity when she met him. And maybe this is where you're meant to be."

"If this is where I belong, why am I so unhappy?" she replied, and he didn't have an answer. He wasn't one to talk about happiness anyway. He existed, that's all. He passed through long days and sometimes wondered what life would have been like if Conner hadn't stolen all their money, if he could have followed Malcolm into the Coast Guard as he'd always dreamed.

"Maybe you're so convinced you're supposed to be unhappy that it's becoming a self-fulfilling prophecy?"

"So you're saying I'm responsible for my own unhappiness? My goodness, I get blamed for everything."

"I'm saying you can make a choice." He shrugged. "That's what I did. I always wanted to join the Coast Guard, so obviously my life isn't what I wanted either, but I have a job and a band and plenty of friends. I get along with my remaining family, and I make it through the day. Can't ask for much more than that."

"Can't you?" She arched an eyebrow at him, and his stomach dropped. Yes, he could ask for more, but he'd never expect to get it.

🌲 🌲 🌲 🌲 🌲

He led her back to the docks, somewhat regretting having made the offer. The bedroom—his crash pad, as he called it—behind the office was small, with just enough space for a twin bed, a mini fridge that doubled as a nightstand, and one beat up old chair. Not only was the space crowded, it was ugly. Not the kind of place to impress a lady.

"This is it. Sorry," he apologized as he unlocked the door and let her into the room.

"It's fine. Lovely, actually. Far better than the park bench I was considering. The bed's a little small though—are you sure we'll both fit?"

Everett swallowed hard. "Are we going to try?" He hadn't thought this through properly. He should offer her the bed and go sleep on the patio. He'd done that before, and the chill night air might do him some good. He could certainly breathe easier outside, without the honey vanilla scent of Amanda's hair wafting over him.

"I wouldn't mind making the attempt." She stepped closer to him, placed both palms flat on his chest, and leaned in to kiss him. The combination of her height and high heels meant she didn't have far to stretch. He twisted his head away and moved back, crashing into the chair.

"Amanda, you don't have to . . ." he began, but she put a finger against his lips to stop him.

"Shush, Everett. I'm not doing this because I have to, I'm doing it because I want to. I get it, you're hesitating because you think I'm just some party girl, but I assure you I am not. I'm sober and willing, and it's too early to go to sleep. We're in an itty bitty room with a bed built for one. Someone's going to have to be on top, and I volunteer for that position."

"I . . . ummm . . . need to take a shower. And before you say anything, no, I'm going in alone. And I'm going to lock the door. You go ahead and make yourself comfortable out here." He slipped from her grasp, fumbled with the bathroom doorknob and practically fell through when it opened. He locked it with an audible click and leaned against the sink, breathing heavily. He was not going to survive this night.

🌲 🌲 🌲 🌲 🌲

Everett took the longest shower possible. He washed everything twice, and considered repeating the cycle a third time. All he could think about was the woman on the other side of the door, the beautiful woman with that goddamn sexy accent and the soft lips, and those perfect, perfect breasts . . . *no! Stop!* He dressed in sweatpants and an old T-shirt, some of the clothes he kept in his locker in here. He and Duncan and his mother all had lockers in the bathroom. They let stranded islanders use the room on an as-needed basis, but no reason to share access to things like their clothing and deodorant and toothbrushes.

Thinking of that made him wonder if Amanda had a toothbrush. He should ask. He should probably offer her something to sleep in too. She sure would look sexy in one of his shirts. Those long legs leading up to that tight . . . *stop! That's enough*, he reminded himself sternly. He'd already made the decision not to pursue anything with her.

"Mandi, do you need a toothbrush?" he asked, opening the door. But then he froze at the sight of her reclining on the bed wearing a silky tank-top, boxer shorts, and nothing else. Where did that outfit come from? And holy shit, how was he going to handle this? So much for his earlier decisions to protect himself from her.

She looked up from the book in her hands and smiled. "You don't think a runaway would remember to pack a toothbrush? If we were in a horror story, do you think you'd be the psychopathic killer, or would there be some kind of monster trapping us both in this tiny place?"

"What? What does that have to do with brushing your teeth?" At first the question seemed to come from so far out of left field he couldn't process it. Then he remembered her little genre game.

She tapped the cover of the book. "Isn't this yours? It's a horror story I found next to the bed. I started flipping through the pages and then I thought oh my goodness, here is little old me trapped in a tiny room with a man I hardly know. And then I started wondering what my character would be. Obviously, as a blonde woman, I'm either the first one dead, or I somehow survive all kinds of torture and make it to the end, most likely wearing artfully torn clothing. I was just wondering who you were."

"I guess I'd be the one who goes outside to investigate the strange noise and gets knocked out. But not killed."

"No?"

"Of course not. I'd be the hero who comes back to save you."

She rose to her feet in one fluid movement. "You think I can't save myself?" In coincidental but utterly perfect timing, something scratched against the window, and she let out a startled shriek and jumped toward him.

"*Now* I think that. Relax. There's a pine tree out there. I guess I should cut those branches back."

"Don't you dare try and trim them right now. Didn't we just discuss you investigating a noise and getting killed?"

"Yeah, but we're not in a horror story. Or situation."

"Are you sure?"

"Positive. Though I'm getting worried that I might be the one trapped with a crazy person."

"Having an active imagination doesn't make me crazy. It does make me good at role-playing though."

"Stop flirting with me. It's late, I need to rest. I work early tomorrow morning."

"Why are you so resistant to my charms?"

"I'm not. Believe me, I'm not. But you're dangerous, Mandi."

"Am I? Are you scared of me? Such a big man, afraid?" She stepped closer, and he tried to back away, but his legs hit the chair. This room was too small for the both of them.

"Stop. Please stop. I . . ."

"What are you so afraid of, Everett?" She tilted her head and gave him a wicked little smile. She was too close to him, too close for him to handle. And he had kissed her before, so what difference did it make if he did it again, if he took her face in his hands and brought his lips down to hers and indulged his desires?

The kiss went on and on until he realized his hands cupped the smooth skin of her ass under her boxers and he was about to lift her, to raise her up and carry her to bed and go too far.

When he broke away, she gasped. "You sure know what you're doing."

That was the wrong thing to say. Warning bells went off. He did. He knew exactly what he was doing. And he was making a huge mistake. He was about to dive into an abyss. She represented everything he couldn't have and shouldn't try to take. He collapsed backward onto the chair and held up one hand as if to ward her off.

"We shouldn't be doing this."

"Why not?" She studied him for a moment making him feel small and unworthy, especially when the next words came out of her mouth. "Is this a . . . size issue?" She waggled her pinky finger and bit the tip of it lightly. "Because if you've got a micro dick, I can work with that. I'm sure there are other things we can do."

"What?"

"If you're embarrassed about your size . . ."

"I don't . . . I'm . . . I'm proportionate! Jesus! What kind of assumption is that? Who have you been talking to?"

"I was joking to lighten the mood, Sugar Pie. But I'm glad to hear about your proportions. What's the problem? I'm clean, I've been tested. And I'm going to insist on condoms if we go that far. Are you . . . do you have some disease I should know about?"

"Why do you always assume the worst? No, I don't have anything." *Nothing but a terrible fear of what happens if we go forward,* he added silently. She wasn't wearing a bra, and he could swear those pert nipples were pointing right at him. *Don't look, don't look. God, don't look.*

"Hmmmm," Mandi tapped her lips with one finger, considering. "Something's going on here that you're not sharing with me. You're a gorgeous hunk of apparently proportionate man flesh, yet you're turning away a willing woman."

"I'm . . ."

"Hush now, Sugar Pie." Her finger moved from her lips to his, and she had the nerve to sit right down on his lap, straddling him in the chair. Luckily it could support both of them. "I can see that you're nervous. Be honest with me, Everett. Is this your first time?"

"What? No! Jesus, Mandi! Stop making all these assumptions. I'm just . . . this isn't going to work." He kept his hands in clenched fists, firmly at his sides. He couldn't move. If he did, he'd put his arms around her. And if he put his arms around her, he wouldn't be able to stop himself.

And he couldn't let himself touch Mandi. She frightened him too much. She threatened to his way of life, the careful balance he'd created between what he'd always wanted and what he was stuck with. She was too much for him, too bright, too beautiful, too out of place here. Amanda rocked her hips and he tried to keep from groaning. The feel of her rubbing against him sent lust coursing through his veins. He should throw her off, just shove her away and run outside and jump straight in the lake. That's what he needed to do. Immerse himself in cold water. For an hour. Or all night. Or the rest of his life.

"Really? Because this feels like it will work just fine. I'm not asking for a commitment, Sugar Pie. I'm asking for a chance. And a few hours of fun, on a long night."

"Hours?" He swallowed. She was wearing down his resistance. Her very presence intoxicated him. Would it be so bad to give in? To bury himself inside of her? To find out if she was a moaner or a screamer or some combination of the two?

"Hours," she whispered, her eyes dark pools of promise. "All night, if you can handle it." Her lips gently brushed against his, and that was the end for him. It was all over. She won. He surrendered.

Chapter Fourteen

Amanda had made many walks of shame before, during the worst of her drinking days. She'd stagger home the morning after, still in her going out clothes, smelling of alcohol and cigarettes and bad decisions. This was different. This was a *ferry ride* of shame. Everett had rushed her out of the back room at the crack of dawn as though embarrassed by her, telling her she couldn't be there when the ferry arrived. She wondered if it had less to do with avoiding gossip and more to do with hiding her from his mother. It was a family business, after all.

She didn't have time for a shower, so she'd pulled her hair into a loose braid, hoping the casual messiness of it looked deliberate. She couldn't do anything about replacing her make-up, which she had scrubbed off last night. She hadn't packed any, thinking she'd just use Nikki's when she got to Austin. Facing the world barefaced made her uncomfortable. Cosmetics were the masks she used to make herself look confident on the outside, hiding how she felt on the inside. But since she couldn't pretty herself up with powders, she squared her shoulders, held her head high, and reminded herself to fake it till she made it—something that would be much easier with a shot or two. But the coffee shop didn't offer whiskey as an option, unfortunately.

You are strong and beautiful, she told herself as she boarded, carrying her coffee and pretending as though she hadn't a care in the world—as though she wasn't up at an ungodly early hour and walking slightly bowlegged from last night's adventures.

"Why, good morning, Everett Ryan," she called out when she spotted him. "So lovely to see you today. It's been too long."

Everett's eyes darted toward his brother and the tips of his ears reddened. She loved having that effect on him.

"Good morning to you too, Duncan." She saluted the Ryan brothers with her coffee.

Duncan gave one of his characteristic grunts, and Everett raised one hand from his loaded dolly to give her a wave. She blew him a kiss.

Unfortunately, it was apparently Everett's turn to captain the boat, so she didn't get to talk to him during the trip, and when she debarked he was deep in discussion with a very serious-faced clipboard carrying man with inspector written across his hat. Too bad. Amanda waved, but he didn't acknowledge her. She hoped that wasn't a sign of things to come. After last night, he wouldn't blow her off, would he? They hadn't discussed it, but was it possible he thought of it as a one-night stand? Oops. She hadn't considered that before, but it made sense.

🌲 🌲 🌲 🌲 🌲

Luckily, both of her roommates were at work when she got home, so she didn't have to answer any uncomfortable questions about her whereabouts the prior day. She had plenty of time for a long relaxing shower and a nap.

Around lunchtime, when she woke up to get ready for work, she heard Sam moving around in the kitchen. He jumped when she entered the room.

"Damn, you startled me." He immediately grabbed a sponge and started cleaning up the spill from the blender he'd knocked over. "And now I need to make another. That's a waste."

"Was that for me? Awww, you're so sweet."

He answered with a withering glare. "It was a protein shake for Cara. My wife, the future mother of my child. The woman you upset by disappearing yesterday. She thought you'd run away or something."

That was an accurate prediction. But there was no way Amanda would admit it. "Of course not. Don't be ridiculous. I was hanging out in Ferry's Landing. You do want me to focus on my sobriety, right?"

Sam's icy blue eyes narrowed, and he glared at her like he didn't believe her. "You know phones work on the mainland. You could have called. Cara was worried about you."

"I . . . honestly didn't think of that." She'd been so distracted by Everett that it hadn't occurred to her to check in with her cousin. Her cell—which didn't have signal on the island—had been in the bottom of her purse the whole time. Apparently, she adjusted easily to living a technologically-isolated existence.

"Next time, call." Sam's annoyance radiated from him as he began making another smoothie.

"There may not be a next time."

"Good." Sam's shoulders relaxed and he flashed a white toothed grin. He sure was attractive when he smiled, but he rarely directed it at anyone besides his wife. "Sit, I'll heat you up some leftovers"

"Thank you kindly, Samuel. You're a sweetheart."

He rolled his eyes at her overly exaggerated gratitude as he pulled some food from the fridge and fixed a plate for her. He might not like her much, but he was a decent roommate—and an excellent chef.

She ate and changed into her rather comfortable but dull work uniform and headed down to the inn, where she found her cousin at the reception desk, sipping a shake. Sam had been here first, so that meant Cara knew she was back.

"I didn't think I'd be seeing you today, since you didn't come home last night." Cara's tone was proof that she was ready for parenthood. She had the nagging mom thing down already.

"I stayed on the mainland." Amanda came behind the desk to start her shift, logged into the computer, and ignored her cousin's eyes boring into her back.

"Were you drinking?" Cara finally asked, voice carefully controlled, in a manner Amanda recognized from their mutual grandmother. Cara pulled it off better than Amanda ever could.

"Nope. I'll even do a piss test if you want."

"Watch your language while we're at work."

"There's not a soul who can hear me." Amanda gestured expansively at the empty lobby.

"Still, Mandi, be professional."

"Yes, boss." Amanda checked to see how many rooms were expected to arrive that day. Not many. It would be a slow shift. Well, slow for check-ins. There were always guests that needed something. Then she leaned against the reception desk with a sigh. "Anyway, if you were curious, I spent the night with Everett."

"Really?" Cara smiled broadly. There may have been relief on her face as well, now that she knew Amanda was with a sober friend. "How was it?"

"Don't ask naughty questions. You said I had to be professional at work. What if one of these non-existent guests happen to overhear our dirty conversation?"

"I didn't know it was naughty, and now I'm more interested. Let's talk later. I want the abridged version."

"You've changed. I thought you'd want *all* the interesting details. But I'll save them for—" She was going to say Nikki, but that wasn't happening. "When you're tired of thinking about Sam and need something to fantasize about. Little preview: his foreplay game is on point."

"Alright, on that note, I'm off. I need to go lie down." Cara's shift only overlapped Amanda's by enough time to coordinate and pass on information.

"Quick question before you go." Amanda tried to keep her tone cool and casual. "How well do you know Everett?"

"I've known him since he was fifteen and just started working on the ferry. He was leaner back then. You wouldn't have liked him."

"I was never attracted to teenagers," Amanda confirmed. "Not even when I was one."

"Yes, I'm well aware of that. I remember when you came and visited Amy and me in college."

"Ugh, don't bring up those sorts of stories around Everett. That's who we're supposed to be talking about." She definitely didn't need him hearing about her somewhat wild younger years. Or her more recent ones, for that matter. He'd made it clear he wasn't down with the party scene.

"Right, so? What about him?" Cara looked at her watch and yawned. That baby sure was sucking all the energy right out of her. Who wanted to put themselves through that? At least Cara's pregnancy was easier than both of Amy's. After suffering a traumatic miscarriage, Amanda's poor big sister later spent months on mandatory bed rest, and still gave birth to her rainbow baby prematurely.

"Just wondering if he's the kind of guy who calls after a hookup. Or if he's more of the pretending it didn't happen type." Amanda twirled a lock of hair and pretended not to care, but her cousin could see right through her.

"Aww, don't worry. He's the type to call. I bet he's a show-up-with-flowers kind of guy too. He likes you, Mandi. It's pretty obvious." Cara gave her a reassuring smile and a pat on the back before picking up her drink and walking out.

A few minutes after Cara left, Tyrell arrived. As he walked behind her to clock in, he nudged Amanda with his elbow. "Rumor has it you didn't make it home last night."

"Does everybody know everything around here?" Amanda asked, annoyed. Small towns produced too much gossip.

"Cara called down to the bar last night looking for you. Tim swore up and down that you hadn't been in, but at first she didn't believe him. Duncan happened to be there and he mentioned that it was Everett's night in Ferry's Landing, so I guess some people made assumptions. By your blush, I'm guessing the assumptions were correct."

"A lady doesn't kiss and tell," she responded primly.

"A lady doesn't aggressively make-out with someone on the porch of their home in front of an open window during a party either," Tyrell said. "Or so I've heard."

"Don't you have some guests to help? I think I heard a report of some toilets overflowing or something." She turned back to the computer, but she couldn't keep the smile off her face.

Chapter Fifteen

That evening, Amanda was involved in a long drawn out conversation with a guest about the dining options in town, when she felt a sudden change in the air, as though the barometric pressure had dropped. She put a hand to the back of her neck to find the hairs standing up. And that's when she turned from the rather uninteresting discourse about the merits of the various local restaurants to see Everett entering the lobby.

His presence as he sauntered over to the desk was a distraction. She had spent all day thinking about seeing him again and wondering if she would. Well, she obviously would, unless she wanted to charter a boat every time she needed to go to the mainland. But she did wonder if his interest would continue, or if he viewed her as a one and done.

"I promise you, any of our local chefs will provide a delicious meal. You can't go wrong with any of them," she said in a rush, trying to conclude the discussion with the guest.

"But how will I know if I'm getting the best food?" the middle-aged man asked for the dozenth time. "Maybe you should come with me, give me tips on what to order."

"The best food is right here at the inn, as I've said," Amanda told him, with as bright and fake a smile as she could stretch her lips into. "But why don't you take these menus back to your room and discuss it with *your wife*? I'm sure she'd love to have some input in the decision-making process."

That worked, that got rid of him. She was finally able to turn to Everett. "Well, hello sailor. Welcome to the Inn at Whispering Pines. How may I be of service?"

"Hello yourself, beautiful." He leaned on the desk. "What time are you off work?"

"My goodness, customers are being all kinds of inappropriate with me tonight. Asking me what time I get off work as though there was something you wanted to do with me afterward?"

"I apologize if I'm moving too fast," he said, the cadence of his speech matching hers. "I can leave if you want me to." He turned as if to go, and she caught his sleeve.

"Sugar Pie, I'm off at eleven. What did you have in mind?"

"Too bad. I was guessing nine. I was going to invite you on a walk or something."

"A walk? Are we courting? Shall I bring a chaperone to safeguard my honor?" She picked up a piece of paper and fanned herself. "My stars, you are forward, sir."

"Oh, stop. The last ferry run is at nine, and it comes back here. There's not many places I can take you at night. But you're working, so never mind."

"I don't mind a midnight walk." That sounded lovely, holding hands in the moonlight, strolling around the island, stopping to make out on the bench on the northernmost tip.

"I work at 5:00 a.m. tomorrow," he said, "So I kind of do. I didn't get much sleep last night. I've been stealing naps all afternoon."

"Stealing naps? I knew you were a scoundrel, but a thief too?"

"Very funny. When can I see you again? For real?" She felt gratified by the intensity in his eyes and the urgency in his question. She was the same way, itching to get him alone again. One night was not enough to learn the intricacies of that body. She needed time to study and practice and play, and let him do the same with her.

Unfortunately, the two of them had incompatible work schedules. Amanda's days off were Tuesday and Thursday—because Cara didn't trust her not to go on a bender if she had multiple days off in a row. Everett's schedule varied, but he rarely had a day off at all.

"You work too hard," she said, with a small pout. Sure, his job was the reason he had those powerful muscles, and she appreciated that aspect. And she did like watching him work. But she also really wanted some private time with him.

"Yeah, I do." He frowned. "But I can take a couple of hours off. I don't have to go on every ferry run. How about lunch tomorrow before your shift? We can go to Harbor Snax and eat all the fried fish we can handle."

"You do know the way to a woman's heart, don't you?"

"So that's a yes?"

"Absolutely."

When he left a few minutes later to go back to the docks, he gave her a gentle kiss on the cheek. Good thing Cara wasn't around to lecture her about professionalism at work. And too bad she couldn't call Nikki. She desperately wanted to talk to her twin and ask her to clarify exactly how she'd felt when she met Griffin. Because Amanda thought she was starting to understand.

Chapter Sixteen

There was nothing she wanted more than to call her sister. *He's tall and has light brown eyes, and I can't close my hands around his biceps*, she wanted to say. *Also, he listens to me and gets my sense of humor, and he kisses better than any man I've ever met.* Nikki would laugh and point out that Mandi had never said such things about anyone before.

But Nikki would also be helpful, choosing appropriate clothing for a lunch date and doing Mandi's makeup for her, and telling her not to be nervous. Why was she nervous anyway? She'd spent enough time with Everett that she should be comfortable with him, and they'd slept together before, so the 'will they/won't they' pressure had already been relieved.

Still, though, she couldn't help it. She checked herself out in the mirror a dozen times. Half of those times were making sure she looked alright, and half were her pretending it was Nikki on the other side, and that Nikki was giving her a pep talk. *You're fine. Take a shot*, mirror Nikki suggested. *It'll calm your nerves. One shot, that's all. Vodka, so it doesn't give you away. Just take a shot.*

But there wasn't any in the kitchen. Amanda dug through all the cabinets and there wasn't a single bottle of alcohol other than some cooking sherry, and since she most assuredly was not an alcoholic, she wasn't going to try that. And besides, it might show up on her breath.

Then she started examining the lock on the beer fridge. It really wasn't necessary to install it, Amanda always complied with basic roommate etiquette—don't eat or drink other people's food without permission. All the beer came from Sam's little brewing business and was therefore not hers to take. Though he was making it to sell, so he probably should be soliciting opinions. Marketing research was important for product launches.

The cheap-looking lock couldn't be hard to pick. And Sam wasn't very bright, he probably hid the key to the best of his abilities nearby, so she didn't even need to pick it. She could just unlock it. If the key was handy, why, that was practically an invitation.

But the damn thing wasn't in any of the kitchen drawers. There wasn't anything wrong with looking in the bedroom was there? Cara was her cousin, so they were family. And they never said their bedroom was off-limits to family. It was only fair Amanda check in there before possibly damaging the lock.

She hadn't been in that particular room before, but it was small like hers, definitely easy to search quickly. One wall was lined with baby things: a stroller, a crib, a changing table, all still unassembled in boxes.

She can't make the nursery while I'm here, taking up space in this house. A twinge of guilt hit her, but she couldn't let that get to her now, not when she had limited time. And besides, there was no way Sam mixed the key in with the baby gear.

The room was painfully tidy and uncluttered—Sam's touch, most likely. Where would a neat freak hide a key? It wasn't visible on any surface, nor was it in the drawer of the night table next to the bed. She started to search the dressers, when the sound of someone clearing their throat interrupted her.

"Looking for something?" Sam stood in the doorway, still in his white chef pants and wearing the bandana he used to cover his curls while cooking. His arms were crossed and he was frowning, and for the first time ever Amanda realized he might be slightly intimidating.

"Breakfast service is over already?" Amanda asked lightly. "Sorry, I was looking for a cardigan to borrow from Cara. Do you know where she keeps them?" He'd fall for that, wouldn't he? If he even knew what a cardigan was. "It's a type of sweater, one with buttons up the front."

"I know what cardigans are and where my wife keeps them. But you don't wear the same size," Sam said, glaring suspiciously at her before scanning the room as though checking to see what was out of place.

"Tighter is better when trying to look hot for a man, as you should be well aware. But fine, never mind, I'll wear my red one," Amanda said. "Thanks for nothing." She stepped around him and went back to her room, where she sat on her bed until her heart stopped racing. That was foolish. She almost got caught. And what a stupid lie to come up with. Regular Cara might wear a smaller size, but borrowing maternity clothes for a date? Ludicrous.

🌲 🌲 🌲 🌲 🌲

She waited on the front porch, completely sober, with jittery nerves and a hollow feeling in the pit of her stomach. Everett would show up, wouldn't he? It wasn't just a one-night stand. She tucked her hands under her thighs to keep from biting her nails, a nervous habit she thought she had broken a long time ago, but one that reemerged with Nikki's abandonment. She tried to stop herself through careful application of nail polish, reasoning that if she put the effort into making her hands look nice, she'd work harder to keep from chewing them off. The manicure wasn't helping at the moment.

There, she spotted movement along the path. Everett was coming, with a large pink bouquet in his arms. When was the last time someone brought her flowers? Other than the maid of honor bouquet she'd been forced to carry at Nikki's betrayal ceremony, the last flowers she'd received were a couple of years ago, and they certainly weren't from a romantic partner. Her brother Danny had given her yellow daisies as a thank-you teacher gift when his oldest graduated from Amanda's pre-school. That was it.

"Oh my goodness, Sugar Pie, did you bring those for me?" she asked, trying to sound overly dramatic so he couldn't see how deeply touched she was by the gesture. As he got closer, she could smell the sweet scent of the peonies, and it made her heart skip a beat.

"Actually, these are for Sam." Everett gave her a teasing grin.

"Too bad he left for the gym. If you hurry, you can probably catch him though."

"Well, in that case, I guess they're for you." He held out the bouquet, and she rose to her feet to take them.

"Thank you, they're lovely. How did you know peonies were my favorite?"

"Are they? That's lucky. I asked Nessie what to bring, and she said roses were cliché, carnations were cheap, and peonies were symbols of beauty and lo . . . stuff like that." He ducked his head bashfully and couldn't seem to make eye contact.

"Beauty and stuff? How flattering. Let me take them inside and put them in water." Her heart sang as she filled a vase and placed the flowers in the center of the table. She should have known not to worry about being stood up. She was going out with an amazing man who not only showed up, he did so with a touching gift.

He's a keeper; you better not mess this up, Nikki's voice whispered. Damn it, Nikki. The nervous fluttering started in her stomach again. Did she have time to quell it? A quick glance at the door to Cara's room revealed that it was shut, and when she tested the knob, she discovered it was locked. Why didn't Sam trust her? Jerk. Didn't matter, she'd be fine anyway, or at least that's what she told herself as she squared her shoulders and marched out the door with false bravado. She'd be fine.

🌲 🌲 🌲 🌲 🌲

Harbor Snax's patio overlooked the lake and the part of the harbor where the yachts tied up. Not fancy yachts, of course. Not like the oil-money yachts some of her friends' dads kept in the Caribbean and allowed them to use over spring break. These were beaten down and almost industrial looking, owned by travelers who passed their summers navigating the cold waters of the Great Lakes. Were they not aware of the existence of the tropics?

"Could we get the family platter?" she heard Everett asking the waitress, snapping her out of her yacht staring reverie. Then he looked at her. "Wait, that's okay, right? I promised all the fried food you could eat."

"Of course it is," she said, and ordered an iced tea for herself, though she really wanted a light beer. That always went down well with greasy food. A light beer with a squeeze of lime. Or a simple lemon drop cocktail, that'd be perfect. But she didn't need those, seeing as she wasn't an alcoholic.

"So . . ." Everett said, nervously drumming his fingertips on the tabletop. "I guess we're on an actual date."

"I guess so." She smiled back at him.

"That's it? No long dramatic sentence? No teasing?"

"Oh, Sugar Pie, if you want me to tease you, I will. And if you want me to talk until you beg me to shut up, I can do that too. Believe me, I can fill a silence."

"I know. But you don't have to." He reached across the table to take her hand. "Can I ask you something and get an honest answer?"

"I'm always painstakingly honest," she said. Slight exaggeration. But she spoke her truth, and whether that lined up with other people's truths or not was a matter for debate.

"Are you still drinking?"

"What?" She thought he was going to ask if she was seeing anybody else, or if she had any feedback on their prior intimacy. Something more relevant to their potential relationship. Plus, it was a stupid question. Hadn't he listened to what she had ordered?

"I like you, Amanda. I like you a lot, more than I should, maybe. But I'm not interested in getting involved with an active alcoholic. I need to know before this goes too far."

She sat back, withdrawing her hand from his. "I'm not an alcoholic. I made one mistake, and I'm paying for it. Don't tell me you breathalyze your girlfriends to make sure they're stone-cold sober all of the time."

"I don't mind dating women who drink. I don't have any issues being around people who are drinking. But I don't want to go out with a woman who gets drunk all the time. There's a big difference between someone who has a couple of drinks, and someone who blacks out and vomits and can't control their alcohol consumption. I told you before, my dad had a drinking problem, and I saw what it did to his relationship with my mom. She had to pick up the pieces all the time, especially after he died. I'm not going to follow the same path."

If she didn't like him as much as she did, if she didn't desire him as much, if she didn't have the urge to jump his bones right now, she would have ended this immediately. She would have accused him of judging her based on her worst moments and tried to make him feel guilty. And then she would have thrown her iced tea all over his coveralls and left. But she decided that—for perhaps the first time—she would make a mature decision and not sabotage herself.

"Well, Everett, I appreciate the warning," she told him with dignity. "I admit I sometimes used to drink too much. I admit that I still get the occasional craving for one drink—just one, mind you. But I don't need it to function. And I don't intend to get wasted again."

He didn't look convinced. "Okay. Good. I just wanted to get that conversation out of the way early."

"Do you always ask your dates if they're terrible drunks? Or did you do it special for me?" She was still mildly offended.

"No, but . . . sorry." He wouldn't make eye contact with her, and she wanted to let him squirm for a moment. Unfortunately, the food arrived, causing a distraction and a change of subject.

The meal the waitress set down in front of them consisted of an enormous platter of golden fried goodness. It was piled high with what Everett called lake whitefish. There were also onion rings, mushrooms, and delightful little balls.

"Hush puppies! I love those!" She grabbed one, dipped it in tartar sauce and took an enormous bite, while Everett laughed. Turns out it wasn't a hush puppy.

"Mac and cheese balls," he said. "I don't think they go well with tartar sauce."

"That may have been a mistake," she confirmed, taking a swig of her tea to get the taste out of her mouth. "I'm sure they're better plain."

"So," Everett began after they'd begun eating and she had a chance to sample the whitefish. "I told you my deal breaker. What's yours?"

Amanda considered it for a moment. "Don't ever try to sleep with my sister. Or say she's prettier than me. Or make any jokes about how once you've seen one of us naked, you've seen us both."

"That's . . . that's really easy to not do those things. Have you seriously had problems with that in the past?"

"You'd be surprised." Amanda couldn't count the number of men who'd treated her and Nikki as interchangeable. One of the greatest difficulties dating as an identical twin was finding someone who liked them for themselves as individuals and not as whichever part of the set they were able to get. No matter who she dated, she could never shake the uncomfortable suspicion they might have chosen her due to availability, rather than preference.

"Nah, I'm a man. I probably wouldn't be surprised. I can guarantee though, I will never make a move on your sister. I can barely handle you alone. I can't imagine two of you."

"Since she's not allowed to talk to me, you don't have to worry about it coming up."

"I thought *you* weren't allowed to talk to *her*."

"Touché." Amanda took another sip of her iced tea. The food settled heavily in her belly. Eating Sam's gourmet cuisine all the time may have destroyed her fondness for grease. "But since you brought it up, are you sure being out with a criminal like myself isn't a deal breaker for you? You being such a fine upstanding citizen and all, I fear I might be damaging your reputation."

"To be completely honest, I've been arrested too," Everett admitted.

Be still your heart, Nikki's voice shrieked excitedly. *Muscles, tattoos, and he's a reformed bad boy? Me-me, you've hit the sexy jackpot!*

"Excuse me, what?" Amanda asked. She was not expecting that. Not staid, serious Everett Ryan.

He scratched the back of his neck in embarrassment. "It happened a couple of years ago. Some stranger at Shore Leave started a fight with me. He was harassing a group of women, and they were getting really uncomfortable. I stepped up and told him to leave them alone, and he took issue with that. I let him punch me twice before I did anything."

"And then?"

"Then I beat the crap out of him, and when his buddies tried to get involved, Duncan pulled them off of me and slammed their heads together. The three of them all got taken to the hospital, and Duncan and I were arrested. We spent the night in jail before the cops reviewed the security tapes."

"How on Earth did you get so much sexier?" Amanda murmured, before realizing it came out loud enough for Everett to hear. She didn't like the real bad boys, the ones who were in and out of prison and always out of work because their records kept them from holding down a job. But a solid responsible man with a dark past? A hero who wasn't afraid to step in and rescue damsels in distress? Yeah, that worked for her.

🌲 🌲 🌲 🌲 🌲

Everett was a gentleman and escorted her home after their lunch, and he gave her a long drawn out delicious kiss that sent tingles through her whole body. And then, regretfully, rather than dragging him to bed, they both went to their separate jobs.

Cara was stony-faced behind the reception desk when Amanda breezed in. "Aren't you going to ask about my date with Everett?" she asked. "No? No desire to know any details of my burgeoning romance? No inquiries as to how—"

"Shut up." Cara's icy voice cut through her. "Sam came by. He seems to think you're a junkie. He says you were going through our room, trying to steal money."

"I am most certainly not on drugs!" That sure took the wind out of her sails. All of her confidence and happiness evaporated in an instant. "I cannot believe your husband would accuse me of such villainous infamy. Why, if he—"

"Seriously, stop talking Amanda." Cara interrupted her again. "You weren't looking for money. You were looking for this." She held up the chain she wore around her neck, the one with her wedding and engagement rings that no longer fit her swollen fingers. There was something else there, something that it took Amanda a second to identify. The fridge key.

"I was just—"

"No. Don't insult my intelligence. I know what you were doing. I'm surprised you didn't crack open the cooking sherry—which, by the way, Sam got rid of. We don't have any rubbing alcohol either. Amanda, you have a serious problem."

"I was only—"

Cara raised a hand to stop her.

"I don't want to hear it. You have a problem, one you won't admit to. I'm letting you live in my house and work in my inn. I need to be able to trust you. I don't like being forced to start locking everything up. You're lucky there's a guest walking over here right now. I'm going to help them, while you sit in the staff office quietly and think of how you're going to apologize."

That's exactly what Amanda did. She went into the office, sat down, and asked herself what Nikki would do in this situation, because she would probably have the more rational response. The Mandi response would be to wail and cry and carry on about how maligned she was, how misunderstood, how devastatingly injured by these unjust accusations.

"Me-me, tell me how to say I'm sorry," she whispered to her twin. *Paddy keeps whiskey in his office*, the Nikki in her mind responded instead. Nikki was slightly less than helpful. She closed her eyes and tried to think, but it was Everett's face that appeared.

I don't want to date a drunk, Everett's voice said. *You need to take responsibility for your actions. Do you like when I do this?* Okay, that last one was not relevant, since he'd said it to her in the other night, right in the middle of bringing her to a screaming climax. But the rest? He was right. It was time to take responsibility.

When Cara finished listing the art galleries for the guest, she waved her back out, and Amanda was ready for it. She stood up, straightened her shirt, fluffed her hair, and plastered a contrite smile on her face.

"Cara, you're right. I messed up. I was looking for the beer key, because I was anxious about my date and I wanted something to take the edge off. It was wrong, and I know it. I'm sorry."

Cara's eyes widened. "Amanda, I believe that's the first time you've ever admitted fault in anything, ever. That's a huge step for you."

"Forgiven?" Amanda held out her arms to take her cousin in a hug, but Cara stepped back.

"Tentatively. But you have to make some changes."

"I already am. I'm going to the meetings, like I'm supposed to." The meetings sucked. They were boring, and lots of people smelled like smokers, and the cookies always tasted stale. But she could force herself to sit through them.

"More than that. You need something else to focus on. That's why I volunteered you for a couple of jobs."

"You can't do that. Slave labor was outlawed almost two centuries ago." She could only imagine what kind of punishments Cara and Sam had come up with. Were there spiderwebs in the attic that needed cleaning? Maybe someone needed to evict the snake that had taken up residence under the porch? It looked like a harmless rat snake, but that didn't mean she wanted to touch it.

"But doing volunteer work as an alternative to getting kicked out of your housing is legal, as far as I know. I called the community library. You're going to be doing a toddler story hour on Friday mornings at 9:00 a.m., and a preschool one at 10:30. You will also spend your Tuesday afternoons at Golden Shores Retirement Community."

Amanda laughed with relief. Cara had signed her up for things she actually would enjoy doing. "That sounds fantastic. I wanted to contact the retirement home anyway, I just hadn't gotten around to it yet."

"Fill your days with activities, and your nights with Everett, and maybe you won't think about drinking so much," Cara said, showing Amanda that, while Cara might not forgive her yet, she still had her cousin's support.

"Oh, believe me, I plan to." As many nights as she could, at least. Too bad their schedules were so incompatible.

Chapter Seventeen

"What are you doing after this?" Amanda asked Tyrell as they shut down the reception desk for the night.

"It's eleven o'clock, what do you think I'm doing? I'm going home to my husband."

"I thought he was at work."

"We live above the bar. I'm going to flirt with him until closing time, then we'll go home together."

"Oh. I was hoping you wanted to hang out or something." She needed some kind of distraction. Sometimes she didn't want to be alone with her thoughts, and it was too early for a night owl like her to go to sleep.

"The Digs is the only place open, Mandi," Ty told her in a gentle tone. "And I don't know if that's a good place for you right now. I heard what happened earlier."

"How? How did you hear that?" The gossip in this town was completely out of control.

"I stopped by to drop something off this morning, and it was right when Sam came in to tell Cara he caught you snooping around. Look, it's no big deal. So you had a relapse. Tomorrow is a new day."

"I didn't have a relapse!" That statement angered her more than anything. If people were going to talk about her, she'd prefer accuracy. "Fine, never mind. I'll just go to bed."

🌲 🌲 🌲 🌲 🌲

She made her way back to the staff house and sat down on the porch swing. Cara and Sam were already sleeping inside, so she couldn't even go in and watch television. She was stuck, isolated, and bored.

Everything in her craved a drink. Why? What was wrong with her? *Everett doesn't want to date a drunk,* she reminded herself.

He doesn't have to know, Nikki's voice whispered. *One drink never hurt anybody. Besides, it's been a long day. It'll help you relax. You need it.*

"I don't need it," she told her twin out loud. "You're wrong about me."

Nikki's laugh burst out in her mind, but there was something odd about it. Nikki had a musical laugh, like bells tinkling. Amanda was the one that sounded like an asthmatic under attack. When did Nikki's laughter turn so wheezy?

Amanda's stomach twisted. It wasn't Nikki's voice she'd been hearing all along. It was her own. Devious devilish Nikki wasn't the one encouraging her to break her sobriety; she was doing it to herself.

But how could she escape herself? How could she make herself shut up? Well, there was one thing she could try. Endorphins produced by running were a healthy alternative to alcohol, or so she'd been told.

Opening the door as quietly as possible, she tiptoed into her bedroom and found her sneakers. Sam had said the loop around the island was five miles, but she wouldn't go the entire way—that would take her through town, passing the bar. Instead, she'd just go halfway in the direction opposite the village, then turn around. A five-mile run would be a good distraction from everything else.

Chapter Eighteen

O'Connell Family Chatroom

<AMY has joined the chat>

Amy: Anyone here?

Kenny: Yep.

Danny: Yep.

Nicole: Been waiting.

Amy: Sorry, V needed nursing.

Danny: Gross.

Amy: You have three children. Shut up.

Kenny: I heard from Cara.

Amy: Why isn't she here?

Kenny: Sibling chat.

Danny: Sibling chat.

Kenny: We were typing at the same time.

Danny: We're typing at the same time.

Kenny: Stop doing that.

Danny: Stop doing that.

Nicole: Both of you stop. Only one of you is allowed to contribute at a time.

Kenny: I can't help when he's typing.

Danny: I can't tell when he's typing.

Nicole: Danny, ask permission before you say anything.

Amy: Can we focus? How's Mandi?

Kenny: C says she's making progress.

Nicole: Is she drinking?

Kenny: Do you care?

Nicole: Don't be an ass. Of course I care!

Kenny: Then you should have let her live with you.

Danny: That wouldn't solve anything, and you know it.

Nicole: I'm not responsible for her actions.

Kenny: Still. Her recovery would be easier with you.

Nicole: I think it would be harder. She's mad at me.

Danny: For getting married?

Nicole: For choosing to get married. And moving away.

Danny: That's stupid.

Kenny: I didn't get mad when Danny got married.

Amy: Mel was pregnant. He didn't have a choice.

Kenny: Demanding a DNA test and paying 18 years of child support was always an option.

Danny: F U!

Kenny: Just saying it was an option. I like Mel. Usually.

Nicole: This isn't about you two idiots! Focus.

Kenny: Cara said Mandi's hooking up with some guy.

Amy: WHO????

Kenny: Emmett Fairy

Amy: WHO????

Kenny: She said you'd know him

Amy: WHO????

Kenny: The younger Fairy brother. She made it sound like there's a lot of them.

Amy: FERRY you dumbass. Everett Ryan, youngest of the family that owns the FERRY service.

Kenny: F-ing homophones.

Nicole: You know him? And define young.

Amy: He's your age, Nik. I think. Of course I know him. Small island. I worked there for years.

Kenny: Did we meet him at Cara's wedding?

Amy: No he had the flu or something. He's very tall. And muscular. And smart.

Nicole: And? Is he going to be good for her?

Amy: I don't think he drinks.

Nicole: Well, that's something.

Kenny: So she can replace alcohol addiction with sex addiction. Cool beans.

Nicole: Don't be an ass.

Amy: ^^^ Most overused words in our chats.

Nicole: Most necessary.

Kenny: Do you want the rest of the update or not? She's going to meetings regularly, she's starting to do volunteer work, and she seems happy. Cara even said she's started running again.

Nicole: How happy?

Kenny: Ask Cara. Or call Mandi.

Nicole: I can't. You know that won't help.

Kenny: It might.

Danny: It might.

Nicole: It's part of the terms of her probation. If she gets caught talking to me, she goes to jail.

Kenny: Don't you miss her?

Danny: Don't you miss her?

Nicole: STOP DOING THAT!

Nicole: I miss her every day. But I'm also trying to live my life too. And she blames me for her problems.

Kenny: It is your fault. If you'd just let her use your identity, you'd be the one on probation, and she'd be fine

Nicole: FU! It is not!!

Kenny: Chill, I was joking.

Nicole: How would you like it if Danny got arrested in your name?

Kenny: Awesome! My wife's a lawyer. We'd make so much in our civil suit against him. Set for life, baby!

Danny: Can't squeeze blood from a stone

Kenny: You have homeowner's insurance. That's where the money would come from.

Danny: That doesn't cover criminal acts, and identify theft is a crime.

Kenny: I'll have to rethink my strategy

Danny: You mean the one where you get arrested while pretending to be me pretending to be you? Why rethink it? You're a criminal mastermind. I can't wait to testify against you.

Amy: Stop typing gibberish and derailing the chat. This is supposed to be an update on Mandi. And a plan for helping her.

Nicole: What is the plan? I thought it was just wait?

Amy: I guess. But that makes me feel useless.

Danny: She hasn't hit bottom yet. And if she's going to her meetings and dating some guy and getting her life on track, maybe she won't.

Nicole: I rather think getting a DWI and losing her job was her hitting bottom.

Kenny: I don't. She still got bailed out. And she's never once acknowledged there was a problem. C says she's still blaming you.

Danny: Me?

Nicole: No, idiot. Me. She's blaming me.

Kenny: I wouldn't worry too much about that. She'll get used to the idea of having a married twin. It's weird, I get it.

Danny: It's not weird. MEL WAS PREGNANT!

Nicole: Stop making everything about you.

Amy: Baby's crying. Got to go.

<AMY has left the chat>

Kenny: Me too. I've updated all I know and housework calls. Also, I think Javi and Micah just spilled cereal on the carpet. D see you tonight.

Danny: Yeah.

<DANNY has left the chat>

Nicole: K send updates when you get them.

Kenny: You could call Cara yourself.

Nicole: Not if Mandi might answer the phone.

Kenny: Have Griff call Sam.

Nicole: Maybe. Keep me posted, ok? I miss her.

Kenny: Yeah. I know you do. I understand, Nik. Love you!

<KENNY has left the chat >

Chapter Nineteen

Fifteen minutes until her dinner break, fifteen minutes until she could see Everett again. She wished their schedules were more aligned. Also, she wished she didn't have roommates or he didn't live with his mother. They weren't naked together as often as she would have liked. In fact, since that one time—okay, four times—in the back room of the ferry office the day she ran away, they hadn't been naked together at all.

When she heard the inn's front door open, she looked up from her paperwork with a welcoming grin ... but it wasn't him. She vaguely recognized the thirty-something man who entered. At first she assumed he was a guest of the inn, but then he stretched his face into an almost comical look of exaggerated surprise and made a beeline to the desk.

"Amanda? I forgot you worked here!"

"Sorry, remind me where I know you?"

"I'm Kevin. I see you twice a week ... oh, you're just pretending, aren't you? Don't worry, I'm good at keeping secrets. I would never expose yours." He gave her an exaggerated wink.

Ah, that's where she knew him from—the meetings. She honestly didn't pay much attention in those things, so she didn't remember much about him, if he was even one of the people who commonly spoke. Several others were like her, quietly sitting in the back and biding their time until they served out the terms of their sentences. If the person who had to sign off on probationary paperwork would do so at the beginning rather than the end, there'd probably be a lot fewer attendees.

"What can I help you with?" She pulled out her polished customer service attitude to cover up her confusion. Kevin lived in

Ferry's Landing, or thereabouts; there was no reason to visit on the island on a Monday evening.

"I'm here because of you."

"Excuse me?" Oh god, had she managed to acquire a stalker? Already?

He laughed at her discomfort. "Not like that, silly. I've been trying to come up with a place to host my parent's anniversary party, and this inn popped into my head. I couldn't figure out why, until I walked in and saw you. You must have mentioned it at you-know-where, and it stuck in my brain. So how about it? Can we talk about your event packages?" He leaned on the counter and smiled.

"I don't handle any of the events, let me call someone for you." She picked up her radio and paged Tyrell. He needed to come to the desk anyway, it was almost time for her break.

"What a shame. I'd rather work with you. Help you out, make sure you get the commission."

"I appreciate that, but we don't work on commission here, and I seriously know nothing about event planning. I only know how to see what's coming up, but not how to schedule or organize them."

Kevin lowered his voice. "If they don't trust you because of your—ahem—problem, then maybe handling something simple like my party will show your bosses that you can do it. I don't mind letting someone learn as she goes."

"It's got nothing to do with my—ahem—problem and everything to do with having different jobs. I'm just reception and social media. But thank you for your offer." She'd only been working with Cara for a short time, but she was able to channel her cousin right now, and maintain a smooth calm façade. This guy was patronizing and annoying, but she could keep her smile professional.

"Maybe I wanted to work with you so I can keep hearing that accent." Great, now he'd added flirting to this conversation, as if it wasn't awkward enough to begin with. Shouldn't there be a policy against hitting on people from meetings? Fortunately, Tyrell arrived, grabbed the events binder, and took Kevin over to a seat in the lobby.

And even more fortunately, the next person through the door was Everett, carrying an extra-large pizza. Good, he got one big enough that maybe she could have more than one slice. She'd never seen anyone eat as much as him.

"Ready to go?" he asked, setting the pizza box down in front of her. The smell filled the air, making her mouth water. Or maybe it was pheromones that caused that. The way Everett looked at her, she wanted to eat him up.

"As soon as Ty is finished with his customer," she gestured toward the two men in the lobby. Kevin saw her looking and gave a nod.

The meeting dragged on and on. It was just an anniversary party, but apparently Kevin wanted to look at every single brochure. At least twenty minutes passed with their meal cooling and Everett checking his watch and glaring before Tyrell returned to the desk.

"Sorry about that. Go ahead and take your break."

"Thanks!" She tried to leave, but Kevin rejoined them. "Tyrell, I'll see you at our appointment Friday, and Amanda, I guess I'll see you . . . *around*." And he had the nerve to wink at her again before he walked out the door.

"What was all that about? You know that guy?" Everett asked as they went out the back door.

"He . . . sort of. Not well." How to explain? But Everett was smart enough to figure it out for himself.

"Never mind. I assume it's *anonymous*."

"I don't know why he had to phrase it like that though."

"I do. He was trying to make me jealous."

"If this were a romantic comedy, you would ask how I knew him, I wouldn't say because it would compromise the integrity of my meetings, and you would assume I was cheating and storm out in anger, leaving him to comfort me. You know, one of those misunderstandings that could be overcome with ten lines of dialogue."

"But then there'd be no story."

"True. And we all need a good story."

"Oh, and without having a stupid fight for no reason, I wouldn't have an excuse to chase you down in an airport or run after you in a traffic jam."

"And there'd be no makeup sex."

"But I want that part! Maybe I should have let him get to me." Everett looked her up and down and gave her a smile, a delicious sexy smile that made her want to pull him into the nearest private space and drop her panties on the floor.

"We can always pretend he did. If we have time after we eat, we might be able to grab a few minutes for make up sex anyway." She tossed her hair and licked her lips, and it had the desired effect. He took a deep shuddering breath and closed his eyes. Oh, he wanted her, she could sense it.

"If I weren't starving from smelling this pizza for the past twenty minutes, I'd say let's do that first. We'll just have to hope for enough time." Really? Food over sex? But to be fair, she was starving too, and while she was eager, she didn't want a quickie, she wanted time to enjoy it.

"Fingers crossed my roommates aren't home."

But of course they were, and there was no way to be subtle or quiet considering what Amanda wanted to do, so after they ate together on the porch she had to settle for a desperate and handsy make-out session behind the house, before smoothing her clothing and heading back into work. Tomorrow, and the planned night on the mainland, couldn't come soon enough.

Chapter Twenty

In his old life, prior to a few weeks ago, Everett might as well have been color-blind. Everything was gray. There was nothing bright, nothing colorful, nothing happy. He trudged about, doing the same thing every single day. Work, loading boxes, politely speaking with passengers, and steering the ferry across the same cold stretch of gray water. Even his band practices were gray, hanging out in a dingy old garage, playing someone else's songs, and not ones he particularly liked, though he did enjoy the power behind controlling the beat.

No, everything was gray and dull and mundane.

Until now.

Until Amanda burst into his life like a flash of fire. Until her sheer radiance blew all the grayness away. It wasn't just her beauty, though of course that was a factor. But no, it was her, it was her humor, her creativity, it was the way she made him feel.

Everything about her surprised him. As he peeled back the layers of her personality, the outer beauty, he found a frail, fragile, trembling baby bird underneath, one in need of support and protection. He loved the dichotomy, and he loved the way she trusted him enough to reveal it to him. She made him want to be a better person, to work harder, to earn her smiles and her laughter.

But, oh, how that woman frightened him. She could upend his entire world, and he would let her.

He wasn't the only one who noticed a difference in his life. His family saw it too. His mother teased him, but gently. And his niece flat out asked him, "Uncle Ev, why are you so bouncy?"

"Bouncy?" There had been more of a spring in his step lately, that was true. Along with being able to see color again, a heavy burden had been lifted from his shoulders. "Pumpkin, grown men aren't bouncy."

"Yeah, you are. Like this." Joy did an exaggerated series of steps.

"I have a better question," Everett replied. "Why are you so squealy?" Then he picked her up and tickled her until she shrieked.

When he finally set her down and she ran off to play, Nessie walked up and poked him in the ribs. "Nice way of dodging the question."

"I don't bounce," he informed her.

"No, but you are happier than I've ever seen you. I like it."

Everett liked it too. He liked the change in himself, the electricity that powered him now. Kissing Amanda was the best decision he had ever made.

🌲 🌲 🌲 🌲 🌲

After band practice, Everett had to stop himself from sprinting to the restaurant where he was meeting Amanda. His drumming had been off rhythm, slightly too fast all night, because all he could think about was seeing her again, having actual privacy with her. The faster he could rush through practice, the sooner he could get his hands on Mandi. Is this what addiction felt like?

She was already seated at a table, reading a novel while waiting for him. "Sugar Pie!" she squealed when he entered, and his face turned red. He secretly loved the nickname, loved that she had a nickname for him, though given how soon she had bestowed it upon him, he suspected she used the same one for every guy she dated.

He sat down across from her and took a moment to drink her in. She was far too pretty for him. But if she didn't know that, he wouldn't be the one to tell her.

"Have you been waiting long?"

"About a half hour. I got here early because the library closed and kicked me out."

"Oh, is that the errand you were running?" He'd invited her to watch his practice, but was a little relieved when she turned him down. She'd be too much of a distraction. Hell, her absence was a distraction too.

"I had my first day volunteering at the retirement community," she reminded him, "And I needed to update my reading matter."

"I don't follow."

She sighed. "One of my assignments is reading to the residents. Since I didn't know what they'd like, last week I stopped by the library and borrowed three books: a thriller, a cozy mystery, and a somewhat naughty romance. Can you guess what they chose?"

"Thriller?" That'd be his preference. He didn't know exactly what made a mystery cozy, but he didn't like them anyway. They were either too obvious and therefore boring, or too convoluted. If you missed the one word clue on page seven, you'd never figure out the damn thing. And romances? Reading them definitely didn't hold his interest—he preferred to be more hands on.

"It was a close vote, actually. So what I did was spend forty-five minutes on the thriller, and then took a break to rest my voice—even I can't talk all the time—and then read the romance. It was hot." She fanned herself to prove her point. "Some of the audience made special requests for next time. I had to go check out some more books. I like to read them in advance. Helps prepare me, plus, I can look up any words I don't know."

"You read dirty stories to a bunch of old people?" He didn't consider himself a prude by any means, but the idea of a crowd of geriatrics listening to verbal pornography kind of grossed him out.

"Everett Ryan! How dare you! Getting old doesn't dry up the sex drive. Did you know that the population with the highest rate of increasing STIs is over age 60? Those old folks get it on. Think about it, no need for avoiding pregnancy, and everybody's single. These are the survivors, their spouses are dead, and they still need some love and attention. Pack all these ancient horndogs into a building full of beds, of course they're going to have sex. It's worse than a frat house."

"I know you're joking."

"I am not! Everett, I'm working with human beings. Humans are sexual creatures, no matter how old. And don't you dare make that face! When I'm ninety I hope to still be getting action too."

She was serious? A sudden image of his grandmother, staying in that same retirement community, popped into his head. Had she been sexing it up with the other residents? He didn't want to think about that.

"Anyway," she continued. "I picked up a naughtier book for next time. They have a surprisingly decent selection, and the librarian told me they can place discrete orders from other locations. I guess people need entertainment in the winter, what with the cold and misery and all."

"It's not that miserable. You actually like those books, don't you?"

She shrugged. "I like romance novels, especially the steamy ones. I like good sex and a happy ending. That's what I aspire to, of course."

"Good sex and a happy ending? I'll give you that tonight."

Amanda's laugh rang out, attracting attention from some of the few other diners. "Sugar Pie, that had better be a promise."

"It is. And will you read me one of the books?" She looked surprised by the question, but in truth, he surprised himself. He never thought about it before, but suddenly the idea of laying down next to her, listening to her tell stories in her sexy drawl, was something he very much wanted to do.

"You want me to treat you like my Gran?"

"You don't have to." Now he could feel embarrassment set in, so he took another bite of food. That was his habit, eating to cover discomfort.

"I think it sounds kind of hot. I'll read to you, but you better do something for me in exchange."

"What?"

"We'll work the details out later." Her wicked grin and the way she licked her lips sent shivers down his spine. Yes, they would work it out. All night long. He bit his tongue, because if he didn't, he'd blurt out the wrong thing. Something like, 'my god, I love you woman,' or perhaps 'stay with me forever.' And this wasn't the right time for either of those sentiments.

Chapter Twenty-One

Sitting outside a cafe down by the lake almost made Amanda feel like she was on a vacation. A vacation to an overly chilly place not of her choosing, but a vacation nonetheless. It helped to have an attractive man seated across from her as her lunch companion. This 'thing' happening between her and Everett was working. When they were together, she didn't even want alcohol. When the waitress took her order, water was the first thing that popped into mind. Not a vodka tonic, not a lunchtime martini. Water with lemon. See? Everyone was wrong about her so-called addiction.

Everett reached across the table to take her hand. "You look distant. What are you thinking about?"

"I was thinking how content I am," she smiled at him. "I'm doing better than I expected here, since I met you. If this were a thriller in which you were the hero, this would be the point when a bomb would go off and I would tragically die."

"I assume I would avenge your death?"

"Well, I certainly hope so. Otherwise, the plot lacks an emotional element. You can't go after terrorists, or mad bombers, or whoever without an emotional connection. Though I expect a love interest would show up to replace me."

"I doubt you can be replaced so easily," he said. Smart man.

"Easy for you to say. I'm sure in the movie version of my life, I'd be replaced by a certain identical twin of mine. You'd work together to avenge me, and as you stand watching the fiery inferno of the burning enemy base, you realize she was the one for you all along."

"You've thought this scenario through. I suspect you're testing me right now."

"Perhaps." She tossed her hair and gave him a coy grin. "There is a right answer."

"Of course. Mandi, I don't care what your sister looks like, she isn't you. You're the only O'Connell I'm interested in, even if you die in a terrorist attack right in front of me. I think the movie would end with me dropping your killer's head on your grave and walking away alone. Probably into the sunset."

"Oooh, I like that imagery. Very bloody and dramatic. You're good at this, Sugar Pie." He was. He was good at everything. It made her wonder when she'd find his flaw, when all of this would go up in metaphorical smoke. Or worse, when he found hers and inevitably discovered that the bright confident person she pretended to be was just an illusion.

Maybe nothing will go wrong. Maybe it will all go right, Nikki whispered. Clearly, the voice actually belonged to Nikki this time—she was the optimistic one.

"I'm good at lots of things," he replied, with a wink. Too bad she had to behave herself in public. She knew exactly what she wanted for dessert.

"But surely you're bad at some things. Tell me something terrible from your past."

"I've already told you about my dad and brother, those are pretty much the only awful things."

"I'm sure there are others. Why don't you tell me about your worst relationship? I'm sure there's something dark and horrifying you could share about that."

He leaned forward, elbows on the table, mouth quirked in amusement. "You first."

"Challenge accepted. How about a competition? Loser pays for lunch."

"Is the winner the one with the worst or the best?"

"Isn't that the same thing? We're talking terrible stories here, Sugar Pie. Not any of that 'we drifted apart' or 'we're still best friends' nonsense. I'll tell you my worst, and if you can top it, I'm buying lunch."

"Go for it. But I think I have a winner." He crossed his arms and waited for her to start. She grinned at him.

"Okay. His name was Brad and we were together for eight months. One day, I decided to spice up our sex life . . ."

"Whoa! I don't know if I want to hear this," Everett warned her.

"I'll be vague. It's relevant, I promise. Anyway, I read a trick in a magazine and thought I'd try it on him. He loved it. And when we were done with our bedroom activities, he called me Nikki. Do I win?"

"Not yet. I know there must be more, but I'm still sure mine tops yours."

"Fine. So he called me by my twins' name, and I was like, excuse me, what did you just say? He chuckled and told me he knew I was Nikki because Mandi was too vanilla to try something so dirty. Then he assured me he wouldn't tell on me, and I was welcome to service him anytime. He even suggested a twin sandwich."

"What did you do?"

"See this?" She tilted her head at an angle and drew a finger along the underside of her chin. "Nothing there. Nikki has a scar from a childhood accident. I pointed out the lack of a scar and kicked him out. He tried to pass it off as a joke, but I'm not stupid."

"That's it? He just left?"

"Not without an argument and getting some shoes thrown at his head. Also, it's entirely possible that someone keyed the hell out of his car and slashed all four tires, but of course neither Nikki nor I know anything about that. Your turn, Sugar Pie."

"I think Brad would win for worst breakup."

"I think Brad deserves what he got."

"I'm not saying he didn't. Please tell me this was years ago."

Amanda sighed. "Yes, I was younger and less capable of concealing my anger back then. And perhaps some of the vehicular damage was caused while I was under the influence of a now forbidden substance." Sure, she had been drunk at the time, but wasn't that how people dealt with breakups? Alcohol, ice cream, sappy movies and lots of tissues when blindsided by it; tequila and vandalism—alleged, not proven—when the breakup was due to finding out the ex-boyfriend's scumbag tendencies.

"Leaving aside Brad, since he's not here to claim his free lunch, I still think I have you beat. My most recent relationship ..."

"Ex, not current, right?" Amanda interrupted.

"Oh, is this a relationship?"

"If it's not, I'm going to start seeing other people. Duncan has been looking mighty fine lately." She folded her arms across her chest and gave him a dirty look, but she wasn't able to maintain her glare. She started giggling, which turned into her embarrassingly wheezy laugh. Everett laughed right along with her.

"Stay away from my brother, though I'll be sure to pass along the compliment. Now, would you like to hear my story or not? I'm starting to think you're interrupting me to prolong this whole discussion, so the check will arrive and I'll lose by default."

"Are my strategies so transparent? Fine, I'm listening. No more interruptions." Well, possibly no more interruptions. Amanda could never guarantee what her mouth would do. She tried to focus on finishing her meal, so at least she could distract herself from talking.

"As I was saying, my most recent ex. We dated for a few months, but didn't go out often, because I work too much. You know how that goes." Fortunately, she had a mouthful of food, so she nodded rather than informing him how deeply she understood and how, while she respected his work ethic, she mildly resented it as well, since it kept them apart.

"She used to come by and sit on the docks and stare at me while I worked," he continued. "I'm not going to lie, I found it flattering at first. I mean, I'm a boring guy, so it felt gratifying to have someone interested like that. She came to every concert too, screaming her head off in the front row. She liked the band and really liked telling people she was dating the drummer. She had the idea that we'd make it big someday. And she'd be right there with us."

"You had yourself a groupie." Amanda clapped her hands in delight. "I hope she wore a T-shirt with your face on it!"

"She . . . did, actually. It was creepy. And she started getting clingy and talking about how she was in love with me and we were soulmates, that sort of thing. Like what we would name our children and should we honeymoon in Europe or go someplace more exotic."

"My goodness, I have to hear this. What are your future baby names?"

Everett looked down at the table uncomfortably. "Maybe you and I should have had this talk sooner. I . . . don't see myself ever having children. I love being an uncle, but I don't want to be a dad. I understand if that's an issue for you."

Her jaw dropped open. Everett didn't want children! How could he become even more perfect? Children were messy and time consuming, and while she loved every single one of her nieces and nephews and would no doubt love Cara's baby just as wholeheartedly, there was no way she would ever have one herself.

"Sugar Pie, I meant what names did your ex come up with? But while we're on the subject, perhaps it's time I informed you that I am also firmly child-free."

"You are?" Surprise and possibly relief washed across his face. "I avoided mentioning it before because you taught pre-school and I assumed you loved kids."

"Oh, I do, I love kids. I also love elderly people, tigers, and dolphins. But my affection for them doesn't mean I want any of them living in my house with me. Or springing forth from my lady parts, for that matter."

"No tigers in your lady parts. That might interfere with some of my plans for later . . ." He grinned, and her heart melted yet again. Here was a man who liked to joke around with her. He gave off such a serious vibe, but then his playful side would come out. She'd never met anyone who got her humor before.

"Well. I'm relieved to learn that we're on the same side of the baby-making issue. But I am sorry to inform you that you will be paying for this lunch, because my story was far worse than yours."

"Only because you won't let me finish."

"Oops." She made a zipping motion across her lips and gestured for him to continue.

"I was about to end things with her for other reasons, when her best friend called me up to warn me. Apparently, my ex was poking holes in condoms and planned to baby-trap me."

"Unzip," Amanda said, rather than bothering to mime it. "That's horrible! I mean, I understand her reasoning—rumor has it if you get knocked up by a Ferry Brother, you get free rides for life. But still, what an awful thing to do to anyone!"

"That deal was limited to Nessie. Doesn't matter, I dumped the ex immediately. And she stalked me for a few weeks, then started sleeping with the bass player so she'd have an excuse to come to band practices. She stares at me the whole time, but then drapes herself all over her new man to try and make me jealous."

"I can't wait to meet her. You did invite me to watch your practice sometime, didn't you?" She laughed at Everett's obvious discomfort.

The waitress arrived with the check and placed it in the middle of the table. They both stared at it.

"Well?" Amanda finally asked. "Aren't you going to pick that up?"

"Me? I had an obsessive woman who turned into a stalker. You got called by your sister's name. Better luck next time, Mandi."

"Fine." She pulled out her credit card. "Though I do disagree with the ultimate judgment, I will concede. As long as you promise me there is a next time."

"There will be a lot of next times with you," he promised, and an excited feeling stirred in the pit of her stomach. He was planning for a future, one that she was starting to hope for as well.

Chapter Twenty-Two

The worst thing about commuting across the lake for her meetings was the schedule. She always arrived too early, but not early enough to go sit in a café and read or otherwise occupy her time. No matter how slowly she walked, she was among the first to arrive. In some ways, it was a blessing—she was guaranteed a seat in the back where she could zone out and think naughty thoughts about Everett.

Right now she was daydreaming about his tattoos. She loved to trace them with her fingers and admire their artistry atop his beautiful muscles. She should ask why he chose those. *Why crows? Or are they ravens? What do they mean? Can I lick them?*

A voice snapped her out of her reverie. "Sorry I ambushed you the other day."

She looked up to see Kevin dropping into the seat next to her. A polite person would have asked if the seat was taken first.

"No big deal. I shouldn't be surprised to run into people outside of these meetings." She took a sip of her barely lukewarm coffee just to have something to do. She didn't want to make friends with anyone here. She wanted to survive the summer and walk away.

"Was that one of the Ryan brothers bringing you food last week?"

"You know him?" He couldn't know him that well, if he couldn't tell Everett and Duncan apart. And besides, they were collectively known as the Ferry Brothers. Nobody called them by their last name.

"I know *of* him. Everybody does. This town is called Ferry's Landing for a reason."

"Makes sense." She tried to stick to non-committal answers. Amanda enjoyed gossip as well as the next person, but she had no desire to discuss her boyfriend with a stranger at an AA meeting. She wanted to keep her personal life separate from her probation obligations.

"You aren't dating him, are you? I've heard things about him from some of his ex-girlfriends that make me uncomfortable."

"We are seeing each other, and I'm not overly concerned about his past. I'm sure my ex-boyfriends have plenty to say about me as well."

Kevin chuckled knowingly. "I bet they do."

She tried not to shudder. Kevin was a perfectly nice man, but she had no interest in having him flirt with her. She had no interest in anything at all with him, or anyone else here for that matter. These were not her people, despite what her probation officer said. Fortunately, the meeting was starting with the usual sob stories and tearful confessions, so she had an excuse not to talk to him anymore.

At the first break though, he started in again. "Listen, I know you aren't from around here, but the Ryan family can be trouble. You need to be careful with them."

"They've run the ferry for generations. His mother has served on the Whispering Pines village council for two decades. I haven't the faintest idea what kind of trouble you're talking about."

"Alcoholism, gambling, brawling. He and the gigantic lumberjack looking one who works on the boat have gotten arrested for fighting several times."

"And I don't believe they've been charged with anything."

"Because his mom is powerful. You think if he ever hurts you, you'd have any recourse?" Kevin acted like he was providing new knowledge. Maybe he was, Everett had only mentioned one arrest. But rumors did tend to fly unchecked in small towns, and that one minor kerfuffle several years ago could have morphed into a dozen heinous crimes in the retellings.

"He's not going to hurt me." Everett was a gentle giant, huge and intimidating on the outside, kind and tender on the inside. There was no violence in his thoughts or actions.

"I'm not trying to upset you or insult your taste in men, I just wanted to warn you. I'm trying to help you, Mandi." She hated when people used her nickname like that. She'd never given him permission to call her Mandi.

"That's sweet of you, but I'm fine." She knew exactly what Kevin was doing. She wasn't born yesterday. He, like so many men before him, wanted to get in her pants. No thank you. She made a mental note to start arriving late to meetings, or always sit in between others so he couldn't trap her in conversation again.

Chapter Twenty-Three

Everett sat waiting in the park for Amanda. Lunch was the highlight of his day—that and riding the ferry with her. Having her stand next to him in the wheelhouse while he was at the helm made him feel powerful. With her at his side, he could do anything. Well, almost anything. He did have his limits. For example, he wouldn't let her touch the controls no matter how much she cajoled him—he was smitten but not reckless.

She showed up, carrying her lunch and glaring over her shoulder in an annoyed manner. Even with her face scrunched in irritation, she was the most beautiful woman he'd ever seen.

"Something wrong?" he asked, after giving her a quick peck on the cheek.

"Just making sure I wasn't followed."

"You're the one with a stalker now? Why am I not surprised?"

"Not a stalker, I hope. You remember the guy who winked at me in the lobby at work the other day? He's taken it upon himself to tell me what a terribly dangerous man I've become involved with."

"Who, me? I'm big, but not dangerous."

"Don't worry, Sugar Pie, I know that already. I can see through his manipulations. He just wants me to leave you and cry on his shoulder, so he can make a move."

"Good. I mean, good that you know I'm not dangerous, not good you have someone hitting on you." He ate one-handed, so he could drape his other arm around her shoulders. He couldn't help it; if she was within reach, he wanted physical contact with her.

"Men have been hitting on me since before I grew breasts. I'm used to it. I hardly notice them anymore." The way she flung her hair and stared off into the distance demonstrated the lie in her statement.

"That's disturbing."

"That's why you acting disinterested was so intriguing to me. I'm not accustomed to men not wanting me." Her fingertips played out a rhythm on his thigh as she spoke, and electricity surged through him. Someday, he'd have to figure out how she did it.

"To be fair, I thought you were a hard partier, and no matter how attracted to you I was, that's not what I wanted." He still worried that her irresponsible drunk persona lurked under the surface, but she was clearly working on improving. Plus, once he'd tasted those sweet lips, he had no power to resist her.

"And now you know me better."

"I sure do. And I was thinking perhaps it's time for my family to get to know you better too." Hopefully it wasn't too soon.

"Sugar Pie, don't be silly," she said, lightly patting his leg. "I have news that may shock you. I know your family. I see your momma and brother almost every day. And that sister-in-law of yours and I had coffee together when I happened to run into her last week."

"You happened to run into her?" Nessie hadn't mentioned anything.

Amanda shrugged. "Maybe I was following her. I don't really remember. What's important is that we sat down and she filled me in on all kinds of stories from your childhood."

"How ... interesting." Nessie would have portrayed him a positive light, wouldn't she? He'd told her how much Amanda meant to him. *I think I'm falling in love* were his exact words. And Nessie had expressed her support.

"Your face is turning red. You think she told me something embarrassing. It sounds like I'm going to have to take up knitting so I can pester her in her shop. Piney Islands Yarn-works, right?"

"You've been doing your homework." He couldn't picture Mandi having the patience to knit. She'd get frustrated quickly, give up, and make some excuse like the needles were too pointy or the yarn was too flimsy.

"I might stop in there anyway. I have to buy some yarn for Rose."

"Who?"

"One of the lovely women at the retirement home. She told me she loves knitting, but all anyone donates to the home for the residents to use is cheap, scratchy acrylic, and nobody wants to work with that. I thought I'd pick her up some fancy wool, and while I was there, I could perhaps pick up a little more gossip about the adventures of young Everett."

"There are no adventures you need to hear about," he said. "Until you came along, my life has been nothing but piloting the ferry back and forth to the island."

"And playing in a band, and getting sexy tattoos, and getting in bar fights," she reminded him. "Don't pretend you do nothing but hang out on an old boat."

He chuckled and tried to deliver a kiss to her cheek, but she turned her head, and he couldn't help but move to her lips. Making out in public was hardly appropriate, but this wasn't a popular park, and her stunning vibrancy made him throw caution to the wind.

"Sugar Pie," she whispered, breaking away. "How terrible would it be to visit your little crash pad right now?"

"Pretty terrible, since my mom is in the office. Speaking of my mom, I was serious about what I said, I want to properly introduce you to my family. What are the chances you can trade shifts with somebody on Sunday evening?"

"That's Tyrell's night off. I'm sure he'd be open to swap. Why Sunday?"

"Once a month we do a family dinner. It's not much. We grill out, and Nessie and Joy come over. It's no big deal. I just thought . . . you don't have to though, if you can't take off work . . ."

She put one of those magical fingers on his lips to silence his babbling. "Sugar Pie, I'd be happy to attend your family's festivities."

That was the other thing he needed to address before she spent any time with them.

"Great, but regarding the whole pet name thing . . . could you not call me that on Sunday? Just not in front of my mom and Duncan?"

"Everett Ryan!" Her tone was rife with indignation. "It is my understanding that, though we are close to an international border, the Constitution of the United States still applies, and I have the freedom of speech. You cannot censor me!"

"Freedom of speech means the government can't censor you. I'm not the government. I'm just a lowly dockworker asking a beautiful woman a favor."

"While I appreciate the compliment, I am fully aware that your momma is on the village council. She *is* the government, and you're telling me I must censor my language in her presence."

"Because she's my mom."

"Oh, you know I'm teasing you. I won't call you Sugar Pie in front of your family." She gave him the smile that twisted his insides up, and he knew that while she would keep her word, she may be more of a letter of the law rather than spirit of the law kind of woman.

Chapter Twenty-Four

Everett walked down the road to meet Amanda when he saw her coming. She strode along, looking beautiful and powerful. He never understood the appeal of high heels before, always thought them impractical and silly, but seeing the way she walked toward him . . . damn. He'd like to see her in nothing but those ridiculous shoes.

"You never told me where you lived. I had to ask Cara," she said, after breaking off their greeting kiss.

"It never occurred to me to tell you. I assumed you knew," he admitted rather sheepishly. On a tiny island like this, everyone always knew everyone else's business. He never once thought about giving her his address.

"Lucky for you, I was willing to get directions. I could have given up, taken a seat at the docks, and handed my surprise off to anyone walking by."

"Your what? Is that a euphemism?"

She held up a bakery box tied up with string. "I brought something special. My great-grandmother would come back to life to smite me if I showed up at a family meal empty-handed. Much as I'd love to see her again, I'd like to avoid a zombie attack."

"Is it from Margaux's?" he asked hopefully. There was only one bakery on the island, and everything that came from there was delicious.

"A purchased treat? How dare you impugn my baking skills! I am a proper lady, I made it myself," she told him indignantly. Then she deflated a bit. "Well, Sam helped. I like to bake, and I make a hell of a cupcake, but he took issue with me using his kitchen, so he basically stood over my shoulder and lectured me on technique and cleaned everything up."

"That was nice of him, I guess. Anyway, here we are." He opened the front door for her and led her in. He didn't want to admit it, but he was nervous about showing his home to her. He got the impression she came from a wealthy family, and he certainly did not. He didn't want her to judge him.

"Is this the same house you grew up in?" she asked as she scanned the entry way.

"We moved here when I was six and my grandfather died. It was my mom's childhood home, and it was much bigger than the place we were living." His father's alcoholism and inability to hold down a job meant they'd lived in a tiny house, little more than a shack, until his mother inherited this one. With three bedrooms and a finished basement, there had been plenty of room for the whole family, even if Everett and Malcolm still had to share.

"I love it. You'll have to give me the official tour. I especially want to see where you sleep," she said, with a suggestive lift of her eyebrows. Goddamn, this woman was sexy.

"Later. Let's get this to the kitchen for now." His mother was finishing chopping vegetables for salad when he brought Amanda in. "Mom, I'd like to introduce you to my girlfriend, Amanda."

"Hi Mandi," Vivian replied. "My son seems to think we haven't met."

"Mom, I was being polite." *Please don't embarrass me*, he added silently.

"Vivian, how lovely to see you in a non-ferry capacity." Amanda gave her a winning smile. Everett watched his mother's expression, trying to discern what she thought. She was always a good judge of character, and he really wanted her to like Amanda.

"She brought dessert." Everett placed the box on the counter, and he caught his mother's approving nod.

"That was kind of you. You didn't have to bring anything." Vivian wiped her hands on her pants and picked up a knife to cut the string sealing the box.

"I wouldn't dare show up without something to share. My Gran taught me better than that," Amanda said. He noticed that whenever she mentioned her Gran, she subconsciously fingered her necklace. The rare outward show of vulnerability made him love her even more.

"What is it?" Vivian asked, opening the lid and looking down at the pie inside.

"I don't know if I'm allowed to say. Everett, dearest darling, am I permitted to tell your momma what it is?" She turned her blinding smile to him.

"Of course. Why wouldn't you be able to?" The second he asked, he knew. This was a set up.

"Why, it's a . . . sugar pie. I got the recipe from one of my favorite residents at the nursing home where I volunteer. I'm just crazy about sugar pie, aren't I?" She nudged him with her elbow and heat rose in his face. He should have known she'd find a way around his admonition.

"Okay, we're done in here. How about we do that tour now?" He took her hand and dragged her away from the kitchen and the knowing smirk on his mother's face.

Chapter Twenty-Five

In Amanda's past, she would have considered 'still lives with parents' as a major deal breaker, but in her current boyfriend's case, it seemed to be reasonable. Especially since he worked at the family business, and they weren't in the best place financially. *He helps out his momma*, is how she'd explain it to her brothers, when they inevitably found out and mocked her for dating a dependent child. *He's a good man and he cares about his family.*

There was an entire wall of photos, and she examined all of them, with particular enjoyment of the childhood ones, from long before Everett achieved his size and bulk. He was a skinny little boy, knock-kneed, with hands and feet far too large for his body.

"Is this your daddy?" she asked, pausing in front of a portrait of a grinning man in full fishing gear. "He was a hottie."

"Yep. That's my dad. And there's Malcolm and Conner," he pointed out the two she hadn't met. She studied them. She could see bits of Everett in them, though he was taller and his hair was lighter. He took more after his mother than the others, with the exception of his height. They were all big men, like their father.

"Is this your brother's wedding?" She recognized petite little Nessie, looking like a child among the sea of enormous Ryan brothers.

"That was the last time we were all together. Malcolm was home on leave." There was always a discordant note in his voice when he mentioned his older brother. She suspected it was envy. Everett didn't seem like the type to be happy tucked away on this tiny island forever. She could imagine him standing proud in a Coast Guard uniform, achieving his long-forsaken dream.

"You're definitely the best looking of the bunch," she told him, pressing a kiss on his cheek. "Now, show me the rest of the house. Where's your bedroom, for example?"

"We can't . . ." His discomfort melted her heart. Her poor gentle giant, worried about what his momma would think.

"I just want to see," she assured him, though of course when he led her to his basement bedroom she did take a moment to lie on the bed and test the mattress out. "Mmmm . . . bouncy, and much bigger than the awful twin you have in your back office. And I like the headboard. I know exactly where to attach the handcuffs." Oh, how she loved the way he blushed. Men like him were supposed to be tough, but he was an old softie at heart.

"You want me to handcuff you?" he asked, discomfort evident.

"Other way around, Sug . . . Darling." She gave him her most wicked smile.

He ducked his head and looked away. "Please get up," he told her in a strangled voice. He was clearly having difficulty keeping his composure, a fact that amused her greatly.

"But this is so comfy. Don't you want to join me?" She stretched her arms over her head, making sure the movement caused her shirt to rise, exposing a flash of the soft skin underneath.

"Mandi, my mom is right upstairs."

"Aww, you're such a momma's boy. I'm fairly certain she suspects we're doing naughty things down here right now, so we may as well live up to her expectations." She sat up and removed her top.

"Mandi!" He sounded horrified, but as she expected, he was quickly all over her, murmuring things like 'we shouldn't be doing this,' but he certainly wasn't stopping himself. Before too many articles of clothing could be removed, he pulled back, cocked his head to listen, and started rebuttoning his pants and smoothing his shirt.

"Quick, put your bra back on," he said. "We're out of time."

Ordinarily, Amanda wasn't one for obeying orders, but the urgency in his voice and the way he looked at the stairs convinced her to comply. Good thing she did. The upstairs door flew open and a small child came pelting down yelling "Drum time!!!!"

Everett swept her up in a hug, using his body to block her view while Amanda made sure her shirt wasn't on inside out. "Pumpkin, let me introduce you to my girlfriend first."

Joy peeked around him. "Oh, that's just Mandi. She talks funny and buys chocolate buttons every Thursday."

"Hi, Joy. Thanks for keeping my favorites in stock." She couldn't help but smile at the little girl. Joy was such a charmer, parading around the crowds on the ferry with her box of candy and winsome smile. There was nothing of her father's side in her at all, besides her height. She looked like a leggy stretched-out version of her petite mother.

"No problem. Mom says I have to earn my college fund." Joy grinned widely, showing off missing teeth. "Uncle Everett, Grandma said we only have twenty minutes."

"Then we better get started. You don't mind, do you Mandi?" He gave her an apologetic look, which she waved off. She didn't know exactly what they planned to do, but she wasn't going to come in between her lovely man and his only niece.

"Of course I don't mind. She's the one who controls my access to chocolate on the ferry, I can't risk getting cut off."

The door Amanda had assumed lead to a closet turned out to open into a small soundproofed room, complete with two drum sets, one of which was sized for a child. Everett and his niece sat down and picked up their sticks.

"You think Mandi should watch?" Everett asked Joy, winking at Amanda.

"Yeah. But she should cover her ears, it's gonna get loud in here," Joy shouted gleefully, and Everett pointed Amanda towards a set of noise-canceling headphones hanging on the wall. She put them on and settled down on the floor to endure the show. Joy counted them off, and they started drumming.

Everett had drumming skills, she remembered that from her first evening at Shore Leave, but what she didn't know was that he was a talented teacher as well. He yelled out instructions, and Joy gamely kept up with him. By the end of the allotted time, they were both sweating, and, despite the headphones, Amanda felt the beginning of a headache.

🌲 🌲 🌲 🌲 🌲

"You don't mind if my brother has a drink, do you?" Everett asked when they first came back upstairs.

"I'm not an alcoholic," she reminded him in an icy voice.

"I know, but if it bothered you ..." He gave her hand a squeeze. "Never mind, obviously, it's not an issue."

Of course it wasn't. Why would she have a problem being around other people drinking? Sure, she'd love a nice cold beer. This was the perfect environment for it, sitting out on an Adirondack chair with her man on a beautiful evening. Yeah, a beer would taste great. But she didn't *need* one. The pitcher of lemonade Nessie brought out was just fine. Possibly better with vodka, but it tasted equally fine without.

"I love your yard," she told him, looking down the small rise to the view of Lake Superior. The neighborhood consisted of about twenty small houses in neat rows. Everett's was one of the older ones, a two-story with a deck overlooking the lake.

Because of the slight hillside, his basement room did have a window, but not a door leading to the outside. The yard sloped down to a flatter area, where Joy was running back and forth in some elaborate game that Amanda had yet to figure out.

"It's a pain in the ass to mow the slope," Everett said. "But yeah, it's pleasant sitting out here in the evening. We have a family of crows who live in that tree over there. I like to feed them, and they talk to me."

"You talk to animals? If this were a fantasy, they would be enchanted. One would probably be a dark-haired princess that needs you to rescue her from a curse."

"And you'd be the evil peasant girl keeping me from her?" Everett raised an eyebrow, then laughed. "If this were a horror movie, more and more crows would gather, and . . ."

"There'd be a murder?" she finished for him, giggling at her own joke.

"Murder of crows, ha ha," he said.

"Are they the inspiration for your tattoos?" She'd been meaning to ask about the crows that started at each shoulder and pecked at his chest. They were done in black, with gradient shading on the wings, clearly expensive and inked by an expert.

"One for sorrow, two for mirth," he said. "You know the old nursery rhyme?"

"I thought it was one if by land, two if by sea?"

"That's the American Revolution . . . oh, you're joking aren't you?"

She giggled. "Sug . . . I mean, Everett, of course I was joking. Now please, satisfy my curiosity. How did you come to have nursery rhyme-based tattoos?"

"I wanted something personally meaningful. Two crows are symbols of good luck and change. And that's what I needed in my life. I got the first one to express my regrets after Conner stole from us, and the second when I realized I carried too great a burden. One for sorrow, for my dad's death and my brother's betrayal. The second one was meant to change my luck, shift the trajectory of my life."

"That's fascinating. I like how you're such a deep thinker." She gently traced the feathers that peeked out from under his short sleeve. Everett was quite possibly the most sensitive man she had ever dated, and these glimpses into his rich emotional life made her feel slightly inferior. She hoped he didn't ask about the tattoo on her lower back, the one she and Nikki had chosen from an artist's portfolio on a whim as part of their eighteenth birthday celebration.

He rolled his sleeve up to his shoulder so she could see it better. "I like the way you trace them," he told her. "It's sexy."

"Then I'll continue." Her finger followed a meandering path down to the black bands encircling his arms beneath the crows. "Tell me about these. What do they symbolize?"

"Those are just for decoration. I like getting tattoos. I want a large piece on my back, but they're so expensive."

"I get it; I've been wanting another too." She'd considered getting a new one, maybe on her shoulder, but since her twin didn't want to, she never went through with it. No sense in making it easier for people to tell them apart.

"Talking about your magpies?" Duncan dropped into the chair on the other side of Amanda.

"Ignore him. He's being pedantic," Everett said.

"I'm being historically accurate," Duncan corrected. "The original rhyme was about magpies."

"Meanings evolve over time. Crows and magpies are both corvids. And the use of the rhyme in the United States has traditionally referred to crows." Everett's tone made it sound like a familiar and well-practiced argument. Amanda waited for him to finish with a 'so there,' but he was much more mature than her.

"I still prefer my wolf." Duncan rolled up his shirtsleeve to show the snarling wolf on his bicep. "But I didn't come down here to talk tattoos. Mom says it's your turn to help with the fish."

"Be nice to my girl," Everett warned. "Mandi, don't listen to anything he says about me."

"I won't." She blew him a kiss as he made his way over to assist his mother at the grill. She didn't expect Duncan to say anything to her at all. His little crows versus magpies argument comprised more words than she'd heard him speak all summer. Duncan was known to be silent and somewhat standoffish.

"Want a beer?" Duncan offered her the unopened bottle in his hand.

"No, thank you." Was he testing her? It sure would taste good, especially right now. She had thought she'd be able to handle a social event with Everett's family, but at the moment she felt very uncomfortable. A beer would help her relax, but she couldn't risk Everett seeing.

"You sure?" Duncan held it out temptingly. Then he shrugged, twisted off the lid, and took a swig. "That goes down well."

"I don't drink," she informed him, lacing her fingers together and positioning her hands firmly on her lap. She would not let herself be tempted. An alcoholic would be, but not her.

"Our dad was an alcoholic," Duncan told her conversationally. "I'm sure Ev told you about him. He was tons of fun. Always the life of the party. Sometimes, in the winter, he'd wake the four of us up in the middle of the night and take us out to Lesser Lake to play hockey."

"Oh, how fun!" She herself wouldn't enjoy the cold, but Everett and his brothers probably loved it.

"Once we tried to tell him the ice wasn't thick enough, and he wouldn't listen. He tried to make us go out on it, but we could see cracks, and we refused. He got mad, took all of our shoes, and left us there in the woods. One of his funny pranks, or that's what he claimed later. We had to hike out in our skates. Malcolm injured his ankle, so Conner gave him a piggyback ride most of the way."

"Everett never shared that story." They'd exchanged many childhood tales, but his always featured his brothers and rarely included his father. If all of his memories of his dad were like that, it made sense he'd keep them private.

"He was young. I imagine he remembers the night differently. He couldn't keep up, and I ended up carrying him. He fell asleep in my arms before we got home. He might think it was a dream."

"Did your dad do that kind of thing often?"

"It wasn't the only time he abandoned us in the woods, if that's what you're asking. But he never got physically violent with any of us. Mom put up with a lot from him, but she had her limits. She kicked him out half a dozen times, but he'd start treatment, and she'd give him another 'last' chance. But whiskey keeps you warm in the winter, and Dad liked to stay warm. Or so he justified it anyway."

Amanda mulled this over. Everett must have spent his childhood watching his father drift in and out of his life. These were things he'd never mentioned to her. No wonder he was so concerned with her potential-but-not-actual alcoholism. He probably had abandonment issues.

"Why are you telling me this?"

Duncan shrugged. "I'm just talking. Can't a man talk to his houseguests?"

"I've never heard you say a word before."

"Never needed to. But I think now I do. See that pine?" He pointed to the same tree Everett had shown her, the one housing the crow family. "When Everett was seven, Dad found a baby crow on the ground. He brought it home to show us and told us since it fell out of the nest it was going to die. You know what my brother did? He nursed that ugly thing for two months. Round the clock feedings. And every day he took it out to the tree, hoping its parents would take it back. Eventually, the crow did rejoin its family, but it had imprinted on Everett. For three years, that bird was his best friend. Every time Ev walked out of the house, here came the crow, begging for food and attention. Sometimes that ridiculous creature would ride to school on his shoulder."

"Does it still live there?" Amanda didn't know much about birds, but she thought crows had long life spans. She smiled, imagining her man as a little boy, pet crow perched on him, a Great Lakes version of a pirate's parrot.

"It disappeared about a month after dad died. Everett looked for it for years afterward. He used to sit out here in the evenings, staring at the tree, always waiting for his little buddy to come back."

"That's so sad." She pictured sweet little Everett, leaning against the trunk, watching the branches and hoping for a miracle.

"Everett was always a good kid. But he developed a bad habit of finding broken things and trying to repair them. That's what he did with the crow, and that's what he's been doing for the family since Conner robbed us. He's trying to fix everything. What's he doing with you, Amanda?"

"Excuse me? What are you implying? I'm not broken."

"Aren't you?" Duncan stared at her and slowly raised his beer to his lips and took another long sip. She closed her eyes to keep from fixating on the bottle, on that enticing drop of golden liquid dripping down Duncan's beard, on the smell of alcohol filling her nostrils.

"I'm not broken," she repeated, more firmly this time.

"Do you know how many times you get to shatter my brother's heart? Exactly one."

"I'm not planning on causing any sort of damage to his heart at all."

"Good, because if you do, there's no coming back from that."

"Everett doesn't believe in second chances?"

"*I* don't believe in second chances. Everett's my brother. I don't let people hurt my family. Believe me, Amanda. If you hurt him once, that's it for you."

"You're threatening me!" She'd never been treated like this by the family of anyone she'd dated.

"It's not a threat."

"Food's up!" Vivian called from the deck.

"Is this the part where you tell me not to tell Everett we had this discussion?"

"I don't care what you tell him." Duncan's toothy smile gleamed through his dark beard. "Let's go eat."

🌲 🌲 🌲 🌲 🌲

Everett stood smiling next to the table on the patio. "Getting along with Duncan?" he asked as he held her chair for her.

"I guess so." She felt a little shaky after the conversation. Should she tell Everett what he had said? It wasn't really a threat, since she didn't plan to hurt Everett anyway. He was her Sugar Pie; she kinda suspected she loved him.

"He must like you; he usually doesn't talk to people." Everett looked so happy that she appeared to get along with his brother that she couldn't bring herself to correct him. "Right Duncan? You don't talk?"

Duncan made his characteristic grunting sound and seated himself directly across from Amanda. Was that meant to be an intimidation tactic? If so, he picked the wrong target. She'd survived hundreds of O'Connell family events. One glowering dockworker was nothing compared to them.

"This meal looks delicious," Amanda told Vivian politely, surveying the spread. Fresh salmon, grilled potatoes, and a massive pile of marinated vegetables. Yum.

"Thanks, help yourself," Vivian passed her the first dish as they all began piling food on their plates.

After the initial clatter of passing platters around and asking for salt and whatnot, the table became strangely silent. Amanda could hear people chewing, but none of them made any attempts at conversation. What was wrong? Was this because of her presence?

She finally couldn't take it anymore. "Are y'all always this quiet?" she burst out.

"Quiet?" Everett repeated. "We're eating. It's rude to talk with your mouth full."

"Oh. Sorry. I guess I come from a much louder family, where nobody knows how to shut up." Full mouths never stopped an O'Connell, though perhaps it was sheer numbers that also contributed to the loudness of her family affairs. Growing up in a household of nine extroverted people spanning four generations skewed her perceptions of what family should be and how they should comport themselves.

"I've met them," Vivian said. "I was at Cara's wedding, though I don't think you and I spoke at all. I saw you and your twin, along with your brothers." Did Amanda detect a hint of disapproval in her voice? Probably. Duncan had just described their father as a loud happy drunk; the O'Connell siblings tended to be the same way.

"And you still allow me to date your son?" Amanda asked. She'd gotten a little drunk at the wedding. Okay, a lot drunk. But the rest of them did too. Amy was healing from a miscarriage at the time, and desperately needed her family's love and support, and that was always accompanied by alcohol. It was the O'Connell way.

"He's a grown man, he makes his own decisions." Vivian's words did not convey support for the relationship. Well, it didn't matter. Amanda was good at winning people over. She'd be able to sway Vivian into a more favorable opinion.

🌲 🌲 🌲 🌲 🌲

After dinner and Amanda's homemade dessert—the name of which she managed to use a dozen times, as Everett's face grew increasingly redder—they moved to chairs surrounding a firepit. Duncan built up a fire. Joy got out sticks for marshmallows, and the brothers disappeared into the house. When they returned, Everett carried a blanket, bongo drums, and a guitar. Duncan also held a guitar, and a violin case, which he handed to his mother. They sat next to each other, heads together, and began to tune them.

Everett brought the blanket to Amanda. "You looked cold," he said, gently draping it over her shoulders.

"Thank you. Am I about to get a concert?"

"Maybe." He set the bongos on the ground beside Joy and admonished her to wipe the sticky marshmallow off her fingers before he joined Vivian and Duncan's tuning session.

"Do you play any instruments?" Nessie leaned over and asked.

"I took piano as a child, but no, I lack all skills when it comes to music."

"Me too. But luckily Joy took after her father, in this one respect."

"I didn't know Everett played guitar."

"He prefers drums, but he's multi-talented. You know he's in a band, right?"

"I saw them perform my first night in Ferry's Landing and knew I needed to get my hands on that drummer," Amanda said, avoiding the fact that she'd hit on him rather drunkenly.

"I'd heard something about that night," Nessie replied, leaving Amanda to wonder exactly what she meant. Rumors about her drunken escapades? Specifically, her *absolute last final* drunken escapades? She'd been stone-cold sober since then.

"Joy, you ready?" Those were the first words that came out of Duncan's mouth since his pre-dinner chat with Amanda.

Joy scampered over to sit cross-legged at Everett's feet, and after some quick instructions, fed them the beat. Amanda wrapped the soft fleece blanket more closely around herself and closed her eyes to listen. They strummed quietly, perhaps in deference to their neighbors, but she was sure nobody would have minded. A deep bass voice started singing, and she opened her eyes in surprise—but it turned out to be Duncan. Then Everett joined, a rich tenor. Not what she'd expected, given his speaking voice, but they sang beautifully together.

You are my everything, but I am your nothing . . .
I would give anything to make you feel something . . .

"Wait! Oh my god! I remember that song," she whispered to Nessie, not wanting to interrupt the performance, but needing to verify what she thought she heard. "Is it *One Thing* by the Last Barons of Sound? Are they seriously singing old boy-band pop?"

Nessie laughed. "Not what you'd expect, eh? It's the Ryan family's embarrassing secret. I'm surprised they let you hear it so early in your relationship. When they get together they jam out with acoustic versions of cheesy old pop songs. My ex used to pretend to be cooler than the rest of them and acted like he only played along because Vivian picked the music, but I caught him watching the videos and practicing the dances. Everett, too. You should ask him to show you his moves later."

"They can dance?" Amanda thought about the photographs inside of teenage Everett with his brothers and tried to imagine those big serious boys lined up and dancing. She couldn't picture it at all, just like she couldn't reconcile what she was seeing now, dour Duncan smiling and singing, Everett trying to hit falsetto notes, Vivian playing violin with her weather-worn hands.

"You haven't noticed? My experiences with Conner showed me that their talents translate well horizontally."

"Oh my, I didn't realize that's where it came from," Amanda feigned fanning herself. Nessie was right. The way Everett moved his hips sometimes, the smoothness with which he controlled their mutual pleasures ... yeah, he could definitely dance. She should have guessed he played the guitar too, with his fingering skills ... oh the things that man could do.

Everett saw her watching and winked. She smiled back, and when the song ended, she stood and clapped. "That was amazing! Did y'all write that?"

The brothers revealed a clear familial resemblance as they both tipped their heads at the exact same angle and cast their eyes to the side before making matching winces.

"I think we heard it on the radio," Everett said, and Duncan gave one of his communicative grunts. Beside her, Nessie turned an amused snort into a cough.

"Play another, boys. Ev, your girlfriend seems to like your music."

They did launch into another, and she recognized another Last Baron's cover.

"You weren't kidding, were you?" Amanda exchanged another look with Nessie, who stifled a giggle and shook her head. This live version was good, a different, slower acoustic interpretation of rather awful dance pop. When they finished, Amanda applauded louder.

"Y'all are fantastic. It's strange, but this is reminding me of the very first concert I ever attended. For mine and Nikki's twelfth birthday, Amy took us to see the Last Barons of Sound in El Paso. I don't know why, but somehow I was just thinking of that. Don't worry, you're nothing like those boys, up on stage wiggling about. Funny how music makes us go places in our minds, isn't it?"

"Yeah, funny," Everett mumbled. But his seeming embarrassment was short-lived. They started playing yet another cheesy pop song, and Amanda sat back and watched with a smile on her face and lightness in her heart. This was better than any night of drinking.

Chapter Twenty-Six

After reading yet another decidedly naughty novel to a roomful of geriatrics—many of whom kept interrupting to ask her to repeat some of the most salacious passages—Amanda took a break. She planned to read from a mystery next, but the schedule gave her forty-five minutes to rest her voice. Not that she needed resting. Sometimes, it seemed she'd trained her whole life for a job like this.

But she took advantage of the break and wheeled her favorite resident outside to the grassy lawn overlooking Lake Superior.

"Have you ever noticed how all these sorts of places have golden in the name?" Rose asked her, gesturing back toward the building that housed the Golden Shores Retirement Home. "My son came up from Duluth this weekend, and he brought brochures from Golden Acres and Golden Years Village. He wants me to move down there."

"I used to volunteer at one called Golden Ranch," Amanda said. "But I've seen just as many with Silver or Peaceful in the name."

"That's what they want, peace. They want us to go quietly. Nice little place to shut us away. The only reason my son thinks I should move is to make him feel less guilty. He hates making the drive all the way up here."

"Maybe he'd visit more often if you lived closer." Personally, Amanda couldn't understand why anyone would dump their elderly relatives off in a home. Her great-grandmother had lived with her family for Amanda's entire life. Her grandmother too. Multi-generational living was common in other cultures; it was a shame more people didn't practice it here.

"No, he'd visit the same amount, it would just save him mileage on his precious car," Rose said. "Speaking of my son, I told him all about you."

"What on Earth would you tell him about me?" Amanda asked, hoping it wasn't in a fix-you-up kind of way. Not only was Rose's son way too old for her, she was happily taken.

"I said that there is a lovely young girl who comes every week to read smut to us old fogeys. He did not approve. But he did remind me of something. Your man is one of the Ryan brothers, right?"

"My man sure is." She loved talking about him possessively. *My man, he is my man. All mine. For as long as he can handle me.*

"I knew his father, Sterling Ryan. He played hockey with my boy for years. Almost won the state championship."

"Really? Was it a close game?" She was ready to press for details to take back to Everett. After hearing Duncan's stories, it might be a comfort to him to learn that others remembered his father with kindness.

"Not by a long shot. Sterling was their star player. He was a demon on the ice, when he was sober. But he showed up drunk as a skunk, threw up in the rink, and got red-carded. The team spent the whole game down a man. It was an embarrassment for the entire town."

"You know, if this were a dramatic family saga, this would be the point where you reveal to me the hidden secret that you were Sterling's real mother." Amanda smiled at the fantasy.

"And then you marry Everett and I'm your new grandmother? I assume it turns out that I'm quite wealthy and I die soon after your wedding, leaving my vast estate to the two of you."

"And your other son sues us, and later hires the mafia to kill us and get his money back."

"You started that as a legal thriller, but I think you're conflating your genres there," Rose said. "Anyway, I assure you, I only had the one child. And I'm not wealthy at all, though I do have a bracelet I want to give you. It's got camphor glass, it'll match your necklace. My daughter-in-law doesn't appreciate that kind of thing."

"You're so sweet. I will wear it with pride." Amanda gave the older woman a gentle hug. Rose reminded her so much of Gran it made her heart hurt.

"You're a good girl, Mandi. Not many people would do what you do."

"Volunteering?"

"No, treating us like human beings. Do you know most of the volunteers that come through here want to do crafts? And I don't mean interesting ones either. They want us to glue together popsicle sticks and puffballs like preschoolers. I'm tired of being talked at and told what to do by people who think we all have the mental status of a six-year-old."

"I can have a chat with the other volunteers," Amanda offered. But she really shouldn't. She was already on thin ice here. Just last week the director had pulled her aside and told her she needed to do her readings in a less dramatic manner because it was getting the residents 'all hot and bothered.' Specifically, "we don't need pornography," were the words she'd used.

"No, don't. Don't rock the boat, or we'll lose you," Rose patted Amanda's arm with one frail hand. "If you must do something for us, contact erotica publishers and inform them that large-print editions would sell like hotcakes."

"I'll make a couple of calls." Amanda checked her watch. Almost time to return to her reading. Too bad, she enjoyed being out here. The cool breezes were starting to grow on her.

"You aren't taking me anywhere until you tell me how your dinner went. Isn't that the real reason you brought me out here? To tell me how my sugar pie recipe went over?"

Amanda giggled. "It tasted delicious, and Everett's face turned red every time I said the name. So I'd call it a success."

"And the dinner?"

"I don't know, it was weird. I couldn't tell if his mother liked me or not. And the meal was eerily quiet. I'm used to my family, where you can't get a word in edgewise and every conversation is a battle." She loved her family, truly she did, but every gathering was stressful, requiring days of prep and another day to recover. The O'Connells always had to be on their toes, ready for anything. Mental alertness was key. If anyone spotted weakness, they pounced. It was one of the things her sister-in-law Mel always complained about. *I just can't with you people,* she'd say, before giving up and going into the kitchen or backyard or anywhere to get away from the bickering siblings constantly needling each other.

"I'm sure Vivian loved you. She must appreciate a strong woman coming in and taking one of her boys off her hands."

"I'm not taking him anywhere." That was the problem, right there. What was going to happen when summer ended? Amanda was certainly not going to stay in Minnesota for a winter. That would be absolutely insane. Who would ever want to do that? And Everett, with his family loyalty and concern about the ferry business, how would she ever convince him to leave? Maybe they could try long distance, but she didn't like letting days pass without touching him, how could she go weeks or months?

"Aren't you tucking him in your suitcase and hauling him off to Texas when you've served your time here?" Rose's voice turned sharp. "Amanda Jean, didn't you tell me you thought he might be the love of your life? You aren't going to leave him here, are you?"

"We haven't talked about it yet." They needed to, soon. But she dreaded that conversation. She dreaded the moment Everett told her he didn't love her enough to go with her, and the moment she told him she couldn't make herself stay.

"If this were a love story, it would all work out in the end," Rose smiled knowingly. "I'm sure that's what you've got."

"We'll see, won't we?" Amanda responded, forcing her voice to sound cheerfully optimistic. "I'd better take you back inside before there's a riot. The next book isn't going to read itself."

Chapter Twenty-Seven

"What'd you think?" Everett finally asked his brother. It had been a couple of days since Amanda's visit, and Duncan still hadn't said a word about it. He'd never mentioned Amanda at all, nor had he ever asked about any of the women Everett dated.

"About what?" Duncan grunted. Most people misinterpreted his general lack of conversation as a sign that he wasn't very bright, but nothing could be further from the truth. Duncan was the smartest of the Ryan brothers. Not smart enough to predict what Conner would do, but at least smart enough that Conner didn't try the same trick on him that he pulled on Everett and Malcolm. That's why they only lost sixty percent of the value of the ferry rather than eighty. *Mom said sign here* would never have worked on Duncan.

"About Amanda, obviously. Dinner the other night. At our house. Remember?"

Duncan glared from beneath his heavy brows. "She's loud."

"She does talk more than we're used to."

"Not what I meant. Did you forget my bedroom is right above yours? Next time she visits, stay in your drum booth."

"Crap. I thought you were in your office working." If he had known, he would have taken her to his soundproofed room. No need to make his brother listen to that, especially since Duncan had been single for years.

"That's what I ended up doing when I got tired of listening to the many ways she has of calling your name. It's fine. I finished another chapter." Duncan was writing his second book. His first, about shipwrecks of the Great Lakes in the 1800s, was sold locally and had achieved minor success among the tourists, and he was following it up with another about more recent maritime disasters.

"Sorry," Everett apologized. "But other than her volume?"

"Fine."

"Fine? That's it?" He couldn't help but keep prodding. He just wanted to hear an honest opinion. Though perhaps he was better off seeking Nessie's impressions instead.

"Pretty, I guess. Kind of annoying."

"She's different, right? Different from most of the women out here?"

"She's definitely different. What is she to you?"

"Besides being my girlfriend?"

"Is that what she is? Or is she a symbol?"

"Of what?"

"I don't know. Freedom? Escape? Are you in love with her, or in love with what she represents to you?"

"I don't know what you mean."

"Yes, you do. She doesn't belong here, and you desperately want to leave."

"Since I can't leave, that doesn't matter. But that's not what I love about her. She's funny, and interesting, and comes across as confident and strong, but I can see this vulnerability inside her that makes me want to protect her." It came out sometimes, when they were talking about their pasts or their families, or even how she felt about her current living situation. She'd get this look in her eyes that made him want to wrap his arms around her and promise to take care of her.

Duncan snorted. "She's another one of your injured crows. Only I think you'll be a lot more heartbroken when this one takes off."

"You're being really unfair," Everett started to argue, but Duncan dropped the last crate on his dolly and started pushing it toward the ferry. Apparently, this conversation was over, and

Everett already regretted it. Duncan may be a man of few words, but he knew how to use them to cut right to the heart of things.

Chapter Twenty-Eight

"Are you sure you want to come with me?" Everett paused with his hand on the doorknob.

Truthfully, she wasn't sure. She hated walking into social situations without a little bit of mental lubrication, and she was having a difficult time thinking of anything besides how much easier this would be if she could have a drink first. Her comfort level with her boyfriend did not extend to his band. But she smiled anyway and patted his arm.

"Sugar Pie, you know I do. I even baked cookies." She reached into her enormous tote bag and pulled out a Tupperware container. She'd been carrying the thing around all day, fighting the temptation to sneak a few. It wouldn't do to show up with a box of crumbs.

"You aren't showing up with my eponymous dessert this time?"

"I think I made my point with that already. No, I made cookies because my Gran always said if you want to win your man's friends over, supply them with fresh-baked goodies. I make a helluva good Texas cowboy cookie, thanks to her. Almost made me homeless today though, when Sam saw what I was doing in his kitchen." The horror on Sam's face when he returned from the gym to find her using his oven unsupervised was priceless.

"If he kicks you out, you're welcome to stay in my basement." Everett's offer was kind, but it was never going to happen. Not that she particularly enjoyed her current housing arrangements, but she couldn't handle the stress of moving in with her boyfriend's family. Everett on his own, that would make for a lovely situation though. She could imagine renting an apartment with him somewhere, a place with a king bed and a kitchen she was allowed to use without someone standing over her shoulder offering 'helpful' suggestions.

"Ugh. Call me a snob all you want, but a drafty underground hole is not my idea of satisfactory living quarters."

"I would never call you a snob for that," he assured her. "Besides, anyone willing to spend nights in my little ferry office can't be too stuck up."

"Your office is cozy. I look forward to going there tonight. But I'm even more excited about meeting your friends and watching you play. Should I clap and scream like a true fan?"

"No, you should sit quietly, hands in your lap, and don't say a word. Also, no requests." They'd had this conversation earlier—he'd made sure to extract a promise to keep some of his musical tastes a secret.

"But there are some pop songs I'm dying to hear," she teased. "Mandi . . ."

"Sugar Pie, I will keep my requests to myself during band practice, but I expect a private concert later." She would never out him as a cheesy pop music aficionado to his friends, especially when his friends were part of a band that played 90s grunge covers. He'd lose all street cred.

"It's a deal." Everett opened the door to Colton's house and led her through to the bass player's soundproofed garage.

"Guys, this is Amanda," he announced to the men already gathered there. "There's Colton on bass, Jesse on lead guitar, and Lucas sings."

"It is so nice to finally meet y'all. I hope everybody likes cookies." Amanda made a quick survey of their faces. Colton blatantly stared at her chest, Jesse appeared indifferent, and Lucas immediately fixated on the container in her hands.

"And now we know why Everett sprints out of here after practice," Lucas said, grabbing a handful of cookies and taking a big bite of three at once.

"How'd you two meet?" Colton asked, eyes still where they didn't belong. Amanda struggled to pretend she didn't notice. Nikki's voice gave her a pep talk: *Have courage, you're here with Everett. He's got your back. You can do this.*

"I came to one of your shows. I saw y'all playing at Shore Leave and thought to myself 'oh, I'm gonna bag me a drummer' and I did." Amanda tossed her hair and smiled with a false confidence. "I always get what I want."

Before they could start playing, the door leading from the house to the garage opened again and a woman entered. From the way Everett stiffened, Amanda knew that this must be the ex-girlfriend he'd warned her about. He said he checked with Colton to make sure she wouldn't be here, but plans must have changed.

"Hello, Everett. I see you brought a rebound." The woman walked right up to them, ignoring her new boyfriend. Amanda studied her. She was a brunette with a smattering of freckles. Not pretty, though Amanda did look through biased eyes.

"Well aren't you adorable?" Amanda replied. She nudged Everett with her elbow. "Sugar Pie, aren't you going to introduce me?"

Everett swallowed audibly. She felt tension emanating from him. "Amanda, this is Aubry."

"Lovely to meet you, Audrey." Amanda extended her hand, palm down, fingers curled under as though she expected it to be kissed.

"Aubry," the ex corrected. "With a B."

"Oh! Bless your heart, you Midwesterners come up with such interesting names. Like I said, it's lovely to meet you, Baudrey. Shall we sit and enjoy the show?"

"Is this some kind of joke, Ev?" Aubry asked, her mouth set in a disgusted frown. Amanda could swear the air temperature dropped by about twenty degrees. "Why would you invite her here? Are you trying to make me jealous? You know I'm dating Colton now."

"My goodness, did you and Everett used to have a little thing going?" Amanda asked as if just realizing it. "Sugar Pie, you should have said something! I'm terribly sorry I didn't know about you, Baudrey, but then again, Everett and I have only discussed our significant exes. May I say congratulations on your relationship with Colton? He's such a cutie, and he plays a mean bass." Minor exaggeration—Colton was a husky guy, with one of those asymmetrical faces that only looked attractive in certain lights, and garage fluorescents were not one of them.

"Damn, I like her. You can bring her back to my place anytime," Colton stage whispered to Everett, and was rewarded by a fierce glare from Aubry.

"Yeah, if she's got more of these cookies, she's always welcome," Lucas said with a wink at Amanda. "You guys want to get started before I finish them off?" The men took their places at their instruments, and Amanda took a seat on the couch across from them. She thought she felt a draft coming from under the garage door . . . or perhaps that emanated from Aubry.

"You know it's not going to last long, right?" Aubry said in a snide voice.

"This practice?" Amanda widened her eyes. "Everett said two hours. Now, if you'll excuse me, my man is on drums, and I need to pay attention. I don't want to miss one second of the show."

Two long hours of repeated verbal jabs later, practice ended, and Amanda sauntered over to Everett, aware of the eyes on her. He was mopping his face with a sweat towel and when he was done, she delivered a swift kiss to his lips. "Mmm, I like it when you're sweaty. We better get you out of here and clean you up, so I can get you dirty again."

"Do you want to stick around, have a couple of beers? Or pop for you Ev?" Colton invited. He sounded like he was talking to

Everett, but the question was asked directly to Amanda's boobs. What a sleaze, doing that in front of his girlfriend. From the expression on her face, Aubry didn't like it much either. Colton was in for a bad night.

"Aww, you're sweet, but I've got to get my man home and out of these clothes." Amanda fluttered her eyelashes flirtatiously as she spoke, a move carefully designed to enrage Aubry. "Maybe next time."

"Yeah, next time." Everett was a smart man; he could probably sense the animosity brewing. "We should take off now."

When they left, Everett directed her away from the road. "There's a different way we can go, if you think you can handle it in those shoes."

"I've been wearing high heels since I was fifteen. I could run a marathon in these." One thing coming into her full five-foot-ten inches of height in the ninth grade had taught her: own it. *You can't change your height, but you can change how you feel about it. Be proud*, Gran had told her and Nikki. Gran was right. Nothing provided the illusion of confidence more than towering over people, especially men. They got flustered in her presence. Except for Everett, of course. In her heels, she could look him right in the eyes, and he was definitely not intimidated.

"I doubt that, but when you do decide to run a marathon, let me know. I'll be waiting at the finish line with a first-aid kit to repair your feet. Seriously though, you'll need to be careful; the steps can be slippery."

He took her a few blocks away to a stone staircase leading down to Lake Superior. They were steep, but she managed the descent without stumbling. She did hold tightly to Everett's arm though, just in case.

"My goodness, it is beautiful down here," she told him when they reached the rocky beach. "And so private." The shoreline held a dark sort of beauty, with all the inky gray stones scattered to the edge of the grayish blue waters. The sun had already set, but the sky still glowed purple, and the stars glittered brightly.

"Most people go to the public beach a little farther north. This stretch is used as a shortcut for getting to the docks." And as a place to dump litter, apparently. Amanda made a mental note to bring a trash bag to band practice next week so they could clean up some of the garbage on their way to his office.

"Does it count as a beach if there isn't white sand?" she asked teasingly.

"If it's alongside a body of water, it counts. And since I've never seen a sandy beach, for all I know, this is the only kind there is."

"I could take you to one someday. Imagine laying out in the hot sun, surrounded by sand. We could sip mocktails brought to us by cabana boys and stare out over the waves. And then a monster arises from the deep . . ."

"Mishipeshu."

"Bless you."

He laughed. "That's our local monster. Mishipeshu. It's an underwater panther that sinks ships. What do you think took down the *Edmund Fitzgerald?*"

"My guess would have been a storm, but I learn something new every day. Do you see that ship all lit up out there? Should we call out a warning? Watch out for the misha . . . what?"

"Mishipeshu. And that's the *Alder,* a Coast Guard cutter from Duluth. They're armed, I'm sure they can take care of themselves. I wonder where they're going?" His voice took on a wistful tone, as it always did when he mentioned the Coast Guard. She wrapped both her arms around him, giving him a hug.

"I don't care that much about what people are doing out there. I'm more interested in what's right here in front of me, protecting me from vile lake creatures." His shirt was still damp from drumming, but she didn't mind. His body heat radiated through and kept her warm.

"I'll always protect you." He pressed his lips against hers and kissed her deeply.

When they broke apart, she giggled. "If this were a romance novel, I've found our cover image."

"What, us kissing by the lake?"

"Yep. Except you'd be shirtless, and, since I'm Texan, I'd be wearing tiny little denim shorts that don't cover my ass, and a crop top. Also a cowboy hat, to really drive the point home."

"And if this were a romance novel, would this be the moment I tell you I love you?"

Her heart nearly stopped. Had he actually said that? He ... loved her? Nobody had ever loved her, other than her family, and they had a genetic obligation.

"Shush, Sugar Pie. You don't want to tell me you love me in a romance novel."

"Why not?"

"Because they say it at the end of the book. That's when they have their happily ever after and we're left to imagine their futures. I want you to tell me in real life, so we can go on and have more of our story left."

"Mandi, this is real life. And I do love you, so much." He stared into her eyes and she felt the power of his emotion coursing all throughout her body. He did, he loved her. He saw her for who she was, and somehow still loved her. If she were the fainting type, this would be a good time to do it. But, given the rocks on the ground, it was a good thing she wasn't.

She took a deep breath. "This is not something I've ever wanted to say to anyone before, but in real life, Everett Ryan, I love you too."

Chapter Twenty-Nine

For once, life—even without Nikki in it—was perfect. She had a job, she had a man, she was on top of her bills, and she didn't miss drinking. Well, not much. Sure, she missed the fun of going out to bars, but staying in on the nights she had Everett was way better, and on the nights she didn't, running turned out to be an acceptable substitute. She could make it around the entire loop of the island without stopping now.

"You look chipper today," Tyrell said as she joined him behind the reception desk.

"Are you saying I normally don't?" she replied teasingly. "I'm in a good mood."

"Being in love suits you." Ty gave her one of his slow grins. She'd found through working with him that he had several different kinds of smiles. There was the *don't worry, I'm not scary* one he used with some of their elderly guests. Then there was the *I'm listening, but you're still an asshole* one that stayed fixed on his face when dealing with aggressive or demanding guests. And then he had a private one, a slow and sly quirking of the lips combined with a twinkle in his eyes. That was the one he used when talking about his husband, and that's the one he was using now. He was thinking about being in love, just as she was.

"It does, it suits me fine."

"What are you going to do in six weeks?" he asked, and her happiness evaporated.

"I thought it was seven." When she'd first moved here, she'd put a countdown on her calendar. Two actually. One to the end of summer, and the other to the end of probation, when she'd be able to call her sister and give her a piece of her mind. *How dare you choose a man over me*, she had planned to say, maybe even in person. She pictured herself showing up at Nikki's work and making a huge dramatic scene.

But plans change. Being with Everett, being loved by Everett, had made her understand her twin's point of view for the first time. They couldn't spend their lives permanently entwined, not when there was someone else out there. Someone they loved, someone they couldn't live without. Nikki would be her sister no matter what, but they had to grow up sometime. And if that meant growing apart, perhaps it was for the best.

Tyrell shrugged. "Six, seven, whatever. I'm not the one counting. Everyone is wondering what you're going to do though."

"Who's everyone? Tyrell Diggins, have you been out chitchatting about me?"

"You know. Everyone. Tim, Duncan, the people who hang out at the bar, my knitting circle . . . hold on, let me get this." He interrupted his list to answer the phone. "Sorry, I have to take this in the staff office." He transferred the call and left her to handle the desk by herself.

She stared after him. It wasn't the gossiping that surprised her, that was part and parcel of living in a small town. When he finally came back, she ambushed him.

"Knitting circle? Seriously?"

"Just a minute, I need to open my email. Amy said she sent me something," he responded, brushing past her to reach the computer.

"Amy? My sister, Amy?" She felt her voice rising in a shriek and tried to modulate it. "Why were you talking to my sister?"

"She called to check on you. And to tell me about Violetta. She's getting her first tooth. She apparently sent another set of pictures, and now I have to look at them and pretend I can see the tooth popping up."

Amanda couldn't believe it. Her family had cut her off entirely. None of them returned her calls. Not that she had tried calling much. Or at all, if she was going to be honest. The first week she'd been here, she'd left an angry message on Kenny's voicemail, but that was her only one. They all acted like they were mad at her anyway, so why bother? But they were checking up on her? Or one of them was?

"Tyrell, how long has this been going on?"

"I don't know, a couple of days, maybe. Believe me, I'd rather hear about what's going on in that baby's mouth than what's going on in her diaper. New moms go into way too much detail."

"Not the tooth, the phone calls."

"Amy and I have been friends for a few years. When I first started here, we shared this shift."

"Are you being deliberately obtuse?"

Ty ducked his head. "Sorry. I forgot I wasn't supposed to tell you I was talking to her until it already came out of my mouth. She calls every week, usually when you're on your dinner break."

"I had no idea. Do the others call?"

"That's up to Cara to tell you."

That sounded like a yes. Warmth suffused her. She wasn't alone. Well, she wasn't anyway, but this meant she still had her family. Someday she'd like to introduce them to Everett. And since she was thinking of Everett . . .

"What were you saying about sitting around and knitting and gossiping about me and my man?"

"I wouldn't call it gossip. It's more speculation. And I guess it's not all the knitters, mostly just me and Nessie."

"You really do knit?"

"Why would I make that up? It's a great stress release. It's like meditation, but when you're finished you get a sweater."

"I just never thought of men knitting, that's all."

"Don't stereotype me. Your boyfriend knits too, you know."

"He does not!"

Tyrell smirked. "Ask him yourself."

"Don't think I won't."

The phone interrupted them again, and this time Amanda grabbed it, in case it was Amy or another O'Connell, but the caller was better than that.

"You have the sexiest phone greeting I've ever heard," Everett's voice said in her ear when she finished the usual *thank you for calling* spiel.

"Which part?"

"This is Amanda, how can I help you. That part."

"Then I'll be sure to say it again later, Sugar Pie." She shot Tyrell a glare when he guffawed. He called his massive bear of a husband 'baby', so what gave him the right to judge her choice of endearments?

"Speaking of later, you're off Thursday evening, right?"

"I am. Does your question mean you might actually have the evening off as well? Dare I say it, are you about to invite me on a proper date?"

"I'd prefer an improper one." Everett sure was in a flirtatious mood. "Listen, I have to make a delivery in Duluth. Duncan usually does it, but I offered. I thought if you wanted to come along for the ride, I could take you out to a restaurant, you pick the cuisine, and we would come back the next morning."

"Asking a lady to spend the night? Improper date indeed, Everett Ryan. What time shall I meet you at the ferry?"

"We can head out after your meeting in Ferry's Landing, if that works."

"I will say yes under one condition. You need to tell me if my coworker"—she winked at Tyrell—"is a gosh darn liar. He's told me things about you that I just don't believe."

"I'm not sure where you're going with this," Everett said, with a cautious note in his voice.

"Tell me, Sugar Pie. What are the chances you could knit me up a sweater?"

Everett laughed loudly. "About zero." But before she had the chance to accuse Tyrell of making up silly stories, he continued. "I only knit socks."

"You do? How is that possible?" She couldn't picture him doing a craft that she—perhaps unfairly—considered the province of women.

"Because one year for Christmas I asked Nessie for some socks, and she gifted me needles, wool, and a card saying your feet are too damn big, make them yourself. It's a perfect hobby during the winter here. Beats the hell out of ice fishing. Maybe I'll teach you."

"Maybe you will," she said. If they could maintain their relationship. Winters here would mean huddling indoors and freezing, suffering through midafternoon sunsets and long dark nights. Even with Everett's warm body in her bed, she wasn't sure she'd be able to tolerate it. As much as she wanted to keep him, they needed to find a home they both could agree on.

Chapter Thirty

Amanda was familiar with the drive to Duluth, though the last time she'd traveled it, her bitter mood left her too miserable to appreciate the scenery. The highway followed along the edge of Lake Superior, through a few small towns and two terrifying but short tunnels.

"Problem?" Everett asked after they passed through the first tunnel and he noticed how tightly she was squeezing her hands together in her lap.

"I don't like caves or tunnels. All that weight of rock above my head, ready to collapse at any moment terrifies me."

"There's another one coming up in a couple of miles," he warned her.

"Sugar Pie, I am closing my eyes now. You tell me when we're through, but don't tell me when we're in it, you understand?"

He did, he more than understood. As soon as she shut her eyes, he turned off the radio and started singing. She sank back into the seat and allowed his voice to carry her away. This man got her, he understood her on such a deep level. He didn't make fun of her like her brothers always did, he didn't scream in mock terror the way Amy would have, no, instead he created a soothing environment to let her relax.

When he reached the end of his song, he finished with a flourish and told her they were long past the tunnel.

"You are my hero." She meant it in all sincerity, and she appreciated the way he stretched over to briefly place his hand on her knee. There was more love in that touch than she'd ever experienced with any man. She had to come up with a way to keep him.

🌲 🌲 🌲 🌲 🌲

The dinner she insisted on in Duluth was Mexican, the cuisine she missed most that Sam couldn't replicate. Well, he probably could, but he was so focused on honoring local ingredients that no matter how many times she suggested tacos, he never took her up on it. Had he never heard of fish tacos? Or did he just not want to satisfy her cravings? This northern version was nothing compared to the real thing back home in Texas, but the view overlooking the lake made up for it. If only she could have ordered a margarita, it would have been a perfect evening.

After polishing off her share of dessert churros, she patted her full belly and sighed happily. "Shall we check into our hotel now?"

"I . . . oops." Everett looked down at his plate, and she got a very bad feeling about this. She'd been looking forward to a king-sized bed. She even brought along some rather scandalous lingerie to drive him wild with.

"Oh, Sugar Pie, did you forget to make reservations? That's no problem. I've got my phone, I'll find us a place."

"We don't need hotel reservations. I'm sorry, I thought I told you. We're camping."

"I believe you failed to mention that part of the plan." Lingerie was out now. No point in exposing that much flesh to the mosquitos.

"Sorry. You hate it, don't you? I thought it would be romantic, sleeping under the stars. I should have asked first."

In truth, Amanda didn't mind, not at all. With five kids in the family, camping was the most common vacation. Sure, her childhood was also full of exciting trips to Europe and the Caribbean, but those were an every other year splurge.

"Sugar Pie," she told him, reaching across the table to take his hands. "I would go anywhere and sleep anywhere with you. Take me camping, and I'll try and make you see stars."

🌲 🌲 🌲 🌲 🌲

Camping didn't turn out to be what quite what Amanda expected. For one thing, there was no actual campsite. Everett drove them into a deeply forested area, where he turned off the little dirt road into a tiny pullout. "Here we are," he announced.

"We are?"

"Yep. Don't worry, this is private land, and we have permission. One of mom's friends owns it. And I've got a hunting rifle."

"You brought a gun on our date?"

"Is that a problem? You're from Texas, I assumed it was standard."

"There you go making assumptions again. To be honest, I'm not all that comfortable around guns. When I was in high school, my graduating class lost a couple of people to them." One was a suicide and the other involved two idiots who forgot the most important rule of gun ownership: every weapon is always loaded. She remembered attending the funerals with her sister, staring at the closed caskets, more angry than sad, because it all seemed so very pointless and tragic.

"It's just a hunting rifle; it is loaded, but I only brought it on the off chance we're approached by an animal that might eat us. I'm not going to play with it. The safety is on, and my father trained me well. He was big on safety. Well, gun safety at least." The unspoken words hung quietly in the space between them: *not boat safety*. He joked about it sometimes, but whenever he mentioned his father's death, she spotted a flash of pain behind his eyes.

"As long as you keep it away from me," she said. She still didn't like it, but she trusted Everett to be responsible.

"I'll keep it on my side, I promise. Alright, get out of the truck."

"Now you're kicking me out? Crap! I know what genre this is. Boy drives girl out to remote location, expels her from the vehicle, draws a gun. You're going give me a head start and then hunt me, and I—because clearly I'm the heroine of my own story—am somehow going to defeat you, take the weapon away, and later go on to be the main character in a trilogy, during which my outfits get smaller and smaller and my sexual escapades become ever more graphic."

"You've really thought this through, haven't you? I just meant get out so we can set up camp."

"I should warn you first, it's been a few years since I've pitched a tent. I'm sure I remember how though."

"Tent?"

"Sugar Pie, tell me there's a tent." She gestured toward the windshield. "There are approximately ten thousand dead bugs that we killed on the way here, and at least seven million more of them outside of this vehicle. You had better have a tent."

That sheepish expression appeared again. "Well, not quite. I have a bedroll for the back of the truck and a mosquito net contraption that my brother and I built out of PVC. It encloses us entirely, but still lets us see the night sky. I've been following the weather forecast; it's not supposed to rain tonight."

"Everett Ryan! We need to discuss the importance of providing details when you come up with plans! This all would have been helpful information when I packed my overnight bag."

"I'm sorry. Would you rather go back to Duluth and rent a hotel room?"

"You think I can't handle sleeping outdoors? Is this because you think I'm too prissy? That's the word you use, isn't it?" Truthfully, she'd much prefer to head straight back to the city, spend the night in a giant bed, and take a long hot shower with her man in the morning. But she never backed down from a challenge, and damned if she'd let him pigeonhole her like that.

"No it's because . . . now you're putting me on the spot."

But she really wanted to know, so she pressed him for a response. "Please, Everett, don't make me beg. Tell me why you keep saying such things."

"I never said you were prissy. It's because you're pretty and rich and I think you're used to more than what I can provide."

She laughed at the utter absurdity of that statement. "Rich? Oh, Everett, you must be joking!"

"I've seen your clothes and purses and hair."

"First of all, my hair is completely natural, which you should know by now. Carpet, meet drapes and all that. Secondly, my clothes and purses? I raid consignment stores for clothing, and I take good care of what I find. And my purses are all knock-offs. A couple of years ago my mom and sisters and I went shopping for Amy's wedding dress in New York City, and I bought five of them for two hundred bucks out of some guy's trunk. Counterfeit, but pass for real. I do appreciate all the attention you pay to my appearance though, assumptions notwithstanding."

"Sorry. You just seem, I don't know, so different from most of the women around here."

"My overall style is carefully cultivated; I won't lie about that. But haven't you realized by now that I'm not some high maintenance princess? I sleep with you in an uncomfortably small twin bed behind an office without complaint, because as long as I'm with you—on top or under, I don't care which—I'm happy."

To prove her point, she slid across the seat and gave him a great big kiss, and a little bit of a grope, until he pushed her hand away.

"Alright, I'm going to set everything up. Why don't you wait in here to avoid the mosquitos? I'll let you know when it's safe to come out." As he bustled around outside, occasionally swearing and slapping at his neck, she decided she had best prepare for the night as well.

Changing into lingerie while in the passenger seat of a pickup truck was not the easiest thing she'd ever done. Trying to maneuver the stockings up her legs without snagging them took real effort and wiggling into the corset while seated made her glad she'd been working out lately. But she managed to get everything in place and covered herself up with a long silky robe—one she'd appropriated from Nikki—in order to do a big reveal moment.

When Everett invited her out, she emerged from the cab and struck a pose. He did not appear impressed, perhaps because everything she wanted him to see was covered by robe, and he, as always, was skeptical of her choice in footwear. True, six-inch fuck-me heels were not ideal on the dirt road, but her cryptic boyfriend hadn't prepared her properly.

"Should I ask what you're wearing?" He took her hand and led her to the truck bed, where he undid the Velcro holding the mosquito net closed. She climbed in awkwardly, and scrambled across the bedroll to the pillows he'd lined up against the back of the cab.

"Would you like me to show you?" She reclined against the pillows and gave him her best come hither look.

He clambered in after her and sealed the netting behind him. "Hell yes, woman. Show me what you've got."

She untied the belt slowly and let the robe fall open.

Everett stared at her until she started to feel self-conscious. Maybe this was a terrible idea. Wearing something so ridiculous while camping in the bed of a pickup—perhaps she was as frivolous and princessey as Everett seemed to think. This is why she preferred hooking up after drinking. Alcohol used to give her the false confidence she needed to get over her insecurities. This was also why a hotel would have been better. She would have seen herself in the bathroom mirror and realized how foolish she looked. She could have avoided this entire embarrassing incident.

"Sorry, this was a bad idea." She wrapped the robe around herself again.

"Wait, what are you doing? Why are you covering up?" Everett still didn't move. He was frozen in place, one hand still on the netting.

I need a drink, she wanted to say. *A couple shots and then I'll be brave enough to let you look again.* But since she didn't drink anymore, she had to come up with something else. "I should change. This was stupid."

"No, you shouldn't. Amanda, you are the hottest woman I have ever seen. I was literally struck dumb. If we were in a spy thriller, I would tell you all of my country's secrets, and even if you murdered me afterward, I would die a happy man."

"Why do you do that?"

"Do what?"

"Play that game with me. Are you mocking me?"

"Of course not! I think it's fun. I love the way your mind works. I love how creative you are. And you know I love you. I'd play any game you wanted me to."

"For real?"

"Yes. Tell me what would happen if this were erotica."

Amanda smiled. He got her, he truly did. "Okay, here goes. Everett removed his pants and strode across the truck to her, massive thundercock on full display . . ."

"Okay, wait. First of all, I can't even stand up back here, much less stride. And, thundercock?"

"I'm writing this portion of my life story. Would you like to participate or not? Everett *crawled* across the truck bed to her, lust in his eyes."

This time, he followed the narrative, though his eyes glowed more with amusement than the described lust. "And when I arrived . . . I mean he arrived, he opened up her robe to reveal her wearing the naughtiest sexiest scrap of red fabric he had ever seen."

"And he was so taken in, that he didn't notice the weapons concealed around her body . . ."

"I thought this wasn't a spy thriller. Or are there actual weapons? Should I pat you down and find out?"

"Eventually. Let's start with the point where we kiss, and see what happens from there." That was the end of the narration. Amanda quickly found herself far too occupied and involved to continue talking.

Chapter Thirty-One

Amanda had become a regular at his band practices, and Everett had never played better. Something about the way those dark eyes watched him made him feel powerful, like he could do anything. Her applause turned him into a superstar drummer, and her smile turned him into the happiest man on Earth.

But there was always a little whisper of doubt. There were only four weeks left until the official end of the summer tourist season and Amanda's job. He'd been avoiding mentioning anything about it to her, out of fear for what she might say. He expected her to break his heart, but he wanted to delay the inevitable as long as possible.

"I need to pop off to the store, thanks to a fun surprise," Amanda said as they finished their post-practice dinner. "I'll meet you back at the ferry office."

He'd offered to join her, but didn't press when she declined, even though he hated every moment they spent apart. Time was winding down, why give up even fifteen minutes? He sat on the bed, impatiently waiting, with a hand pressed firmly on his leg to keep it from vibrating up and down in anticipation. Since this thing with Amanda had started, she'd turned into a sort of addiction. He needed her, he craved her, he couldn't stop thinking about her every minute of every day. Was this how his father had been with alcohol and Conner with gambling? If so, Everett was starting to understand why they'd succumbed.

For a moment, he considered getting undressed and sprawling across the covers, in an imitation of one of her sexy poses. She might appreciate that. Yeah, she'd probably like that a lot, actually. Why not be primed and ready when she walked back in? She said something about picking up a fun surprise . . .

When he heard the knock on the door, he reclined back, arms behind his head, fully exposed and ready to go, and called out, "Come in."

"Everett? Oh my god!" The face peering around the door frame did not belong to Amanda. He frantically grabbed the blanket and covered himself up.

"Aubry! What the hell are you doing here?"

"Looking for you, obviously. And I've certainly found what I was looking for. Don't act so embarrassed, I've seen you naked before."

"I'm not embarrassed, just surprised. And annoyed." He reached down to pick up his shirt from the floor, carefully keeping his other hand holding the blanket on his lap. "What do you want?"

Aubry sat on the edge of the bed, forcing him to scoot back against into the corner of the wall. He resisted the urge to shove her off with his foot. "I wanted to talk to you about that bimbo you've been bringing around lately."

"Amanda is not a bimbo."

"I think she fakes her accent. I think she fakes a lot of things. And did she tell you she's an alcoholic?" Aubry said the last bit with a smirk of triumph, as though she was delivering news likely to alarm and devastate him.

"Fake accent? Is that the best you've got?" He ignored the comment about alcoholism. If Aubry knew about that, it seemed someone in the meetings was rather blasé about the anonymous nature of the group, but he wouldn't be the one to confirm it.

"I'm sure her boobs are fake too, but I'm sure you figured that out. Everett, what are you doing with her? You're a smart man, you should try to find someone more on your level. You don't need some superficial ditz who's only dating you because you're in a band."

"Is that what you think is going on?" Movement caught his eye. Aubry hadn't shut the door all the way, and Everett spotted Amanda's face peeking through the crack.

"I think you're trying to make me jealous because I'm with Colton now. It's not going to work. I'm not jealous of some bleached blonde faker. You're savvy enough to see through her act. You're going to come crawling back to me soon. Don't think I won't make you beg."

"You've never been more wrong." Everett couldn't stand up, not under the circumstances, but he sat up straight and glared at Aubry. "Amanda is beautiful and brilliant, and so far out of my league I can barely see her. But I'm going to hold on as tight as I can while I've got her. And if she does decide to leave me, I'm not going to come looking for you."

"Because once a man has sampled caviar, he won't go back to canned tuna?" Amanda's Texas drawl caused Aubry to jump to her feet. Amanda strolled in and gave Aubry a dismissive once-over. "Hello Audrey. Don't you think you come off a little desperate, throwing yourself at a taken man?"

"Hello Amanda. Been out drinking?"

"Of course not. Just picking up a few things to help us enjoy our evening." Amanda held up her shopping bag and then leaned over and whispered something in Aubry's ear. Everett couldn't hear it, but he saw the look of outrage on Aubry's face before she fled, slamming the door behind her.

"She's such a pleasant person. How long was she here?" Amanda asked.

"What the hell did you say to her?"

"I told her she needed to keep her thirsty self away from my man or I would mess her up." Amanda grinned and then changed her voice, dropping into a flat Midwestern accent. "And I said it like this."

"You really do have a fake accent?"

"The first time I watched your band practice, she sat on the couch next to me. I think she was trying to be intimidating. So every time I spoke directly to her when nobody else could hear, it's entirely possible that I used my Minnesota accent. Tyrell has been helping me work on it. I'm quite proud that it went over so well."

"You are sometimes diabolical."

"And you're naked. Did that happen before or after your ex-girlfriend showed up?"

"Before. And I was preparing for you, not her. I swear, I thought it was you at the door."

"I believe you. Too bad."

"What's too bad? I want you to believe me."

She held up the shopping bag. "I was buying tampons due to an early emergency situation."

"Oh. I thought you said you were getting a fun surprise." He tried to hide his disappointment.

"I said *thanks to a fun surprise*," she corrected. "I was being sarcastic. Sorry, I'm crampy and unhappy. I suspect my monthly visitor ruins what you stripped down for."

Everett bent over to grab up his pants. "Yeah, sorry about that, I guess I was overly excited."

"No need to get dressed on my account. I assure you I still enjoy the view. I just need ice cream and maybe a heating pad?"

"There's a heating pad under the bathroom sink. You settle in and make yourself comfortable; I'll go get some ice cream."

"No, I bought some, I'm prepared." She pulled a carton out of her bag. "I usually get those bitty little pints, but since I'm sharing with you, I went for the full quart. I know how my man eats. And while I'm disappointed that my bloody misery makes me unwilling to do whatever naughtiness you clearly had planned, at least we have confirmation my birth control works."

"Both methods worked." While he trusted her to take her pill on schedule, it still wasn't worth the risk to go unsheathed. One pregnancy scare when he was nineteen had scarred him for life. Fortunately, in that case, his torture only lasted twenty-four hours before his girlfriend called him to say she'd wrongly misinterpreted her symptoms and had food poisoning.

When Amanda had gotten settled and—despite her protests—he had redressed, they took two spoons and started working on the ice cream.

"Do you want to watch a movie?" he offered. "I can grab the laptop from the office and set it up?"

"No, I'd rather snuggle up against you and talk. Tell me something interesting."

"I don't know anything interesting." Actually, he did. He'd found out that the one-bedroom apartment above the drugstore was going to be available for rent starting September first, and it was in his price range, if Amanda was able to get part-time hours at the inn. But he was too nervous to bring it up yet.

"Fine. Tell me about meat raffles."

"That came from out of nowhere. You consider them interesting?"

"No, I consider them confusing. You're a surprisingly cryptic man, Sugar Pie, and sometimes you drop these little nuggets of regional information into conversation. You told me about them early on, and I keep forgetting to ask Cara or Tyrell what you meant. But when I caught a glimpse of your glorious naked body, it reminded me I had a meat-related question."

"I make you think of meat? Is that supposed to be flattering?"

"Sausage, specifically, but I have no idea why." She blinked innocently.

"Basically, a meat raffle is just like the name says. You go to a bar, you buy a raffle ticket, someone spins a wheel, and if your number gets called, you pick a slab of meat from the table. All the bars do them. Tim puts on one monthly in the winter. Last year, I won a giant haunch of venison. Fed us well for a few days." A couple pounds of elk had been Conner's first raffle prize, the thing that made him go back for more. Elk, his brother's gateway drug leading into a gambling addiction.

"I will never figure you out. I only know summer Everett. Winter Everett knits socks and goes to bars to win dead deer. He's a strange man, that winter version of you."

"Maybe I'll introduce the two of you."

"Maybe you will."

That was it. That was his opening. He could sense the rightness of this moment. He took a deep breath and willed himself to be strong. "Speaking of this winter, where do you plan on spending it?" Sweat broke out on his palms, and his voice came out higher pitched than he would have liked.

She sighed and leaned back into him. "Texas, I suppose."

"Texas?" he pronounced the name slowly and carefully. That's not what he'd been hoping she'd say. "You aren't considering about staying here?"

"You know my job ends with the tourist season. And my whole family is in Texas."

Something painful clenched in Everett's chest. It was already ending. She didn't see a future. This is exactly what he had dreaded, the reason he hadn't been able to say anything earlier.

"There are other jobs," he said, cursing himself for how weak and needy he sounded.

"Oh, Sugar Pie, you know I'd die in a Minnesota winter."

He got up abruptly and walked to the tiny bathroom, wishing he could hide in there. He splashed water on his face to cool off. His thoughts raced and he couldn't think straight. This was it, wasn't it? This was the end. It was happening far sooner than he would like.

"Everett?" she called. She hadn't gotten up from the bed and, horrifically seemed completely oblivious to his pain. Didn't she care at all? "Everett, I would consider not going to Texas. Heading somewhere else. Like maybe New Jersey."

New Jersey? New Jersey? What the hell was in New Jersey? They'd never even talked about anything East Coast before.

"You know what, Amanda, you can go wherever you want." He tried to stay calm as his dreams were dashed around him. "It's obvious it's over between us."

"What?" she leapt to her feet, dropping the heating pad.

"It's fine, I should have known this wouldn't last."

"I don't understand what you're doing right now. Are you breaking up with me? Are you playing a game?"

"No, this isn't one of your games. I'm not interested in long distance. And I'm not interested in wasting my time falling in love with someone who doesn't want to be with me." He looked around, desperately wishing this wasn't happening. Why did they have to have this conversation now, when they were trapped on the mainland with nowhere else to go?

"Everett, just because I don't plan to stay in Whispering Pines doesn't mean we have to break up. I love you; you know that."

"So? That's not enough. I'm temporary for you. You know my obligations, you know I have no choice as to where I live, and you aren't willing to stay with me. I'd rather end it now than spend the rest of the summer with a guillotine hanging over my neck."

"Everett!" she stepped forward as if she were about to put her hands on his chest, and that would have been too much for him to bear. "We need to talk about this!"

"You've already said enough. I'm leaving. You can stay here tonight. Don't ... don't break anything. And you need to be gone before Duncan gets here in the morning."

He heard her calling his name as he stormed out, but he didn't turn around. He couldn't let her see him cry.

Chapter Thirty-Two

O'Connell Family Chatroom

<AMANDA has joined the chat>

Amanda: Hello? Anybody here?

Amanda: Seriously, anybody?

Amanda: Please?

Amanda: I've done it. I've hit bottom.

Amanda: Anyone? No?

<NICOLE has left the chat>

Chapter Thirty-Three

The bottle of vodka settled heavily in the bottom of Amanda's overnight bag. Good thing she'd brought the larger tote when she came to the mainland yesterday—she wouldn't be able to smuggle anything in her smaller one. It weighed more than she remembered, but her entire body felt heavier too. It was like Everett had taken her lightness away when he unceremoniously dumped her.

And what was that snide remark about not breaking things in his crash pad? Did he think she was going to vandalize everything? Go on a rampage and destroy the room? While it may have transpired in the past that perhaps cars of her exes had been keyed or memorably spray-painted with various cuss words, Amanda didn't drink anymore. She'd matured beyond that sort of behavior, and had learned not to burn bridges, especially if she wanted to cross them again.

She still hadn't figured out why he did it. He'd gotten angry that she didn't plan to permanently move to Minnesota, but he never should have expected her to stay. A Midwest winter? No thank you. But he wasn't open to discussing going anywhere else. What, he wanted her to give up her whole life for him, but he wasn't willing to make any kind of sacrifice for her? He said he loved her, but clearly not enough.

She sat down during the ferry ride back to Whispering Pines, bag of contraband clutched tightly on her lap. The worst thing that could happen would be dropping it and having the bottle fall and roll away. Everett would see—if he was even looking and not hiding from her in the captain's cabin. He'd purposely avoided her when she boarded, but it would be just her luck that he would notice the vodka. Actually, no, worse than him finding out, she'd lose her liquor, and she couldn't replace it on the island. Nobody would sell to her there.

When the ferry lurched to a stop, she stood up carefully and debarked with smooth, controlled steps, not giving away that she already snuck a few nips from the secret vodka. She could feel Everett's eyes on her, and she didn't want him to think she was drinking. Hell, she didn't want him to think anything other than regret that he'd let her slip away. She added an extra swing to her hips and flipped her hair. *Look at me. You miss me. You want me back.*

By the time Amanda's shift started, the alcohol was half gone, and she wasn't feeling well. She used to be able to throw back with the best of them. Shot contests with her brothers? No problem. Drink all night? Easy. But this time, the liquid sloshed uncomfortably in her stomach, and rather than lending a pleasant rosy haze to the world, everything felt off. Wrong, somehow.

"Are you okay?" Tyrell asked her, an hour into their shift. She'd successfully evaded him thus far, since she covered the desk and he was out roaming the property assisting guests. But when he came up to help re-key a room—for some reason she couldn't make the card go into the machine properly—he got way too close to her.

"I'm fine," she told him, turning her head away so he couldn't smell her breath.

Tyrell finished fixing the key and sent the guest away. "You're drunk."

"No I'm not. My eyes are just red from allergies. I think I'm allergic to pine."

"My husband owns a bar. You think I can't identify a drunk when I see them?" Tyrell picked up the phone. "I'm calling Cara."

She tried to stop him, she really did. When she couldn't snatch the phone from his hand, she brought up her foot to kick him as hard as she could. She stared at his legs first, trying to remember which one could feel pain.

"You kick my prothesis, you'll hurt your toe, then I'll take it off and beat you with it," he threatened, which stopped her. She didn't believe he'd follow through, but just in case, she backed up, bumped the desk, and stumbled. Damn it, that made her look drunker than she actually was. She wasn't drunk at all, she'd only had a couple of sips. A little vodka to make her stop thinking about Everett, to stop replaying the moment he walked away from her.

"You're such a tattletale," she complained. "I only drank a tiny bit. I'm not driving anywhere. What's the big deal?"

"Besides doing it at work and violating your probation?" he asked. "Cara is on her way down, and she's pissed."

Great. Her stupid cousin with her stupid rules was coming down to yell at her.

No, her situation was worse than she'd feared. Both Cara and Sam came in, and Cara was scarily calm. Amanda recognized that face. She was in real trouble now. She instinctively reached for her water bottle to take another sip, but Tyrell snatched it from her hand. What an asshole. For all he knew, it could have contained plain water and he was making her risk dehydration. It didn't, it was full of vodka, but he couldn't know for sure.

"Amanda, you're done for the day," Cara said, walking around the reception desk to the employee area. "Sam is going to take you on a walk to sober up. I will deal with you later." Amanda could sense the threat in her words.

"I think this is all a misunderstanding," she tried to claim. "I don't know what horrible lies Tyrell may have told you, but rest assured he is sorely mistaken. I'm having allergy problems. I probably should take some medication."

"You're slurring your words. You need to go, right now." Cara turned to her husband. "Sam, get her out of my sight."

"Don't make me drag you," Sam said, though he rather looked like he would enjoy doing it.

"I'm not in the least bit drunk, but I will leave anyway so as to not make a scene," Amanda informed them with as much false dignity as she could muster. She pushed past Tyrell, nearly knocking him over, which served him right. Then she led Sam out the front door, because she wasn't going to go around and leave through the back like an ashamed servant. She hadn't done anything wrong. She knew her limits.

"This way." Sam grabbed her by the arm and marched her down the inn's driveway instead of taking her back to the staff house.

"Are you trying to get me alone? You're a married man. Shame on you, Samuel." She tried to wrench her arm away, but his grip was too strong.

"Shut up. Don't say another word." He practically dragged her down to the main road, and then across to a path leading down to the lake. When they reached the rocky beach, he didn't stop. He kept moving, pulling her toward the shoreline. He only paused momentarily, to slip off his kitchen clogs. That's when she understood his plan.

"Are you going to drown me?" she asked in horror. There was nobody around, nobody to help her, and she was about to get murdered by a madman. She fought to escape, and he merely scooped her into his arms and started walking into the water.

Salvation almost came when she spotted a double kayak within rescue range. The occupants looked familiar. It took her a moment to identify her cousin's friend Matteo and his busty girlfriend with the weird name. Apple? Something like that.

Names didn't matter, what mattered was that they could save her from a deranged lunatic.

"Help! I've been kidnapped! He's trying to kill me!" she screamed at the kayak, and both paddlers halted their rowing. Matteo tapped the top of his head with his fist, and Sam pulled one arm out from under Amanda to repeat the gesture. And then, despite her screams, they kept going.

"Universal everything's okay signal," Sam explained. Then he bounced her in his arms as though testing her weight.

"Sam, please," she begged.

"Cara said to sober you up." His implacability made him more terrifying.

"She didn't say to dunk me in the lake!" Her voice grew high-pitched with hysteria.

"She didn't say not to. I've been wanting to do this all summer." A few more bounces to gain momentum, then that absolute horrible monster of a man tossed her, tossed her like garbage.

The shock did sober Amanda up as she sank beneath the icy water. She struggled, disoriented, and for half a second considered giving up and staying down there. But the urge to live was powerful, and she managed to make it, gasping, to the surface, before sinking again. She flailed, resurfaced, and shrieked for help.

"Put your feet down," Sam suggested, clearly enjoying this. He was a sadistic awful person, and if she survived, she planned to do everything in her power to get revenge on him. This was attempted murder!

"Sam! Help! Please!" She tried to splash her way towards him, but went under again. This time, her thrashing legs hit something solid. The bottom of the lake. Oh. She rose, dripping, to her feet. The water only came up to mid-thigh.

In fury, she splashed Sam, and stomped her foot. "You animal! I hate you!" Filled with rage, she lunged forward, intending to knock him off his feet, but he easily dodged and she fell back under water. His hand caught her and pulled her up by her collar.

"You need to go home and dry off. Don't you dare drip dirty lake water all over my clean floors, either. Go take a warm shower, get dressed, and sort yourself out. Now." He didn't seem inclined to assist her, though he'd obviously been happy to carry her before.

"I can't. I'm too cold." Her Texas blood was too thin for this, and her teeth chattered violently. "You tried to murder me!"

"The water's at least fifty degrees this time of year. I'm standing in it and I'm fine," he told her. "Stop being such a baby, you needed this. You deserved it. Back to the house, now."

He hauled her out of the water and set her on her feet, shivering. She stumbled, freezing and miserable. This was it, the lowest point in her entire life. She was going to catch a cold and die here on this isolated island, and not a single damn person would care. Not Cara, not Nikki, and not even Everett, the man she thought she loved.

Amanda barely survived the walk back to the house. Her skin was covered in goosepimples, and her sopping clothes clung miserably to her. With every step her shoes squelched, until she finally took them off and continued on in her dripping socks.

🌲 🌲 🌲 🌲 🌲

A half hour later, wrapped in a robe with her hair in a towel, she felt a little better. Warmer, at least. And definitely sober. And filled with a crushing guilt that was only made worse when she emerged from her room to see Cara sitting at the kitchen table, the depleted vodka bottle in front of her. She did the only think she could think of: go on the offensive.

"Cara Michelle O'Connell Vervaine! What in tarnation are you doing with alcohol? You're pregnant, you know that's bad for the baby. Do I have to call the authorities? My goodness, why would you . . ." she trailed off when she realized her words had no effect.

"Sit down and shut up, Amanda."

"Listen, Cara, I . . ."

"I said shut up. For once in your life, you will listen to someone other than yourself. I found this in your room. Did you drink all of this today?" She tilted the bottle, revealing that less than a third of its contents remained.

"No."

"Amanda Jean, you better not lie to me!" Cara's voice never rose, she stayed deadly calm, which was far more frightening.

"I didn't! Some of it is still in my water bottle." Amanda wilted under Cara's stare. She collapsed into the chair across from her cousin and put her head in her hands. "I fucked up, didn't I?"

"You think?" Cara sighed. "Mandi, if you weren't family, I would fire you, and you'd be packing right now to leave on the next ferry."

"Technically, you can't kick me out. I have my rights as a tenant, and you would have to evict me through the court system." She knew all about housing law, having been evicted from her previous apartment when Nikki moved out and she couldn't make rent on her own. Her stupid brother Kenny was rich enough that he didn't work at all, but he wouldn't help her out. Neither would Danny. Even Grandma refused, and she once gave Amy a thousand dollars for emergency airfare. How was that fair to anyone? So much for family support.

"Legally, I can have you trespassed from inn property after firing you. Read your employment contract. And don't even think about arguing with me. You won't win, and it's just going to get worse for you."

"Nothing can make this worse. I've officially lost everything. Everett dumped me yesterday, I don't have a twin anymore, I have no career prospects, no future, and my whole family treats me like an embarrassment. There's nothing left Cara, nothing at all." She surprised herself by crying real tears. She wasn't faking for sympathy, and it wasn't because of the alcohol.

"You know I've been there." Cara's voice took on a comforting note, and she came around the table to hug Amanda. Amanda embraced her tightly, angling over the pregnant belly, and allowed herself to sob. When she pulled away, Cara's shirt was wet with her tears.

"You couldn't possibly understand," Amanda said, wiping her eyes with her sleeve.

Cara got her a glass of water from the sink. "I do understand. Mandi, do you remember when Phil died?"

"Yes, of course I do." How could she forget? Cara's former fiancé had committed suicide in Uncle Alan's garage. Mandi and Nikki had gone to the funeral and taken Cara out for a long night of shots afterward. Cara had been a pale shell of herself.

"But you don't know what I went through after that. I blamed myself for his death, and the way I coped was through drinking too much. I drowned myself in alcohol so I wouldn't have to think or feel anything. But when you're in your twenties, people assume you're just a party girl, not an alcoholic. Nobody ever staged an intervention for me, even though it reached the point that I was lying to my therapist about it, and my friends started to express their concern and notice that I had a problem. I was trying to numb the guilt."

"What changed?" Amanda hadn't known about any of that. Sure, Cara had been drinking heavily every time Amanda saw her in the year after Phil's death, but they were only together at holidays and that's how their family celebrated. It would have been more unusual if she wasn't drinking.

"Sam. He changed things for me."

"That's ridiculous." Amanda had been hoping for a real solution, not this trite love nonsense. "Don't pull this love solves all problems crap with me. I know better. Sam doesn't have some magic dick that fixes everything."

"What makes you think he doesn't? In all seriousness Mandi, I'm not saying you need a man, or that love heals all wounds. What Sam did for me was taught me that I was worthy of love and compassion. He taught me that I had value. Or, rather, he reminded me. I had forgotten for so long. Once I learned to love myself again, I didn't need to crawl into a bottle and hide. I'm not saying I'll never have another drink—believe me, when this baby is out I'm trying some of Sam's latest beers—but I am saying I won't have a problem again."

"You can't know that. Maybe you're the alcoholic, and your projecting right now." Amanda couldn't help her instinctive need to argue. But Cara's words were starting to break through the defensive layers she had been building up for years.

"I'm not. My drinking problem was situational, a coping mechanism I developed to avoid my feelings. For you, it's probably different. You have an addiction. That's biological. You have to face the fact that you cannot drink again. But that won't matter, once you learn to love yourself. When you start to care about yourself again, you'll be able to heal emotionally and develop the strength to fight your alcoholism, and control it."

"But how?" the words came out more anguished than Amanda intended. "How do I love myself when I'm all alone?"

"You aren't alone. You never have been. You still have your family; we've never left."

"Haven't you?" Amanda didn't bother to hide her bitterness. "Cara, you barely tolerate me, and the rest of them decided I had an alcohol problem and cut me off entirely."

"No, Mandi, you told the boy twins to go fuck themselves and stay out of your business. You told Amy she was a terrible sister and not to call you again unless she took your side against your parents. And your plea agreement prevents you from contacting Nikki after you stole her identity. Stop blaming everybody else. Your entire family has been patiently waiting for you to acknowledge fault. They've all forgiven you already, but they're giving you the space you need to figure things out."

"I . . . I . . ." Amanda couldn't come up with an argument. It was true; she had said all of those things. "Cara, you're right. I've ruined everything, haven't I?"

"No, not yet. But now would be a good time for you to do some real reflecting. You need to focus on figuring out who you are—you, Amanda, not you Nikki's twin. Not half of a set. Once you're secure in yourself, things will improve. Maybe you'll stop blaming everybody else for your problems. And you'll get your life back together."

"I hope you're right." *And I hope it's not too late.*

Chapter Thirty-Four

When times were difficult, there was one person Everett had always been able to count on. As soon as he could take his lunch break, he headed up to Piney Islands Yarnworks. Fortunately, it was empty of customers. Well, not fortunately for Nessie, she could use the money, but Everett was glad of the privacy.

"If you're looking for Joy, she's doing the day camp at the school this week." Nessie perched on a stool at the counter with a rat's nest of yarn in front of her, apparently trying to detangle it. She held it up to him. "Can you believe this happened when I tried to wind this skein? I know one vendor I'm never dealing with again."

"That's quite a mess. I wasn't looking for her, I was looking for you. I brought you a sandwich," he said, offering up a bag from the bakery.

"I'm suspicious. What do you want?" she asked, but she gladly accepted it, peeking in the bag and smiling.

"A neck rub? I slept in the truck last night and now I'm all messed up." He twisted his head from side to side. The movement hurt.

"Shouldn't your girlfriend do these kinds of things for you?"

"I don't have a girlfriend, and that's why I ended up in the truck. Please?"

"Fine, sit on the floor in front of the couch." The yarn shop was set up with comfortable furniture for knitting. A couple of times a week it filled with happily crafting people, a circle he occasionally joined in the winter.

Nessie sat cross-legged on the couch behind him and started digging her knuckles into his neck. Her hands and forearms were strong and he relaxed into her touch. Finally, she let out a long sigh. "Why aren't you talking, Ev? Tell me what happened."

"We broke up, that's all. It happens."

"Too bad. I liked Amanda. I thought she was good for you, and you were going to fall madly in love with her."

"I did. But that's the problem."

"Yes, falling in love is awful, you poor thing."

"It is when it isn't reciprocated." He'd been dreaming of a future together. She was just waiting out her sentence.

"Are you sure it wasn't? I saw how the two of you interacted. She was crazy about you, and you were . . . how did Joy put it? Bouncy over her."

"She used me for sex and entertainment."

"Why? No comment on your sexual prowess, but you're not that entertaining."

"I'm a drummer in a rock and roll band."

"You're a drummer in a small-town cover band that plays occasional weddings and bar mitzvahs. Not a rock star, sorry."

"I already feel low. You don't have to kick me while I'm down."

"Sorry." Nessie continued kneading his neck in silence, and the knot started to loosen. "Everett, for real, what happened? I've watched so many of your relationships crash and burn, but this one seemed different. For the first time in your life, you were truly happy. She brought out your playful side. I haven't seen that in years."

"I was happy. I was deliriously happy, and that was foolish of me. I was stupid to think something would work out between us. But Amanda never thinks about anyone but herself. Do you know why she came here? She was so mad at her twin sister for getting married that she went out and got drunk and crashed her car. And she has yet to take responsibility for any of it. She blames everyone for all her problems. Like her drunk driving arrest is the fault of the bar for serving her, and probably the stop sign for standing on the corner. She doesn't take responsibility for anything."

"So she has some maturing to do. Some people grow up faster than others." That was a true statement. One of the things Everett admired most about Nessie was her strength and maturity. She'd been a twenty-year-old kid with a newborn when Conner left her, and instead of dissolving in the wreckage or blaming the world, she came back to the island, moved in with her grandmother and worked hard to give his niece the best life she could afford. "That doesn't seem like a reason to break up with someone. I mean, you knew what she was like when you started dating in the first place."

"Yeah, but I'm not going to wait around for her to outgrow her selfishness. I would, maybe, if she were planning on staying here, but that thought never occurred to her. Once the summer ends, she's leaving me, that's been her plan all along. I'm not going to try to maintain a long-distance relationship."

"She said she wasn't going to stay here, so you broke up in advance? Did you shout 'you can't fire me, I quit' at her?"

"If she doesn't want to live here, what's the point? There's no long-term potential. Why would I spend the rest of tourist season with her, when she's counting down the days to abandoning me?" He'd never been concerned about long-term potential in any of his previous relationships. Things like moving in together or getting married had never been on the horizon with anyone else. But since the first time he kissed Amanda he had imagined a future that she apparently didn't: renting an apartment in the village, and taking vacations, and growing old. Childish fantasies, obviously, of a beautiful woman showing up here, on this remote island, and falling for him, and loving him enough to stay.

"I couldn't imagine a city girl like her sticking around," Nessie agreed. "But you don't have to either."

"Yes, I do. Nessie, I'm just as trapped on this island as you are."

"You think I'm trapped? Don't be ridiculous. I'm here by choice. Can you think of a better environment to raise Joy? She goes to a good school, and she gets all the advantages of growing up in a small town surrounded by wilderness. She can run and play and have freedom that mainland kids don't get anymore. Plus, your mom is her only living grandparent. When I was a teenager, of course I fantasized about escaping. We all did, didn't we? Conner and I were going to live in Duluth. Remember my college dreams? And what about you? You wanted to join the Coast Guard, remember, and travel the world fighting pirates and rescuing people."

"And Conner took that away from me." The old bitterness welled up in him again.

"The hell he did. Why didn't you enlist?"

"Because Conner stole all our money. Someone had to pay it back."

"But you still could have gone. The Coast Guard pays a salary. You could have sent money home."

"Not enough. I had to stay and work off Conner's debts. You know that. You've been dealing with his mess for years too."

"He was my husband, so I'm cleaning up my own credit by paying off the debts he created in my name. But you, you don't have that same issue. Look, Everett, there's something you should understand: you are replaceable."

"Well fuck you, too."

"Everett!" She stopped massaging his neck and gripped his head in both hands, tilting it backward and forcing him to look up at her. "I'm trying to help get something through your thick skull. You aren't the only one who can do your job. We live on the Great Lakes. There are hundreds of perfectly qualified dock-workers who would jump at the chance to spend their days loading cargo other than fish. You are replaceable *in your job.*"

"But the money . . ." The way she held his neck was undoing the work she'd done on the knot. He wrenched away.

"Your profits have been going toward fixing Conner's mistakes, but I know you're still getting hourly and benefits. Your mom and Duncan could hire someone else, and you could leave. But you're too scared."

"I'm not scared. I'm obligated to stay. It was my fault. He tricked me, and I signed the papers. I put us in the debt just as much as he did."

"You were barely eighteen and you trusted your brother. It wasn't your fault. But you've been punishing yourself for years. Maybe it's time you grow up, put on your big boy panties, and do something with your life."

"I don't wear panties."

"Maybe that's the problem. Everett, seriously. I love you. Not a whole lot, seeing as how you're the guy who gave my child a drum set, but enough to want what's best for you. We're family."

"And family takes care of each other, I've heard that speech before, Nessie." That's why he had to stay. He had to help run the family business to make up for his part in nearly destroying it.

"Family also encourages each other to take flight. Taking care of someone doesn't mean stunting their life's journey. You were meant for more than this tiny island. But you've spent years playing the martyr to avoid whatever it is you're afraid of in that crazy world beyond our shores. That's why when Amanda came, this beautiful free spirit who would never be content here, you were already prepared to let her go. That's what you've been planning this whole summer, because you'd rather chicken out and push her away than try something new yourself."

"Don't put this all on me! She was planning on leaving me all along."

"No, Everett. Amanda planned to leave *the island*. She might have wanted to take you with her. Did you ask?"

"I don't want to have this conversation. She said she'd rather go to New Jersey than stay here. If that's not a kiss off, I don't know what is." He rose to his feet, towering over his petite sister-in-law. "Thanks for the neck rub. I gotta get back to work." Back to work, where he could lose himself in physical labor and escape both the deep desire and sense of loss that Nessie's words had triggered in him.

"Everett," she called, but he ignored her. As the door shut behind him, he heard one last thing. "Malcolm went to New Jersey."

Chapter Thirty-Five

The scrutiny of dozens of sets of eyes was nothing new to Amanda. Every week she faced similar ones as she cracked open a novel and started reading. But standing in front of this group made her nervous. They weren't waiting for her to share someone else's words; they were waiting for her own.

"Hello, my name is Amanda," she began, gaining strength from the few encouraging smiles. "And I am an alcoholic." There. She said the words. Out loud. She did it. She finally admitted the truth.

The group repeated back a hello, and she took a deep breath. She surveyed the strangers staring at her. She'd seen them twice weekly for over three months, but she hadn't really looked. She should have. She should have studied all their faces and embraced all their stories. These were her people.

"I haven't had a drink in about five days. My boyfriend dumped me, and I did what I always do when I need to numb myself. I decided to drink away my sorrows. And it didn't work. I felt worse, and not just physically. I did a lot of thinking and talking to family members, and I finally realized that my tendency to turn to the bottle whenever I'm in need of comfort is a problem. I've been coming to these meetings for a couple of months thinking that I was better than everyone else—y'all are alcoholics, whereas I was merely someone who liked to indulge a little. I'm so sorry. I was wrong. I've been wrong this whole time. And now I'm ready to begin getting better."

In exchange for her words, she received understanding smiles, supportive nods, and a particularly annoying double thumbs-up. That last one came from Kevin, of course. When she returned to her seat, she reflected on the empowering feeling such encouragement engendered. All along, she'd sat there, bobbing her head along with everyone else, participating in the sea of what she'd dismissed as perfunctory nods, in order to keep up the pretense of active listening. Her heart had never been in it. Until this moment, she never understood the importance, or the warmth and acceptance signaled by the nods and smiles of her peers. In fact, until today, she hadn't even realized they were her peers.

After the meeting, Kevin approached.

"Thank you for sharing today. That was brave of you."

She shrugged. "I guess it was about time I participated." Now that it was over, she sort of wanted to pretend she'd only done it to check off another box on her probation sheet. *Debase myself in front of a group: check.* But she'd promised herself to stop hiding. She needed to tear down this false wall and keep admitting her truth.

"I'm sorry to hear about Everett," Kevin added. "But it's for the best. He's not one of us. He couldn't possibly understand what we're going through. Recovery is difficult enough, especially without a supportive partner."

"That's not why we broke up." Everett was the sole cause of the breakup. Him and his refusal to have a rational discussion about their futures or entertain the idea of leaving Whispering Pines. But her drinking was the reason they wouldn't get back together. If she hadn't gotten drunk immediately afterward, she would have had a chance to win him back. But what was his one deal breaker? *I don't date drunks.* That's what he told her on their first date. And that's what she was, a drunk.

"Want to talk about it? Let me take you out for coffee. You have time, right?"

She did, now that her lunch plans with Everett were non-existent, so why not? Kevin, despite his slightly sleazy motivations, struck her as mostly harmless, and she needed to talk to someone. But at the coffee shop, he kept brushing up against her. When she reached for her cup, he reached for his, and their fingers touched. He smiled. She did not.

"I'm not over Everett," she warned him.

"I didn't think you were."

"Okay, it just seemed like you . . ."

"I'm not making a move, Amanda. I'm your friend, I'm trying to be here for you."

She pretended to believe him, but she was too smart to fall for his little act. She'd met plenty of men like Kevin before, men who would flirt but then deny it. Men who wanted in her pants, while all the while protesting that they were a gentleman and she misunderstood their intentions. They'd make their moves and excuses at the same time.

All she wanted was coffee and conversation. And damn it, that's what she was going to get. "You want to be here for me? I need someone to listen."

"You can tell me anything," he assured her, and she adroitly moved her hand when he tried to take it. Great. She was going to talk his ear off.

Chapter Thirty-Six

The days stretched out, vast and empty. It had been a year since the break-up. A full year.

Or at least that's what it felt like. In reality it had only been one week since Everett had stormed out the office door, masking his tears. One week since he last held Mandi in his arms. Only one week, the longest, emptiest, hardest week in his entire life.

He couldn't face her. When he saw her approaching the ferry, he would quickly duck out of the way, hiding in the captain's cabin or busying himself with cargo and checklists. The others did the ticket taking on those days, giving Everett sympathetic looks (Mom) or grunts of support (Duncan). He couldn't handle watching her walk up, the feel of her fingers as she handed over her punch card. The way she would probably look at him, either like he meant nothing or like she wanted him back. Which would be worse? He wasn't sure.

But he'd been able to avoid dealing with her at all. Lunches in the back room of the office instead of the park, having his brother make any deliveries to the inn, and refusing to answer the phone ever, just in case her voice was on the other end. It was for the best. She intended on leaving at the end of the summer. He meant nothing to her, and if they didn't have a future, he had to end things before he got even more sucked in. His heart was merely cracked, not shattered, because he'd done it at the right time. Or so he told himself.

When he went to band practice, he could feel his whole body thrumming. He needed to hit something. He needed to sit down at his drum set and pound the pain away. Angry, aggressive drumming, something to allow him to work out some of the awful emotions swirling in his brain.

But it was canceled. It was fucking canceled, right when he needed it most. Colton had left a sign on the garage door, a scrawled note. Everett clenched his fists. If he could make it back to the island, he could beat on his other drum set at home.

"No practice?" Lucas arrived right when Everett turned away.

"Apparently not."

"You want to grab some burgers?"

"Sure." Dinner meant he'd miss the last ferry, but he'd rather follow Lucas and his bottomless pit of a stomach to a restaurant. An evening hanging out with a friend—someone who didn't know about his loss—would help. It was better than going home, or sitting alone in the office, on the bed he used to share with Amanda. How they ever fit, he didn't know. Her body on top of his, her hair always getting in his mouth, her delightful wheezy laugh when he grazed his fingers over her ticklish sides. God, there was so much he missed.

Unfortunately, Lucas couldn't stay out late, perhaps because he grew tired of dealing with Everett's moping. He had to admit, he wasn't good company lately. He dragged himself back to his crash pad, dreading it, because everything inside the room reminded him of Amanda, of what they had, of what he'd lost. His broken heart couldn't heal if he had to keep being exposed to memories of her.

And everything outside it reminded him of her too, because damn it, there she was, sprawled against the doorway, as if she thought she had a right to be here. As if she missed the last ferry and thought she could sweet talk her way into a free room for the night.

"What are you doing here?" he asked, though he could guess.

"Everett, I don't feel good." Her words were slurred and when she tried to rise to her feet at his approach, she swayed and abruptly sat back down. For once she wasn't wearing her ridiculous heels, and her bare feet were filthy.

"Because you're drunk." Why was he surprised? Of course she wouldn't follow the plan and stay sober. Of course she'd mess things up. Typical alcoholic. He never should have had higher expectations of her.

"I'm not drunk." She turned to the side and started throwing up in the bushes, immediately demonstrating the lie. God, he did not want to deal with this. He was not going to invite her inside, no matter what. He had no intentions of spending the night babysitting his ex-girlfriend, even if her drunkenness would go a long way toward helping him get over her.

"Not cool, Mandi. You need to get out of here." Even as he said it, he resigned himself to taking her in. Where was she supposed to go? The motel? But then he'd probably end up having to pay for her, and he'd still have to spend the night to make sure she didn't aspirate vomit or anything like that.

"Everett, I . . . my head hurts." He barely understood what she said and had to rush to catch her as her eyes closed and she collapsed.

"This really sucks, Mandi," he told her, and gently moved her unconscious body so he could unlock the office door. He was going to have to take her to the hospital—and let her deal with the legal consequences of drinking—but he wanted to protect the interior of his truck. He got out a garbage bag, cut a hole in the bottom, and put the whole thing over her like a dress to keep the vomit on her shirt from smearing or dripping on the passenger seat. Then he picked her up and, swearing more than necessary, carried her to the parking lot.

She didn't open her eyes on the drive, not that he expected her to, given how wasted she was. Fortunately, she kept the remaining contents of her stomach where they belonged, so he didn't need to scrub out the truck later. Duncan would not appreciate the smell in their shared vehicle. He thought about rolling up to the Emergency Room doors and tossing her out on her ass, but his conscience wouldn't allow that. He carried her from the parking lot instead.

When he walked in, people sprang into action. "It's fine, she's just drunk," he explained to the orderly who ran up with a wheelchair. A nurse handed him a clipboard full of paperwork, and they hurriedly started wheeling Amanda back to an exam room.

"What's going on with the patient?" the nurse asked as he followed behind them.

"I think she's had too much to drink," he said. He didn't want to tell them that she was an alcoholic, though that would probably come out.

"How much did she drink?"

"I don't know. I found her like this," he tried to explain as they lifted Amanda's body from the wheelchair to a bed.

"What's your relationship with the patient?"

"She's my ex-girlfriend." He hated the 'ex' part of that description, but seeing her like this made him not want her back. Was she really so weak that she couldn't stop drinking? How hard could it be? She kept insisting she wasn't an alcoholic, but then she went and did things like this. She knew how he felt about it too, so it was like a slap in the face. A reminder that she didn't care.

One of the doctors who had rushed over to perform an examination looked up at his words. "Take him to the waiting room. He can't be in here."

Everett found himself escorted out, still holding the paperwork. He had to guess at most of it. Like, what was her address? The staff house probably had a street number, but nobody on the island bothered learning such things. In the end, he just scrawled down the name of the inn and listed Cara as the emergency contact.

After he submitted the clipboard at the desk to a person who refused to give him any information—*because he wasn't the emergency contact, damnit!*—he wasn't sure what to do next. Was he obligated to wait around? No, probably not. But he should stay anyway. Sure, Amanda had taken his heart and torn it to pieces, but he couldn't leave her here alone, even if she had brought it upon herself. Fucking alcoholic. It was a shame; he thought she'd be able to maintain her sobriety long enough to complete her probation. But maybe time in jail would be the wakeup call she needed.

After about a half hour with no updates, he considered leaving, but two police officers walked through the doors. That wasn't a surprise—small-town cops didn't have much else to do. They probably considered Amanda a multi-state fugitive at this point.

Everett decided to stick around. An evil part of him wanted to see Amanda get perp walked out of here, but he told himself he was staying to help. She would need someone to make arrangements for her bail. Not that he had any intention of paying it, but he could at least pass the details on to Cara. Though he suspected Cara would punish her by leaving her to sit in a locked cell overnight.

He watched as the officers were taken through the double doors to the exam rooms. A few minutes later, they came out and approached him.

"Everett Ryan?" one of them asked.

"Yes?"

"Would you mind coming with us?"

"Is this about Amanda?" Obviously, it was, but there was no reason to have this discussion anywhere else.

"Please come with us."

"Can we talk here?" He'd give them any information they needed, not that he knew that much. She'd shown up uninvited on his doorstep.

"If that's the way you want to do it, fine," said the same officer. "Stand up, turn around, and place your hands on the wall. You are under arrest for assault and battery, and attempted murder."

He froze in his seat, too shocked to move.

"What?"

"You are under arrest. Stand up, now." The officer placed his hand on his taser and that was enough to bring Everett to his feet.

"I didn't do anything. I didn't give her the alcohol. I don't even know what she drank."

"Turn around. Hands against the wall." Everett complied, maintaining his composure through the overly aggressive pat down. "Anything in your pockets I should know about?"

"There's a box cutter in my right front pocket," he said, and the cop removed it. "I swear, I had nothing to do with this."

None of what he said mattered. In short order, they handcuffed him, read him his Miranda rights, and hauled him off to the police station.

🌲 🌲 🌲 🌲 🌲

Finally, after sitting in a cell for nearly two hours, a detective came and led Everett into a room for questioning. He'd spent that time confused and annoyed. There was nothing illegal about taking a sick person in for medical treatment, and it wasn't like he poisoned her. He kept reassuring himself that as soon as the hospital contacted Cara and learned Mandi's history of overindulgence, he'd be freed with an apology for wasting his time.

The interrogation room contained one table and three chairs. They told Everett to sit in the one that was bolted to the ground. Did they expect him to pick it up and throw it? This was all an overreaction.

"You know Amanda is over twenty-one, right?" he informed them. "She's legally allowed to drink."

The detectives exchanged a glance. "Thank you for that information. So, Everett Ryan. Mind if I call you Everett? I'm Detective Hudson, and this is my partner, Detective Wood." His friendly tone instantly made Everett's hackles rise. Something seemed wrong here. Cops weren't friendly unless they were trying to trick you.

"Call me whatever you want, if you can tell me what's going on." His best guess was that they thought he supplied alcohol to a minor. Maybe Mandi was carrying around someone else's ID again. She did have a history of identity theft.

"Before we start this interview, I want to make sure you understand your rights. You don't have to talk to us. You can call an attorney, if you think you need one. It's up to you. Do you think you did something wrong and need an attorney for this?"

"I don't need one. I'm happy to answer your questions, if you would just tell me why I'm here." He didn't need a lawyer, but Amanda sure would. She might go to jail for her probation violation. Wait, were they going to charge him with conspiracy? Was there such a thing as conspiring to violate probation?

"You're here about the Amanda O'Connell situation. Now, it's my understanding that she's your ex-girlfriend. How long ago did you break up?"

"How is that relevant?" Everett demanded, but he wilted under their stares. "Last week."

"But you kept in contact with her?" Hudson kept looking down at a file folder and nodding, but Wood didn't take his eyes off Everett.

"No, but we both live on Whispering Pines Island. It's a small community, and I work on the ferry. Obviously, we see each other." *From a distance, until I can escape.*

"Want to explain what happened this evening?"

"Amanda was drunk, she passed out, and I took her to the hospital. What's to explain?" What had gone so wrong that they didn't understand that? They'd surely have pumped her stomach and woken her up by now. She wouldn't accuse him of anything, would she? She was always a little crazy, but in a fun way, not in a psycho lying to police kind of way.

"Drunk, you say? Were the two of you drinking together?"

"No, I don't drink. Look, I don't want to talk trash about her, but she's an alcoholic."

"Was that a point of contention between you?"

"Contention? No. Not really. I mean, I didn't want her to drink, but she didn't around me anyway."

"So, what happened?"

Everett was getting sick of hearing that same question.

"I don't know. She was sitting on my steps when I got home. Well, not home. Back to the place I stay when I'm in Ferry's Landing. She was drunk, and she passed out, so I took her to the emergency room." How many times did he have to repeat the same thing before they listened?

"And at what point did you hit her?" Wood spoke for the first time, and the controlled fury in his voice startled Everett, as did the words.

"What?"

Hudson took up the narrative. "We're trying to construct an accurate timeline here. Just tell us, at what point did you hit her? Were you fighting because she was drinking? Did she make you angry? It's okay, it happens. Your ex-girlfriend shows up, maybe says some things you don't like. You got a little mad.

You didn't mean to hurt her. You're a big guy, you don't know your own strength."

As Detective Hudson spoke, Wood rose to his feet, and Everett fought the urge to stand up as well. That would probably be seen as a threat, and he really didn't want to get tazed. Hudson tapped his pen against the table and raised his eyebrows. Everett looked back and forth between the detectives and a chill ran down his spine. Something was seriously wrong here.

"I never laid a hand on her, ever. I don't know what you're talking about."

"Did you think we wouldn't look you up, Everett? We know about your history of violence, even if you did manage to avoid charges. Look, you did the right thing tonight. It was a good move to take her to the emergency room. That demonstrates that you care, and the DA will like that. Remorse is always important in cases like these." Detective Wood's eyes burned with anger as he spoke.

"But I didn't touch Amanda except to carry her to my truck. What's going on here?"

"We need to set up a timeline for what happened tonight," Detective Hudson repeated. "This is important. Everett, I know you still care about her. If you didn't, you wouldn't have taken her to the hospital. We need some honesty from you. It will help the doctors. Don't you want to help them? What did you hit her with? Your fist? Some kind of object? If you cared about Amanda, you'd tell us the truth."

"I didn't hit her with anything, I swear. She's just drunk." Wasn't she? Doubt flooded him. He'd made the assumption, but he hadn't actually smelled alcohol on her. When he carried her, he breathed through his mouth to avoid the lingering odor of bile. Could she have been sober? No, that didn't make any sense.

"Everett, please," Hudson said. He was clearly filling the good cop role. "You're already going to be charged with attempted murder. If she dies, it's going to be a hell of a lot worse for you. But if you cooperate now, we might be able to convince the DA to reduce it down to manslaughter."

"Dies of what? Alcohol poisoning?" He didn't give her anything, and there was no way they had any evidence to the contrary. She'd probably been at Shore Leave, and that place had cameras. There would be plenty of proof that he had nothing to do with any of it.

"Did you think the doctors would take your word for it without examining her? Amanda didn't have a drop of alcohol in her system. What she does have are bruises in the shapes of handprints, and a massive head wound. Someone, Everett, grabbed her and beat the shit out of her. You know what a TBI is, right? Traumatic brain injury. She was in surgery when we arrested you. We're still waiting on a call from the surgeons to determine what exactly we're charging you with. Why don't you cooperate right now, so we can make things go easier on you? If she doesn't make it, what you say now could mean the difference between murder and manslaughter. And believe me, you don't want it to be murder. You're going to go away for a long time, but maybe, just maybe, we can help you out. You give us the info we need for the doctors, and we tell the DA to go easy on you."

All of the air left his body. Someone hurt Amanda, and they thought he did it. She might be dying right now. She might be dying, and all he had done was yell at her for drinking. He'd blamed her . . .

Now Everett stood up, tasers be damned. "You need to take me back to the hospital. I have to see her."

"Sit down. You're not going anywhere near her ever again. We already know what happened."

Detective Wood chimed in again. "Yeah, we know what happened. You knocked her out. Maybe you hit her a little harder than you meant to, and you thought she was dead. But you wouldn't call for help, would you? No, you wrapped her body in garbage bags and were driving her out to bury her. You're familiar with the woods around here. I'm sure you could find some secret place. And hell, maybe you already have. Maybe there are more bodies we need to look for. But what happened with this one? She woke up and you grew a conscience? You realized you hadn't killed her yet and decided not to finish the job? Or did something spook you?"

"I didn't touch her! All I know is she showed up at my place, I thought she was drunk. She threw up in my bushes—go check, it's still there. I put the bag on her so she didn't get vomit on my seats. I would never hurt her, I love her!"

"Yeah, we've heard that one before. Nobody ever hurts the one they love."

Everett put his head in his hands. "I think I want to talk to a lawyer now."

Chapter Thirty-Seven

O'Connell Family Chatroom

<NICOLE has joined the chat>

Nicole: You can't just text that my twin is injured and tell me to log in for details. Why can't you just call me? What happened?

Kenny: It's easier to tell you all at once.

Danny: So do it.

<AMY has joined the chat>

Amy: WTF is going on? I got Cara's message, but I can't reach her.

Kenny: Cara is at the hospital with Mandi. She's in surgery right now. They had to remove part of her skull to relieve pressure on her brain.

Nicole: I feel it. My head hurts. Was it on the right side?

Kenny: I don't know which side. They might have to leave the bone piece off for a few days to keep her brain from over-swelling, then they put it back.

Amy: She has an f-ing hole in her head?

Kenny: Apparently that's a normal treatment.

Danny: It's fine, I looked it up. The technique is called trepanning. It's been used for thousands of years. There are historical records all over the world of ancient peoples doing it.

Amy: NOT THE TIME FOR A HISTORY LECTURE!

Kenny: Read the room, bro.

Danny: Trying to help. Don't you feel better knowing it's not some made up new-age treatment?

Nicole: Shut up D!

Kenny: Hang on, call coming in.

Kenny: SHE'S OUT OF SURGERY! SHE'S ALIVE!!!

Nicole: Now what?

Kenny: They transferred her to the ICU. Cara swears she's not leaving until Mandi wakes up. She'll call back as soon as she has an update.

Danny: She will, right? She will wake up?

Nicole: HOW CAN YOU ASK THAT?

Nicole: Of course she will!

Nicole: She will, right? Tell me she's going to be fine!!!!!!!!

Nicole: Kenny! Answer me right now!

Kenny: You type faster than me.

Kenny: Cara says the doctors are giving an excellent prognosis.

Kenny: We'll know more when she wakes up. Which she will do soon. I promise.

Amy: I'm trying to find flights.

Danny: Me too.

Kenny: Me too.

Nicole: Can I come? I have to see her.

Amy: She's still on probation. She's not allowed to have contact with you.

Nicole: That's BS.

Kenny: You didn't think it was BS four months ago.

Nicole: Four months ago she wasn't having her head chopped open!

Nicole: This is my twin we're talking about.

Kenny: I know.

Danny: I know.

Nicole: I just told Griff to find me a flight.

Kenny: She could go to jail if you show up.

Nicole: And she could die. I'm not letting my sister die!

Danny: You're not a doctor.

Nicole: Fuck you. I'm her twin, I'm going to be there with her. I'll go to jail in her place if I have to.

Danny: You can't switch places. You aren't identical anymore. Unless you want a hole in your head too.

Amy: Not funny, D.

Kenny: Seriously not cool, bro.

Danny: Sorry. I'm worried about her too.

Nicole: Griff booked a flight leaving in the morning. Are mom and dad on their way?

Kenny: They're on vacation in Argentina. I haven't been able to reach them on the phone yet. Don't want them to read about it in an email.

Nicole: I forgot.

Danny: They've posted a million pictures on Facebook.

Nicole: My mind is a little occupied with other things. I'm going to go pack. K call me with updates as soon as you get them.

Kenny: You got it, sis. Love you.

<NICOLE has left the chat>

Danny: Now that she's gone, we need to have a serious talk.

Amy: About Mandi? Is there something you haven't told us?

Amy: OMG! Is she dying?

Kenny: Not about Mandi.

Danny: Not about Mandi.

Amy: What is it?

Danny: Should I take my gun?

Amy: What????

Kenny: Not on the plane.

Danny: Are we road-tripping then?

Amy: WTF are you talking about?

Danny: Mandi's boyfriend put her in the hospital.

Kenny: She's our little sister.

Danny: He's not getting away with that.

Kenny: He's not going to get away with that.

Amy: You're both idiots. Don't put anything about guns in writing.

Kenny: Not like these chats are archived.

Danny: Assume we're joking.

Amy: Is that really what happened? Did Everett do it?

Kenny: The police think he did. They arrested him and might charge him with attempted murder.

Amy: What did Cara say about it?

Kenny: Somebody beat the shit out of our baby sister, that's what she said.

Danny: They broke up last week.

Kenny: He has a record.

Danny: He's the one who took her to ER.

Kenny: And lied about what happened.

Amy: It doesn't make any sense though. He's not a violent person. I know him.

Kenny: You never can tell with some people.

Danny: And it's not his first time.

Amy: He's been arrested for bar fights, but never charged. Self-defense. Not the instigator.

Kenny: I'm sure that'll be his excuse this time too. I bet he'll claim Mandi slapped him, and he punched her in self-defense.

Amy: I don't think that sounds right.

Danny: You've already admitted he's violent.

Amy: In self-defense. And in hockey, I've heard. But everybody fights in hockey.

Danny: Everybody doesn't beat up their ex-girlfriend though.

Kenny: We need a plan of action for when we find him.

Amy: He's in jail, he can't be that hard to find.

Amy: But he's also way bigger than both of you combined. And his brother is a brute. The two of them could take six of you.

Kenny: Sounds like we need to strategize in advance.

Danny: We'll be smart about this. But he's going to pay.

Amy: Go after him legally. I don't need you guys to get hurt too. But wait until we've heard the whole story.

Kenny: When did you become a whole story kind of person?

Amy: When my little brothers started plotting to murder someone.

Amy: I just want to know more.

Kenny: I think we know enough.

Danny: I think we know enough.

Amy: No guns!

Danny: Fine, no guns.

Amy: And let's get the truth first. We need to make sure we're going after the right person.

Kenny: I hope it wasn't him. I hope it was somebody smaller and less intimidating.

Danny: Yeah, then Everett can help us get revenge on the real perp.

Kenny: We'll have Fabio and Griff too, right?

Amy: Don't know. We have a baby; I need to figure out how to travel with her. She doesn't even have a passport yet. And Fabio has to check on his visa waiver to see if it's still valid. We weren't planning on coming out until next spring.

Danny: Don't come. We'll handle everything.

Kenny: I forgot about the baby.

Amy: Yeah? Well I forgot about your kids too.

Danny: Ha ha nice comeback. Mommy brain took away your edge.

Kenny: I'll have to arrange a nanny. Gina has a trial this week.

Danny: I'll call mine. Maybe she can watch all the kids. What do you usually pay?

Amy: Can you discuss this somewhere other than our chat?

Kenny: Fine. I'll update when I hear something.

Amy: I'll send you our ticket info if I can get them. NO GUNS!

<AMY has left the chat>

Danny: I'm researching if my concealed carry permit is valid there.

Kenny: So am I. I'll call you later.

<KENNY has left the chat>

Chapter Thirty-Eight

Her body needed sleep. That's what the doctor told her last night, in her few brief moments of consciousness. *Sleep will help heal you*, and Amanda sank back into a dark, dreamless state.

This time when she woke up, she sensed someone close to her bedside, someone holding her hand who immediately stood up and leaned over to peer in her face.

"You're awake!" Nikki said, relief washing over her features.

"I don't remember anything ... who are you?" Amanda asked weakly. Nikki recoiled.

"You lost your memory? It's me, Nicole, your sister."

"I have a sister? Who am I? Where am I?" Amanda raised her fingers to touch the edge of the bandage across her forehead. "I don't ... I can't remember."

"I'm your twin sister," Nikki said, crying now. "And I promise, I'm going to take care of you."

"Are we identical?" Amanda tentatively reached her other hand to touch Nikki's face as though trying to compare the two.

Nikki cupped her sister's cheek in her palm. "Yes, we're identical. We look exactly alike."

"We're identical? Why didn't anybody warn me that I'm so ugly?"

"What ... Mandi, you bitch."

Amanda smiled. "Hi, Nikki. Thanks for coming."

"Don't do things like that! I was so worried about you," Nikki wiped her eyes. She probably wanted to smack Mandi too—good thing she was already hospitalized. Nikki would never hurt an invalid.

"Hey, don't cry Me-me. I'm sorry. I thought it would be funny. How many opportunities do I get to wake up from a coma?"

"Hopefully, only the one."

"If this were a soap opera, I bet I'd get lots of comas because I'm so good at looking ill. This bandage really brings out my eyes."

"And you and I would be played by the same actress."

"And we'd keep getting killed off and brought back to life."

"You're not funny, you were almost killed off. Mandi, you nearly died. They cut your skull open. What happened? Nobody seems to know anything."

"That's the thing. I don't remember what happened. I . . . there's a gap in my memories. One moment I was having coffee, the next thing I knew I was waking up from surgery. Hours are gone. And the doctor said I won't get them back."

"At all? Ever? So you do have amnesia? You drama queen. It figures you'd get something like that."

"Just a few hours' worth of memories. I guess they were never created. Nobody hit save on that file." In her short waking moments, she had tried to remember what happened. A police officer came in to question her about Everett and suggested that he had done something. She didn't want to believe that, but the size of the marks her attacker left on her upper arms suggested someone of Everett's stature had been involved.

"Can I see your other injuries?" Nikki asked, and Amanda let her examine the bruises. Nikki placed her hands over them to measure.

"These were made by a big guy. Unless he had his fingers spread way out, but then he wouldn't have had the strength to leave those marks." Nikki demonstrated different squeeze strength between having her fingers close together and spreading them wide. "Me-me, I hate to ask, but your boyfriend has large hands, doesn't he?"

"I don't have a boyfriend. We broke up." He dumped her. Could he have been mad enough to attack her? The last thing she remembered was going to a coffee shop with Kevin from her meetings. Did Everett have a jealous streak? Could he have found them and overreacted? It didn't make sense, not her gentle giant, but there was no other explanation.

"Has he ever . . . is this the first time he hurt you?"

"Was it him? Has he confessed?" Her head hurt badly, making it difficult to focus on the conversation. And she was exhausted. Even seeing her twin, having her long-lost sister back after such a terrible and unnecessary separation, wasn't enough to keep her eyes open very long.

"Not yet. He's in jail though. It's too bad this happened. Kenny told me you actually liked this one."

"You've been asking Kenny about me?" Amanda spent months thinking Nikki was ignoring her entirely, off enjoying a twin-free married life. Amy called Tyrell regularly, and she had gotten Cara to admit that Kenny checked in weekly, but nobody ever mentioned Nikki.

"Of course! You're my twin. I miss knowing everything about you, but I don't want you going to jail for talking to me. Kenny's been keeping tabs on you through Cara and passing the information on. I know all about your relationship with Everett, and the breakup. Oh, and the vodka too."

"Can we not talk about that?" Her self-destructive mistake wasn't something she needed to be reminded of right now. She could barely keep her eyes open. Each blink lasted longer than the one before. She wasn't going to be able to continue this conversation much longer. "Me-me, I'm so tired."

"I know, you need rest. Get some sleep, baby girl." Nikki kissed her gently on the forehead, and despite her exhaustion and pain and the nagging suspicion that the man she loved had tried to kill her, she smiled. With Nikki by her side, she felt almost complete again.

Chapter Thirty-Nine

The sun had never felt so good on Everett's face as it did when he walked out of the courthouse a free man. Well, not entirely free. He still faced an assault—but thankfully not attempted murder—charge, and he had restrictions on his movements. The judge released him on his own recognizance, but also slapped him with a no-contact order.

Now what? Besides a shower and some clean clothes, all he wanted was to see Amanda, to change the picture of her in his mind. The last sight he had was of her unconscious and surrounded by doctors. But the no-contact order meant he couldn't go visit her or even ask anyone about her without being tossed back into jail. Maybe his best shot would be to head back to the island and hang out in The Digs, listening in on conversations. Surely people would be talking about Mandi, though they might clam up when they saw him there. He had no idea what the gossip was right now, but he'd probably already been convicted in the court of public opinion.

"Everett Ryan?" The voice coupled with that damned sexy accent froze him in his tracks. He turned slowly, unable to believe his ears. She was here.

"I'm not allowed to talk to you," he said, but he couldn't keep his eyes off of her. She looked much better than expected. Tired, angry, but healthy and well. Her hair had been trimmed a little bit shorter, but there were no bandages, no signs of any head wounds. He realized his mistake immediately. "Nicole?"

"Good guess. Or not really, since I'm the only one of us who can physically stand right now. You need to tell me exactly what you did to my sister." She crossed her arms and glared at him. Her eyes crawled across his face, analyzing everything. Two men, slightly shorter than her, with brown hair and the same dark eyes stood behind her.

"You need to tell all of us," said the one on her left.

"Our brothers, Kenny and Danny," she pointed over her shoulder at them.

"Backwards sis."

"Seriously, sis?"

"I didn't look when I pointed. You rearranged yourselves." Nicole rolled her eyes. "Now, Everett. Start talking. Tell us why you hurt our sister." Her beautiful familiar face wore an expression he'd never seen: hatred.

But he wasn't intimidated by them, this gathering of O'Connell twins staring him down. What he thought, actually, was that this was the worst possible way to meet the siblings of the woman he loved. And yes, he did still love her. That's all he thought about while locked up. How he loved her, and how he needed to find out who attacked her.

"Why don't we go somewhere we can talk?" he asked. Better not to do this out in the open.

"All of us," Kenny spoke up.

"We're not letting you have any alone time with either of our little sisters," Danny added.

"I meant all of us. There's a coffee shop on the corner, we can get a table."

He felt awkward walking with three sets of Amanda's eyes boring into his back. They didn't say a word. Danny bought three coffees, and they all sat, rearranging their chairs in such a way that they all faced him. To an outsider it may have looked like a job interview, but these stakes were much higher.

The men's faces were set in anger. Nicole appeared more open and willing to listen. Each of them reached into a pocket or purse, pulled out a cell phone, tapped the screen a few times, then placed it on the table. Odd behavior, especially given the poor reception out here, but maybe they were expecting a call from the hospital. Was Mandi in surgery again?

"Is . . . how's Mandi?"

"I was in the courtroom, buddy. I know you can't ask," Kenny said. Everett could tell them apart easily. Unless something changed since Amanda had described them, he was the one with the muttonchop sideburns. "You don't get to have any contact with her or communicate in any way at all."

"I'm not supposed to ask, but you could tell me anyway. It seems like you're the ones who want to talk to me, so I won't say anything until I know exactly how Mandi is doing." He crossed his arms and watched them, feeling his heartbeat pounding in his chest. Amanda would appreciate him standing up to her siblings, he just knew it.

"He's standing up to us," Danny muttered quietly.

"Yeah, he is. That's unusual. Hey, Everett, show me your tattoos," Kenny replied, *apropos* of nothing.

"What? Why?" He couldn't roll up his long sleeves far enough, but he did slip a finger into his collar and stretch it to reveal part of a crow.

"Figures," Danny said.

"Of course he has some," his twin said at the same time.

"Tall, huge, tattooed . . . he's perfect," Nikki whispered, in a tone so low Everett suspected he wasn't meant to hear.

"Look, I don't know what's going on, but please, just tell me about Mandi." He'd beg if he had to, he didn't care. The last information his mother managed to pass through the lawyer was that she survived the surgery and the doctors moved her to the intensive care unit.

"I went to see her. She's awake and talking, but she doesn't remember the incident that put her in there." Nikki frowned at him, staring intently with those distracting matching eyes. It hurt to see so much distrust and suspicion in them.

"She doesn't remember? But she must know I had nothing to do with it, right?" She called him her gentle giant, surely she couldn't be blaming him, could she?

The boy twins shook their heads in unison. "Dumbass," they both said, then Danny continued. "If she doesn't remember, how would she know it wasn't you? Obviously, you're the number one suspect."

"They always blame the ex. But I swear, I would never hurt her. Nikki, if this were a detective novel, you would have walked past her attacker in the hospital hallway, and he'd have done a double take. Did you encounter anyone like that?"

He intended to lighten the mood, but Nikki reacted like he'd slapped her. She broke down sobbing, turning to her brothers for consolation. Kenny held her and patted her back, making gentle soothing sounds.

"Wait," Everett said, knowing he'd somehow made everything worse. "What did I say?"

Nikki wiped her tears on her brother's shoulder. "Sorry, I just wasn't expecting that. You play her dumb game."

"The detective thing? I was joking."

"No, but that's it. You were doing her 'if this were a' genre game. It's so goofy and annoying, but you did it like it was perfectly natural. And you're huge and tattooed, and Amy says you're in a band. You're perfect for her, you're her literal dream guy, and instead of Mandi introducing us to you with a shit-eating grin on her face, we're sitting across from you and accusing you of attempted murder."

'Dream guy' would have brought a smile to his face, if it weren't for the 'attempted murder' part of her statement.

"I know it looks bad because it happened so soon after we broke up, but I'm still in love with her and I promise you I would never lay a hand on her. All I know about Tuesday is she showed up at my place, told me her head hurt, then vomited and passed out. At the time, I thought she was drunk. I had no idea she had a head injury until after the police arrested me."

"If you didn't do anything, why'd you wrap her body in a trash bag?" That challenge came from Danny. The coldness in his eyes made him appear to be the more threatening of the brothers.

"There was puke on her clothes. I was . . . I was trying to protect my truck. I know it was a mistake." God, was that ever a mistake. That bag made him look guilty. If he could change one thing about that awful night, he would have let her throw up on his seats. Actually, no, he'd have sought out Amanda earlier, before whatever mugging-gone-wrong occurred so he could rescue her.

"What kind of truck?"

"Danny, focus," Kenny said.

"An old Toyota I share with my brother. Is it relevant? Anyway, the garbage bag got me in more trouble. The cops thought I was on my way to bury her when she woke up and I re-routed to the hospital instead."

"They thought you weren't smart enough to wrap the whole body up? Or unwrap it before dropping her off in the ER?" Kenny smirked. "Dumbest criminal ever."

"You saved her life. If you hadn't taken her in when you did, she never would have woken up." Nikki reached across the table to take Everett's hand as she spoke. "Thank you."

Everett squeezed her fingers in relief. "You do believe me? That I had nothing to do with it?" He didn't understand how he convinced them, but he wasn't going to object.

"We choose to believe you," Nikki said. Then her brothers took over the conversation, volleying their sentences back and forth like a table tennis match.

"If you didn't do it . . ."

"You're the perfect person to help us . . ."

"Find out who did. And if it was you . . ."

"We'll be gathering evidence."

"Keep your friends close . . ."

"And your enemies closer."

"Wow." Everett was almost dizzy from watching them talk. "Do you always finish each other's sentences? Nikki, are you and Mandi the same way?" He tried to envision Mandi, happy healthy Mandi, sitting with her siblings, joking around with them. He couldn't do it. All he could picture was her lying unconscious on the hospital bed, while a nurse shoved him out of the room.

Kenny was the one who answered. "Now I don't think he's met Mandi at all. Who are you again?"

"Hush, Kenny. Everett, you know how Mandi is," Nikki explained. "She opens her mouth, an entire paragraph falls out. I can't finish her sentences; I never know where she's going with them."

"Nikki once went a week without uttering a single word, just to see if anyone noticed," Danny added. "We didn't. Mandi talks enough for the both of them. Hell, she talks enough for the whole family."

"Speaking of Mandi, I want to track down whoever did this to her." Everett may have convinced her brothers and sister, but he needed to clear his name with the police too. Since he couldn't visit her, he had to do what he could to help her from the outside.

"That's our plan too. You're going to be a big help, since you're familiar with her schedule. We can figure out where she went and retrace her steps in order to solve this case." Nikki picked up her phone and started tapping to open a note taking app.

"Yeah, and you can be the one to kick his ass. We'll provide moral support," Kenny said, and Danny nodded.

"Or we'll leave that to the authorities." Nikki shook her head in disgust. "Amy told me what you idiots were planning, and I think it's best that nobody in our family go to jail. Now, talk to me Everett. Where would Mandi have been on Tuesday?"

Chapter Forty

This time when Amanda woke up, her brothers were peering down at her. She blinked to make sure it was both of them and not double vision.

"We brought you chocolates." Kenny placed a box on her bedside table. Hopefully, it contained actual chocolates and not one of her brother's pranks.

"We figured the hospital food sucked," Danny said. Amanda wasn't sure, since she hadn't actually eaten anything. Her head hurt and all she wanted was sleep, not food. Even the meals Sam delivered didn't entice her.

"It might. I don't know. I don't remember." She tried to look weak and miserable. "I just know that I don't feel well."

"Is there anything you need?" Kenny asked, concerned. He was always her favorite.

"There's something going on with my feet. I can't quite feel them. Maybe if you could rub them a little bit . . ." she trailed off and pretended to wipe a tear from her eye as her brothers immediately began massaging her feet. They were good at this.

"Did you both fall for that one?" Cara asked, returning with a pitcher of ice water. "She pulled that trick on Sam too."

"And it worked," Amanda pointed out. "He has strong hands. Lucky score there, Cara."

Danny dropped her foot to the bed with a thump, Kenny set the other one down gently. "You're definitely feeling better," they both said.

"Not really. I'm sleeping all the time. I just woke up and I'm already ready for my next nap. Where's Nikki?" Nothing made her happier than having her twin back with her, nothing. She didn't care that she might go to jail for violating her restraining order. Gina could probably get her out of it anyway. There were extenuating circumstances.

The boy twins exchanged a glance. "She's . . . with Everett," Kenny finally said.

"Everett? But everyone says he's the one who did this to me!" She didn't want to believe that, not her sweet Sugar Pie, but that's what people kept telling her. There was the police officer who came to take her statement, the doctor who saw Everett bring her to emergency room, even Kevin from her AA group who snuck in to visit earlier. They all said the same thing: Everett had hurt her. It seemed so out of character for him, but she had nothing to contradict those statements, especially with such large handprints on her upper arms. Those bruises couldn't have been accidental.

"I don't think he did," Kenny still sounded cautious. He watched her for some sort of reaction.

"We confronted him . . ." Danny added.

"With Nikki, and we asked him straight up . . ."

"If he had done this, and he said it wasn't him."

"And Nikki said she believed him."

"They're off investigating . . ."

"And we came to ask you for more details."

"I hate when they do that," Cara told Amanda. She used the button to raise Amanda to a sitting position and held out a cup of water with a straw. "Here, drink up."

The cold water soothed her throat, and sipping it gave her a chance to think. She'd been trying everything she could to bring back the memories, but they were just gone.

"I can't give you any more information. I don't remember anything. I went to my AA meeting and the next thing I knew, I was here, with Cara crying over me like a big baby. When I realized we were in the hospital, I thought she gave birth or something."

"That was your first thought?" Cara asked. "You were the one in the bed."

"I have a head injury. Don't judge my thought processes."

"And now she's crying again," Danny shook his head and tsked at her. "Good job, sis."

"I'm just hormonal, shut up." Cara wiped her eyes with her shirtsleeve.

"You always cried all the time anyway," Kenny said. "That's why we didn't like watching movies with you ever."

"Or hallmark commercials."

"Or anything involving cute puppies," Amanda joined in the teasing, but she also patted Cara's hand. "We love you, you silly crybaby."

"Stop, I can't help it. I was worried about you. You were supposed to be here under my protection," Cara said.

"I know what this is. It's a mafia tale. Yes, I'm under your protection. Now you need to send your hitmen to punish the rival gang that did this to me."

"You're mixing up the mafia and street gangs," Kenny said. "For real, can we get back to figuring out who did this to you?"

"I don't know! I'd tell you if I did, I promise. I want him to pay as much as the rest of you. But I don't remember and I'm so tired." She wanted to cry like Cara. And she needed sleep. She couldn't control it. Her eyes closed of their own accord.

Chapter Forty-One

O'Connell Family Chatroom

\<FABIO has joined the chat\>

Fabio: Hello, I am here.

Fabio: Hello?

Fabio: It has been ten minutes. It is very late and I am tired.

Fabio: Anyone?

Fabio: I do not like your country's various time zones.

\<FABIO has left the chat\>

\<FABIO has joined the chat\>

Fabio: I am here, for the second time, though I do not understand why I have to do this.

Mel: Me neither. Danny phones me fifteen times a day, I already know everything.

Kenny: This is the easiest way to update everybody.

Fabio: It is the middle of the night, and my love is asleep.

Kenny: I hate when you talk about her that way. You make the rest of us look bad.

Gina: Yeah, Kenny, why don't you call me your love?

Kenny: Because you don't have any sweet nicknames for me. Your dad does though.

Gina: He calls you a lazy freeloader.

Kenny: It sounds better in Spanish.

Griffin: Hi. Is there a point to this? I only get a short break.

Kenny: I said this was to give you all updates on Mandi's situation.

Mel: There better be something new. I'm taking care of three kids by myself right now.

Kenny: The way I do every day? Not impressed. Anyway, the current situation: Nikki has taken it upon herself to track down whoever did this to Mandi.

Griffin: I thought it was the ex-boyfriend?

Kenny: So I guess these updates are important after all . . .

Griffin: I'm at work. I worked all day. I haven't been checking my texts. And Nic hasn't been sending them. She's busy and I respect that.

Kenny: *Nik

Griffin: It's short for Nicole, thus, Nic.

Kenny: Nicole=Nikki=Nik.

Griffin: I'm not arguing with you about how to spell my wife's name.

Kenny: Then spell it correctly.

Mel: Kenny, stop picking fights.

Gina: Nikki knows she can't go see Mandi at all, right? She hasn't been to visit her?

Kenny: Of course she has.

Gina: That's a violation of the restraining order. Mandi could go to jail.

Kenny: Only if someone finds out.

Gina: I'm an officer of the court.

Kenny: Attorney-client privilege. Ha! Lawyered!

Gina: Kenny, I love you, but you have to stop saying that every time we argue. I'm not going to turn her in, but I can't encourage it either. And you shouldn't put in writing that it's happening.

Kenny: She's using Amy's name at the hospital, which reminds me, Fabio, don't let Amy call there directly at all.

Griffin: This family is rife with identity theft.

Kenny: Doesn't count amongst siblings.

Mel: I don't know about that. I'd be pissed if you did that to Danny.

Gina: Or vice versa. And the police sure thought it counted when they arrested Mandi.

Kenny: ANYWAY. Back to Mandi's assault, if anyone cares. Nik and the ex teamed up to retrace Mandi's steps. They're going to find out who it was, and probably murder him.

Gina: Or call the authorities. You know you aren't funny, right?

Kenny: Meanwhile, we've been talking to the doctors about her recovery. They think she'll have no long-term effects, but she won't be 'better' for a few weeks or months. She needs lots of rest and recovery time.

Mel: Is she coming home? Staying with your parents?

Kenny: Mom and Dad are on their way to pick her up. She doesn't know yet, though. But Cara and Sam are handling everything for her.

Griffin: Why isn't Sam included in this in-laws' chat?

Kenny: I don't think he knows how to use a computer.

Griffin: He does.

Kenny: He's a cousin-in-law, not a sibling-in-law, and he's at work right now.

Griffin: So am I. We're both chefs. This is the dinner hour. I wish you'd take that into account when you schedule these.

Kenny: Yeah, but Sam spent the morning at the hospital, so he already knows everything. ANYWAY. Mandi will get released to the folks, but it might be a couple of days. Cara found someone to cover her shifts at the inn.

Mel: Good. Her shifts were the thing I was most concerned about. What's the sarcasm tag again?

Gina: /s

Mel: Thank you.

Fabio: I will tell my love. When she wakes up. Which may be soon, because of the baby. I am leaving this chat now. This could have been put in an email.

<FABIO has left the chat>

Chapter Forty-Two

"Hey! Get away from him!" Everett turned in the direction of the shouting voice and saw Kevin, the guy from Amanda's AA meetings who always pretended he wasn't hitting on her, running at full speed towards them. He stopped right in front of Everett and Nikki, and tried to position himself in between them.

"You're Nicole, right? Amanda told me about you," Kevin asked, between pants. He didn't seem to be in good enough shape for an all-out sprint like that. "Do you have any idea who this guy is?"

"I am Nicole. And I know who I'm walking with. But who are you?" she replied.

"I'm Kevin, I'm Amanda's . . . friend. Listen to me, please, you aren't safe with him. I don't know what lies he's told you, but he's the one who put your sister in the hospital."

"How did you hear about that?" Nicole asked.

"My friend works in the ER and saw him get arrested. I visited Amanda to check on her, but I had to sneak past your cousin to do it. He said she wasn't accepting visitors."

"He?"

"Big guy, dark curly hair? I didn't catch his name."

"Sam. But why do you think Everett is the one that did that to her?" Nikki spoke with genuine interest, and for a moment Everett had a touch of concern that she might believe Kevin.

"Everyone knows his reputation! He's violent and aggressive. It's not the first time he's done that kind of thing."

Nicole turned to Everett and raised an eyebrow. He shrugged. "I was in a bar fight once, the other guy was my size, and he started it. Charges against me were dropped." Had he known that minor incident would come back to haunt him so terribly, he wouldn't have gotten involved. No, that's not true. He didn't regret protecting the women who were being harassed, he only regretted that people found out about it and twisted the story into something less savory.

"Not being charged is not the same thing as being nonviolent," Kevin said. He was posturing an awful lot for such a small man. Well, he wasn't Napoleonic, more average- sized, but that was nothing in comparison to Everett.

"Kevin, I do thank you kindly for the warning," Nicole reached out and clasped one of his hands in hers. Kevin smiled and shot Everett a triumphant look, but Everett knew what she was doing—comparing hand sizes, and not subtly either. She glanced over at Everett and shook her head. Not Kevin.

"Where are you staying in town? Not with him, I hope. Your sister was afraid of him."

"No, she wasn't!" Even though he wanted to convey the nonviolence of his nature to Nikki, Everett had a very strong urge to use his fists to wipe the smug smirk off of Kevin's face.

"She was, she told me."

"You're a liar. And you need to walk away right now," Everett warned him.

"No, I want to hear this." Nikki put the back of her hand against his chest, which he interpreted as a message to stand down and let her handle the situation. "What exactly did Amanda tell you?"

"She said he hurt her and she was scared. Those are the exact words she used."

"Emotionally or physically?" Nikki's question had the effect of making Kevin visibly wilt. He swallowed.

"Well, technically she said emotionally. He hurt her by ending the relationship just when it was starting to be really good. And she was scared . . ."

"Scared of what?" Nikki's tone sharpened. Kevin looked at the ground and mumbled his reply.

"Scared that if they got back together, he'd do it again, abruptly walk away without a backwards glance."

That made Everett's guilt rise up again, but at the time, he didn't see what difference it made, breaking up immediately or waiting until the end of the summer. Since Mandi always planned to leave him anyway, he shouldn't regret cutting it off weeks early, before he could sink in even deeper. He had already reached the point of being madly in love and imagining a future, one that could never happen ... unless Mandi's head injury changed things. Unless somehow finding out who attacked her would earn him a second chance. But was it selfish of him to fantasize about that while she was still hospitalized? Would it be manipulative of him to use her weakened and vulnerable state to convince her to stay?

🌲 🌲 🌲 🌲 🌲

Walking to the Golden Shores Retirement Community with Nicole evoked strange emotions in Everett. Looking down at the blonde hair bouncing along beside him gave him a strange sensation. She moved like Amanda, smiled like Amanda, but some of her mannerisms were different and the tired and wary hesitation that hadn't quite left her eyes was something he'd never seen in her sister.

As soon as they entered, the receptionist rushed from around her desk to give Nicole a hug.

"Oh, Mandi, I thought you were in the hospital. I'm so relieved you're already back on your feet! We need you; the residents are desperately waiting on the ending of that mystery you started last week."

Nicole gently extracted herself from the embrace. "I'm Nicole, Amanda's sister. She, unfortunately, is still hospitalized."

"Are you twins? You look exactly alike! And I'm so sorry to hear that. How is she doing?"

"She's recovering," Nicole said. "But she doesn't remember what happened."

"I heard her boyfriend . . ." the receptionist trailed off, looking up at Everett with a jolt of fearful recognition.

"It wasn't me. I didn't see her until after she got hurt. I swear."

"He didn't do it," Nicole confirmed, patting Everett's arm. "But we need to find out who did. We're retracing her steps from last Tuesday."

"She was here, I can tell you that. She does a story time where she reads aloud to some residents, then she went around and did some visiting. I don't have records of who she talked to, but I can tell you her favorites and you can check with them."

Everett smiled at the thought of bright, beautiful Amanda bringing her sunshine around to this dim place. His grandmother had resided here for four years, until she had to transfer to a facility better equipped to handle Alzheimer's patients. He could remember coming here as a child. The smell of cleaning products and mothballs triggered thoughts of racing Malcolm down the hallways in wheelchairs while old men clapped. The boys thought it was great fun, until the nurses found out. A couple of angry lectures, a wheelchair confiscation, and a forced apology ruined the activity for everyone involved.

The first patient they were directed to was a wizened old woman named Rose. He recognized the name immediately: Rose of the sugar pie recipe.

Rose sat in a wheelchair in the main activity room facing a window, but when the nurse escorting them called her name, she turned and her face lit up. "Mandi! I guess it worked!"

"What worked?" Nicole asked.

"You got him back. This is him, isn't it? Your Sugar Pie? He certainly matches the description."

Nicole broke down in a fit of giggles, and Everett felt the heat spreading across his face. "I'm Mandi's ... sugar pie ... but this isn't Mandi. This is her twin sister, Nicole."

"Nicole. Hmm. Aren't you the one who ran off and married a man you barely knew?" chided Rose. "You left your sister behind. Who does that?"

"I married the man I love. I didn't need her approval."

"Oh, I know, sweetie," Rose reached out to take and pat Nicole's hand. "I was only teasing. Amanda eventually understood your decision. Don't tell her I told you, but she admitted you were right, and that you deserved to find happiness with that short husband of yours."

"Five eleven is not short," Nicole corrected, and Everett tried to stifle a laugh. The glare Nikki shot at him matched Amanda's perfectly, wiping the smile from his face. He sure would like to see the two of them together, but not under these circumstances.

"Didn't you both wear flats at your wedding?" Rose asked. "She showed me pictures. But height doesn't matter when you're horizontal. My husband was short too." She gave them both a wink, and Everett instantly understood why Rose was Mandi's favorite.

"Did you say about something working to get me back?" Everett brought the conversation around to the reason they were there.

"Last time I saw her, she was upset from your little spat. But I told her not to give up, and when you find true love, you seize it and hold on with all your might. She said she understood and knew what she needed to do, but she never reported back to tell me if her plan worked. I've been waiting."

"When did you talk to her? Tuesday?" Everett asked, though when else could it have been? His heart swelled. Mandi wanted to find a way back to him. Maybe Rose convinced her of what he couldn't: that winters weren't as terrible as she feared, and his love would be enough to keep her warm. Wait, that was a line from a pop song.

"Yes, I think so. Days pass oddly in here; you'll have to ask at the desk when she came here last. Is that when you have band practice? She wanted to show up and surprise you. Did she change her mind? Where is she anyway? Why are the two of you here without her?"

"Practice was canceled." A sick feeling developed in Everett's stomach. Colton had canceled unexpectedly, with no explanation.

"Could she have gone there looking for you?" Nikki asked the question that was foremost in his mind. What if she went and nobody was there? Or worse, what if she went and that's where the attack happened? He would have missed her by mere minutes.

"Maybe. It's worth heading over to Colton's to find out." He hadn't spoken to anyone from the band since his arrest. His mom had promised to inform them about it, so they weren't expecting him at whatever make-up practice he was sure they'd scheduled. He hadn't thought to ask them for alibis.

"Excuse me? What's going on?" Rose interrupted them. "What happened to Amanda? Is she missing?"

"No, no, don't worry, she's not missing. It's just she got injured on Tuesday, and we're trying to figure out what happened. She's in the hospital and can't quite remember the details." Nikki used a soothing tone that didn't work. Rose grew more agitated.

"In the hospital? Oh no, will she be alright?" The elderly woman appeared so distressed that Everett wanted to comfort her, but Nikki was better at it than he was. She knelt next to Rose's wheelchair and took her hands.

"Don't you worry about my sister. She's got a teeny bump on her head and a wee bit of amnesia. Just enough to get attention, not enough for concern." Nikki's smile appeared false to Everett, but Rose believed her.

"As long as she's not hurt too badly, she must love this. She's in a mystery novel! Though I think she always pictured herself the detective, not the victim."

"I'm not sure she's enjoying it that much," Nikki said. "None of us are. We need to turn her story into one with a happy ending."

🌲 🌲 🌲 🌲 🌲

They practically ran to Colton's house. Luckily, they found him there, and his reaction told them everything they needed to know. He answered the door to Everett's pounding, saw Nikki, his face turned white, and he attempted to slam the door on their faces. But Everett, even if he hadn't been powered by rage, was far stronger. His fist smashed the door open, sending it crashing into the wall, despite the door stop.

"You can't come in here! You're trespassing!" Colton backed away, looking from Everett to Nikki, almost in a panic. He held his hands up in supplication. "She said you broke up, I swear."

Everett's vision turned red. Amanda had been here. He grabbed fistfuls of Colton's shirt and lifted him off the ground, giving him a violent shake. "What the hell did you do?"

"She told me you dumped her; I wouldn't have tried anything if I thought you were still together! Tell him, Mandi! It wasn't my fault!"

"She's not saying anything. I want to hear your version of events." Everett pressed Colton against the wall. He felt Nikki's hand on his back, reminding him not to do anything stupid. Getting arrested for assault would not help his case.

"She came over before practice and said you'd broken up. I thought she was here for revenge, you know, like Aubry. I figured her goal was for you to catch us in the act. I was wrong, I'm sorry!"

"Tell me what happened next," Everett growled. He couldn't imagine that Mandi would come down here and hook up with Colton for any reason, especially if she, as Rose had said, wanted him back.

"I made a mistake, okay? She made that very clear. And I didn't mean to hurt her." He looked at Nikki pleadingly. "Mandi, really, I didn't. I thought you were playing hard to get."

"You did it! You almost killed my sister!" Nikki launched herself over Everett's arm, clawing at Colton. Her reaction surprised Everett so much he dropped him, and Colton scooted away.

"Your sister?"

"I'm going to rip your heart out," Nikki shrieked. She transformed into a wild animal, and Everett had to wrap his arms around her and catch her before she could claw Colton's face off. He wrestled her away as she kicked at him, swearing and fighting. Now he knew how an angry O'Connell reacted and was glad he wasn't on the receiving end of such ire.

"You put Mandi in the hospital, and I got arrested for it," Everett said, tightening his grip and trying to keep Nikki under control. "I'm calling the police, if Nikki doesn't kill you first."

"Hospital? For what? Who's Nikki?"

"For her fucking head injury!" Nikki calmed down enough to sound coherent, but not enough that Everett trusted letting go of her. "I'm Mandi's twin sister. You bashed her skull open, and she almost died, and you are going to pay for it. I'm telling my brothers, and we'll find out how you like getting your head bashed in! You're a dead man!"

"You aren't . . . I didn't touch her head! Jesus, man, you know I'd never do something like that," Colton's face drained of color and, to Everett's amusement, a wet stain spread from his crotch. "I swear that's not what happened. I just tried to kiss her and feel her up a little, that's all."

"She has handprints on her arms," Nikki said, spreading her fingers. "I measured. You're a match. Everett, hold him down, I'm getting a giant fucking rock, and we'll see how *he* recovers from a TBI."

"Everett, please, you have to believe me," Colton pleaded desperately. "I didn't hit her. Yeah, I grabbed her arms and maybe shoved her around a little, but I thought she was teasing me. I thought she wanted it."

"Did she tell you she wanted it?" Everett was rapidly changing his mind on stopping Nikki.

"She kneed me in the balls, and when I went down, she kicked me in the back a bunch of times, right in the kidneys. I've been pissing blood ever since. That's why I canceled practice. I could barely move. I spent the rest of the night laying on the floor in agony and I've been hiding from you ever since. When she left here, Mandi was fine. Furious, but fine. I knew she'd find you and tell you what we did, and you'd be mad enough to kill me. But if someone hit her, it happened after that."

"Nikki?" She'd gone quiet in his arms, and he started to relax his grip.

"I think he sexually assaulted her, and we need to report this. But I don't think he caused her head injury."

"Report him to the cops, or your brothers?" Everett asked, imagining what Danny and Kenny would do.

"Ummm . . . police, please," Colton said weakly.

"That's probably the safer decision."

🌲 🌲 🌲 🌲 🌲

They left Colton in a sniveling heap on the ground. Everett paced the sidewalk in front of his former band mate's house, wanting nothing more than to punch someone. From the anger on her face, Nikki wanted the same thing.

"Should we call the cops now?" he asked her. He wanted to watch Colton as they dragged him out in handcuffs.

"We can wait. I've got it all on my phone." Nikki patted her purse. "I've recorded every single conversation so far. I'll turn a copy over to the police for evidence. But we need to keep working. Where would Mandi go after leaving here? Looking for you, right?"

"She must have . . . Nikki, I was here. I was here right after Colton attacked her. I must have just missed her." She would have been upset and possibly in tears when she fled Colton's house, and he hadn't been able to protect her. If only he'd come early! A few minutes could have made all the difference.

"Focus, Everett. Where would she go next?"

"The ferry office. I went to grab a bite to eat, and when I got home, she was there, sitting on the steps." That moment would be seared into his mind forever, Amanda telling him her head hurt and then falling over. He hated that feelings of disgust and annoyance were his first response to her when she sought his help.

"So, someone attacked her between here and the office. How would she get there?"

"The beach! She would have gone down the beach route. It's the way we always walked together." She would have followed along the same path they took the night he first confessed his love. Would she have sat down on the rocks and cried? Was someone else lurking in the shadows there, someone violent?

He led her to the stone staircase, cautioning her to be careful on the descent, though her shoes were far more practical than any that her sister ever wore. At the bottom, Nikki stopped and put a hand to her head. "I feel weird. It hurts right here."

"Nikki, check this out." He knelt down by the rocks and gently poked at a dark spot. Smears of dried blood. "Was she bleeding?"

"Mostly internally, but some on her scalp." Nikki sank to her knees and touched the stain with a trembling hand. "I think this might be hers. She fell down these stairs? Or did somebody push her?"

"I don't know. If this were a police procedural, we'd search for signs of a scuffle, but I'm not sure what those would be."

"Broken branches are what they always say, but this is a rocky beach; that won't work here." Nikki stood up, hands on her hips and surveyed the area. "Can you tell if there's there anything unusual or out of place . . . hey! Is that hair?" She pointed to a matted clump on the ground. "It's blonde."

"And there's a shoe," Everett spotted a broken high heel next to the stairs. He wished he'd paid more attention to Amanda's footwear. "Do you think that's hers?"

Nikki picked it up and examined the damage. "No, this is definitely not hers, it's mine! I was searching all over for these! She must have hidden them while I was packing. And there's the other one!" The intact second shoe lay among the rocks a few feet away.

"She was barefoot when she showed up at my place." He'd noticed her dirty feet, but hadn't registered how alarming it should have been. That, if anything, should have been a clue that something had happened to her.

"It's hard to walk with the heel snapped off like this, and the strap is still intact, so she took them off herself. But why not carry them? Doesn't she remember how much these cost?"

"If she broke the shoe, stumbled, and knocked herself in the head, she would have been dizzy and disoriented." Everett was less concerned about the damaged footwear than he was about what it represented. "And she came to me for help."

Poor Mandi. She was injured, but still managed to make her way to him, and he treated her like shit and considered leaving her unconscious on the ground. If he had ... the sickening thought rose up again. He wasn't her attacker, but he could have been the one responsible for her death.

"She fell down the stairs," Nikki started laughing. "All this drama, and she just tripped. Doesn't that figure? Leave it to my sister to do it to herself."

Chapter Forty-Three

The next time Amanda woke up, her twin was sitting next to her bed. "You're back," she murmured, stating the obvious.

"It wasn't Everett," Nikki replied.

"What wasn't?"

"The person who did this to you."

"Oh. That's good, right?" Sometimes she had a hard time focusing.

"I thought you'd be happier."

She should be, right? She should be thrilled to learn that her boyfriend didn't turn out to be a violent psychopath who nearly killed her. No, ex-boyfriend. But it didn't matter if it was him or not, they didn't have a chance at a future anymore.

"I am happy. Who was it then?" The idea that someone else out there hated her enough to attack her was frightening. Was it a mugging? An attempted rape?

"Mandi, it was you."

"Me?"

"You know the stone staircase leading to the shoreline in the neighborhood where Everett has band practice? You fell down them."

"How do you know?" Was it possible she was just a klutz?

"We found your blood. And a pair of my shoes, one of which had a broken heel. You owe me."

"The red ones?"

"No, they were brown . . . how many pairs did you steal?"

"I . . . I have amnesia. Be nicer to me." Amanda sighed and rested the back of her hand against her forehead, in a pose she hoped earned sympathy.

"You have about eight hours' worth of amnesia, and you stole my shoes long before that. But I love you, so I won't bill you for them until you get a new job. Also, when I moved out, I took the sexy mini-dress Amy sent you from Italy. And your leather jacket, the one with the cool pockets."

"I looked everywhere for that!" She rubbed her temples for a moment, to fight her headache. Something didn't seem right. "Where did these handprints come from?"

Nikki traced one of the bruises with her finger. "Those came from Colton."

"The guy in Everett's band? Why would he grab my arms? Was he trying to catch me?" Those stairs were near Colton's house. Maybe he was some kind of hero. She wondered if any houses nearby had security cameras that may have recorded the accident.

"I'm unclear on the exact details, but you went to his house looking for Everett, and Colton seemed to think you came to flirt with him. He said you were playing hard to get, so he grabbed you and tried to kiss you. Or worse."

"So, what'd you do?" Amanda could imagine a few different ways her sister might have retaliated against her attacker, and they were all bloody and satisfying.

"Me?"

"Or are you sending Kenny and Danny to handle him? Somebody needs to." O'Connells stuck together, and they wouldn't let one of their own get hurt without resolving the situation.

"Mandi, you kneed him in the crotch and kicked him in the kidneys so hard he's still peeing blood. You can, apparently, defend yourself against everything but gravity. I did meet with the detective who is handling your case. Colton might end up charged with assault. Your actions would be self-defense."

"And Everett?"

"I expect those charges will be dropped after the police complete their investigation. We turned over the recordings, but there's a process they need to go through. As soon as he can, he'll be here. Don't worry, you'll see him again." Nikki smiled broadly. "You'll get your man back."

"I don't want to. It's over anyway." That was the worst part of all this. She'd destroyed any possibility of repairing their relationship by getting drunk at work last week, committing his one deal breaker. It had probably been her subconscious tricking her into performing an act of self-sabotage. She couldn't be brokenhearted about some guy leaving her if she purposely drove him away.

"It doesn't have to be over. If he wasn't in love with you, he wouldn't have been running all over town with me, trying to figure out who attacked you."

"Since they arrested him for it, he had to help you. It was the only way to clear his name." Everett had been the only suspect; the cops weren't bothering to investigate further. If he hadn't kept looking for the real perpetrator, he would have ended up in jail. His assistance was self-serving.

"He did it because he loves you. I saw it in his eyes."

"Not when he finds out what I did. He had one deal breaker, Nikki, just one. He didn't want to be with a drunk. And guess what I did when he dumped me?"

"Cara told me. Vodka in your water bottle. What are you, sixteen? Me-me, you made a mistake. He'll forgive you one little mistake."

"Maybe I don't want him to." Amanda closed her eyes, not because she wanted to sleep—though she was tired again—but because she wanted to hide the tears. "I think I need to let him go. He doesn't want to leave Whispering Pines, ever. He doesn't love me enough to go."

"And you don't love him enough to stay?"

"I love him too much. If I stay, I'll resent him, and he'll end up resenting me." Before the breakup, she had high hopes she'd convince him to move with her, and they would go off together and start a new life. But now that was off the table, and not only because Everett felt bound to stay here and work the family business. No, now she was damaged and needed someone to help take care of her. She couldn't ask that of him.

Chapter Forty-Four

"This place is tiny. How in the hell did both of y'all fit?" Nikki's voice carried loudly from inside the back room of the ferry office. She'd asked to stop in and use his restroom on the way to breakfast. Apparently, she and her brothers were sharing a motel room, and their grooming habits kept the bathroom occupied, especially Kenny with his extensive sideburn maintenance routine.

"It's not that bad," Everett said. He sat down on the steps outside and waited for her. They were on their way to a diner to grab a bite and get to know each other a little better. It was his idea. If he wanted a relationship with Mandi to work, he needed her family's approval, even more so now. He had to show them that he'd be able to step up and take care of her, or else they might take her back to Texas, and he'd never see her again.

He peeked over into the bushes, and there were no remnants from Mandi's stomach. His mom or Duncan must have sprayed the hose back there. Guilt flared. His family had been working overtime—more overtime than usual—to cover for him. Plus, his mother had bailed him out and paid for his attorney. Where did the money for that come from?

Everything in his life was crashing down on him again. How was he ever going to pay his mother back? Work more hours, he supposed. Though caring for Amanda would cut into his availability. He needed to be by her side.

"Hello, Everett." The greeting startled him, and he looked up to see Aubry. After everything that happened, he lacked the energy to deal with her.

"What do you want?"

"I heard you dumped Mandi, and she went after Colton. Figures. I warned you, didn't I?"

"Did Colton tell you he tried to cheat on you?"

"It wasn't his fault. I watched Mandi leave his place, and I knew exactly what happened. That hussy goes after all my men."

"You saw her?"

"I did."

He looked at Aubry more closely. She wore a chain around her neck, an art deco design, partially covered by her shirt. He wasn't familiar with jewelry in general, but he'd recognize that piece anywhere.

"Can I look at your necklace?" he asked, forcing himself to make the request politely.

Aubry reached up. "No." Her fingers closed around the pendant.

Just then, the door behind him opened, and Aubry gasped. "I see the rumors of your demise were exaggerated. Too bad."

"Excuse me?" Nikki asked in a low voice. "Who the hell are you?" She stood casually, hands in pockets, leaning against the door frame.

"Very funny." Aubry put her hands on her hips. "I can't believe you Everett! Her? Still? Haven't you learned your lesson?"

"That's my sister's." Nikki spoke in a dangerously calm tone, that was somehow far more frightening than the shrieks she'd emitted at Colton's house. "You are wearing Amanda's necklace."

"Sister? Oh my god, is this woman literally insane? Everett, now she's pretending to be a twin."

Nikki made it past Everett to Aubry faster than he thought possible, reaching for the other woman's neck. Aubry tried to duck away, but Nikki wrapped her fingers around the antique chain and pulled. It came off in her hand, a broken link falling to the ground. Nikki examined the jewelry carefully.

"Everett, who is this woman and why does she have Mandi's necklace? Where the fuck did she get this?"

That's when everything became crystal clear.

"Nikki, this is my ex-girlfriend, Aubry. She saw Mandi leaving Colton's place. And she . . . Aubry, it was you, wasn't it? You pushed her down the stairs!" He'd never been so blinded by anger before.

Aubry was completely unrepentant. "So what if I did? That bitch is crazy, Everett! She's been using a fake accent on you, and now she's faking being a different person! She's scamming you, Everett, I had to protect you. And what difference does it make? She's obviously fine. Still crazy, but perfectly fine."

"My sister is in the hospital. She's not fine."

"Yeah, your *sister*, I'm sure," Aubry used finger quotes and rolled her eyes. "I'm not listening to your crap, Amanda."

"Aubry! This really is Mandi's twin. She's still in the hospital recuperating. I was arrested for what you did." Everett felt sick and horrified at this whole situation. Aubry had nearly killed Mandi, and for what? For him? So he did share the blame for her head wound. If he'd been more cognizant of the depth of Aubry's hatred and jealousy, he could have stopped her.

"If you had served time, you would have deserved it for choosing her over me."

Nikki put one hand on Everett's shoulder as if to calm him down. All of his muscles tightened with fury, but he couldn't allow the violent rage to escape.

"What was your name? Aubry? Are you seriously saying that you intentionally pushed my sister Amanda O'Connell down the stairs at the beach and caused her head injury?"

Aubry smiled tauntingly. "I did. And if I ever catch you on the stairs, I'll push you too!"

"Did she even see you coming?" Nikki sounded far calmer than Everett would expect at a time like this. Her reaction seemed oddly subdued compared to yesterday. He would have expected a cat fight—and if it turned into one, he wasn't about to break them up. He'd put money on Nikki.

"I guess not, if she didn't turn me in," Aubry jeered.

"*I'm* going to be the one to turn you in," Nikki said. "And my family is going to sue you for damages. You have a lot of medical bills to pay. "

"Too bad there's no evidence. Your word against mine. Who's going to testify against me? Everett? I'll just say he's the one that did it and you're covering for him. He's got a history of violence, so who do you think they'll believe?"

Nikki smiled coldly. "I hit record on my phone the second I recognized the necklace. I've got your entire confession. So I guess they're going to believe *you*, confessing, in your own words."

Chapter Forty-Five

A cool hand gently stroking her face woke Amanda up. She blinked, hardly able to believe her eyes. "Mom? You came?"

"Of course I came." Her mother delivered a gentle kiss to her cheek. "I'm sorry we couldn't be here sooner. Your father and I were doing a wine tour in Argentina. As soon as Kenny called, we hopped on the next plane."

"Where is dad?" she asked, pushing the button on the bed to raise herself into a sitting position.

"You know him, he can't stay still. He went down with the boys to pick up some coffee. We've got a long day of travel ahead of us."

"Oh. You're going back already?" She tried not to feel too disappointed, but it stung. Her parents had been less supportive than she would have liked these past few months, though they claimed to have good reason. Tough love, and all of that nonsense.

"We're taking you with us, sweetheart."

"Mom? When did you get here?" Nikki appeared in the doorway, face flushed. But she didn't wait for an answer. "Mandi, you'll never believe the news! You're not a clumsy idiot after all!"

"Nicole! Be nice!" Mom warned, defending Amanda for once.

"I thought you were with Everett. Is he here?" Amanda asked, trying to peek past her twin into the hallway. The rooms were not set up in a way conducive to spying on the outside world.

"He still can't come until the judge lifts the restraining order," Nikki explained.

"Like that's ever stopped one of you before," Mom said pointedly.

"There's no violation here. I registered as a visitor under Amy's name," Nikki replied. "But Mandi, that isn't what I came to tell you. Look what I found." She held out her hand, and the light glinted off the camphor glass.

"My necklace!" Amanda reached for it eagerly. "I had Cara scouring the hospital for this. I thought I lost it when they brought me back for surgery." The clasp was damaged again, and one of the links had snapped. She gingerly poked at the sharp metal. Good thing one of Nikki's jobs was at a jewelry store; she'd be able to have it fixed at a discount.

"Actually, I found it around the neck of a woman named Aubry."

"Everett's ex-girlfriend? Why would he give her my necklace? Are they back together?" If her heart hadn't been broken before, it sure was now.

"You jump to the weirdest conclusions, Me-me. It turns out, that bitch pushed you. She's the reason you fell down the stairs and hit your head. That's where you lost your necklace. And my shoes, by the way, which you will pay to replace."

"The black ones with the bows?" She couldn't remember what she wore the day of the accident. No, not accident, assault.

"We discussed that yesterday. They were brown ... seriously, how many pairs did you steal?"

"I forgot. I ... my head hurts." Amanda sank back against the pillows, beloved necklace clutched tightly in her fist. They had talked about this, but it was hazy. Not all new memories remained recorded in her head. It would take time, the doctors said.

"You can't keep using that excuse."

"Girls, no fighting!" Mom interrupted. For a moment, Amanda had forgotten her mother was even there. "Nikki, you can go with Cara to pack up your sister's things. We're leaving this afternoon."

"Are they letting Mandi out already?"

"The doctors cleared her to go, we're just waiting on paperwork, which might take a few hours. But once she's free, we can get started, and see how far we can make it before nightfall. It's a long drive."

"I can't drive," Amanda protested. "Can't we just fly? That'd be so much faster."

"Faster but more risky. The changing pressure can cause a lot of harm to your poor healing brain right now. Don't worry, your father and I will trade off. We'll get a nice hotel room somewhere tonight and finish the drive tomorrow. We rented a big van with comfortable seats. You'll be able to sleep the entire time."

"And I'm coming with you," Nikki declared. "I don't have a return trip booked yet anyway."

"Okay." Amanda closed her eyes briefly. A road trip with her sister used to be her idea of a good time. Spending twenty-three hours in a van with a head injury did not sound fun at all. "But I don't think I want Nikki doing my packing. Cara should do it instead; she knows where everything is."

"Meaning you don't want me to find out what else you stole?" Nikki asked.

"My head is in so much pain. I think I need to rest. Nikki, please stay with me and let Cara handle everything."

"I'm on to you," Nikki muttered, but she climbed into the bed and curled up against her. Amanda let out a deep sigh. Things would improve. She might have lost Everett, but she had her twin back.

🌲 🌲 🌲 🌲 🌲

"Are you sure you're okay leaving like this?" Nikki asked, when Amanda was finally released. An orderly wheeled her outside while her parents went to get the rental vehicle. She hadn't felt the sun on her face in days, but her exhaustion didn't let her appreciate the warmth.

"I guess. There's no other way to go, unless you're offering to pay for a low-altitude helicopter."

"I meant going back to Texas without seeing Everett again." Nikki knelt next to the wheelchair and looked her directly in the eyes. "Me-me, are you sure this is how you want things to end?"

"Things already ended." Amanda said. All of her choices had been taken away. She couldn't go back to Everett this damaged and force him to take care of her. She still had weeks, if not months, of recovery to go through. She couldn't cook or clean. Hell, she barely had the energy to drag herself to the bathroom.

"It doesn't have to be over between you. You could make it work."

"No, I can't. Nikki, I don't want to talk about this anymore. Help me into the van." Her father pulled up, and Nikki held her arm for her few staggering steps to the passenger seat.

This was not how she ever imagined leaving. She thought at the end of summer, she would triumphantly board the ferry and wave to Cara, who would be crying at the docks. Sam and Tyrell would be there too, also in tears. Tyrell because he would miss her, and Sam because he realized how rude he'd been all summer and felt guilty. Everett would carry her suitcases, and his as well, because they were going to ride off into the sunset together.

She hadn't actually fantasized much beyond that. Maybe showing up at Nikki's in Austin and announcing her probation ended and she was moving in. Maybe buying a duplex and living on one side with Everett and having Nikki and Griffin on the other. But that possibility died along with her relationship.

Amanda closed her eyes. She wasn't going to watch Ferry's Landing go by. Better to sleep and pretend this was all just a dream.

Chapter Forty-Six

The wheels of justice turned far too slowly for Everett's liking. Even though he had recordings of both Colton and Aubry admitting to attacking Amanda and causing her injuries, Detective Wood claimed there had to be another complete investigation. Why? Why, when all the evidence was right in front of them, did they need to investigate? All that served to do was drag out the time before Everett's charges were dropped and the restraining order lifted. Days it dragged out, days when he could have been at Mandi's side, nursing her back to health.

He was, fortunately, on the Whispering Pines side of the ferry line when his lawyer called to tell him he was free and unrestrained. "Ma, I gotta run up to the inn real quick," he said, hanging up and already halfway out the door.

"The inn? Wait . . ." she yelled after him, but he didn't stop, not when he finally had the legal ability to go declare his love. Also, apologize. Profusely apologize. He owed her that too.

He expected Mandi to be recuperating in the staff house, but nobody was home. *She must be back at work*, he thought to himself. Nikki had told him when Mandi got released from the hospital, but he'd thought she'd also said Mandi would be bedbound for a while. *Nothing keeps my girl down.*

But the only person behind the reception desk was Cara. Her eyes widened when she saw Everett. "What are you doing here?"

"It's okay, the judge lifted my restraining order. My lawyer can fax you the paperwork if you don't believe me."

"Why wouldn't I believe you? Nikki played me the recordings."

"Can I talk to her? Is she in the office?" Why hadn't she come out when she heard his voice?

"Nikki?"

"No, Mandi. I know she's probably not too happy with me, but I'd like to at least clear the air between us. There are still two weeks of summer, and I just want . . ." he trailed off. Cara's look of pity stopped his words.

"Everett," she said gently, "she's gone."

"Gone where?"

"She went straight home from the hospital. Her parents took her back to Midland. She's got a traumatic brain injury. The recovery takes time. She needed to be surrounded by people who love her."

A knife to his heart would have been less painful.

"Did she say anything about me before she left?"

When Cara didn't answer, he knew everything he needed to know.

Chapter Forty-Seven

Amanda woke up in a hospital bed in an unfamiliar room. Had it happened again? How bad was her memory? She fumbled for the bed controls so she could sit, and the room came into better focus. Gran's old room. She was home.

Automatically, she glanced to her right, to the chair she always sat in when she read to her great-grandmother. If this were a ghost story, now would be the time Gran showed up, probably appearing in Amanda's chair, trading their customary places.

"Gran?" she whispered, just in case her ghost happened to be hanging around. "Gran, I miss you. I could use a little advice about right now."

"Are you awake?" Her living grandmother appeared in the door frame instead, carrying a tray. "I brought you a snack."

"Why am I in Gran's bed?"

"You were too tired to make it upstairs to your own room. Sweetheart, we've had this conversation."

Amanda sighed. Yes, they had. Several times. She remembered now. Her neurologist promised she could form new memories; they just took a little extra effort to recall. "Sorry. I forgot."

"It'll all come back; I promise." Grandma placed the tray next to her bed and seated herself in Amanda's old chair. "Give yourself time."

"I hate waiting. I want myself back. I want my old life back." But what was her old life? First she lost Nikki, then she lost Everett, then she lost her mind. Nothing of her former life remained.

"You're young and healthy. You'll be fine. Nikki's driving down for a visit tomorrow, so you have something to look forward to. And Gina is picking you up in an hour. You're taking a yoga class with her and Mel this evening."

"I can't stay awake long enough to do yoga," Amanda protested. She tried two days ago and embarrassed herself by falling asleep on the mat in the middle of class.

"Amanda Jean, stop with all the negativity." There really must be a ghost, because Grandma sounded exactly like Amanda's great-grandmother.

"Okay, Gran," she muttered.

"It's not an insult to imply that I sound like my mother. You respected her; what do you think she would say about you wallowing in self-pity?"

"She'd say, which one are you again?"

"That's not funny, Amanda." Gran's mind had gone in the last few months. She'd stopped remembering anyone's names and kept mistaking Kenny's little boys for her own grandsons, Amanda's father and his twin brother. Her decline had been rapid and heartbreaking.

"I'm sorry. No, Gran would have said 'and what are you doing to improve your situation, young lady?'"

"And?" Grandma prompted.

"I'll go to yoga. And I'll move upstairs to my old room."

"Good. See, you're making progress."

🌲 🌲 🌲 🌲 🌲

But progress was slow. Even if Amanda could keep her eyes open a few minutes longer every day, still her future stretched out before her empty and meaningless.

"Have you talked to Everett?" Kenny asked on one of his frequent visits. His young daughter sat on the floor at their feet, temporarily occupied with goldfish crackers.

"Nope. Why would I?" Amanda replied. She leaned over to touch Graciela's soft toddler hair. Graci swatted her hand away.

"Mine fishies!" The little girl glared fiercely and shoved another handful in her mouth.

"She thinks you're stealing her food. Never get between my kid and her snacks," Kenny said. "And you should at least call him. He did all that investigating to find out who attacked you, you may as well thank him for it."

"He did it to clear his own name."

"Is that truly what you think?"

She wanted to say no. She wanted to say what she wished: that Everett did it all for love. But if he loved her, why didn't he call? Why didn't he show up with flowers? Why did Cara avoid mentioning him every time they video chatted? Well, that last one might be because Cara was busy showing off newborn baby Cindy, but an equally plausible situation was that Everett had moved on and started seeing someone else. Someone who never drank, who never put herself in terrible situations. Someone mature and stable and deserving of a man like him.

"Mandi," Kenny eventually said, when it was obvious she didn't plan to answer. "What did you see in that guy anyway? Honestly? Is he worth sitting around being depressed about?"

If Graci hadn't been at her feet, Amanda would have responded with some choice swear words.

"Kenneth! How dare you talk about him like he's nothing. Not only is he the most gorgeous man I've ever seen, with the most perfect body, he's caring and considerate and smart and funny and understands me. He works hard and he's loyal and determined. And he sings and plays music, and rumor has it he can dance, and I never got to see that. He . . . he was my Sugar Pie, and I let him get away. And then I sabotaged everything so he wouldn't want me back."

"Is that why you haven't called him? Because you think you sabotaged things?"

"You know me. I'm an O'Connell, we burn the bridges and salt the earth. I'm not going to call just to get rejected. He broke my heart once. I'm not letting him do it again." And it would be worse if he did want her back. She wasn't the person he'd fallen in love with in the first place. Instead, she had transformed into a muted, tired version of herself. She wouldn't force an unwanted long-distance relationship on him, especially when she lacked the energy to maintain or even participate in it. He deserved to find someone else, anyone else. Except Aubry, of course. That bitch could rot.

🌲 🌲 🌲 🌲 🌲

Nikki's weekly visits were the thing she looked forward to the most, even if she did often bring her husband. Nikki seemed to think that if Griffin came around enough, Amanda would soften her stance toward him, forgive him for taking her twin away. The truth was, Amanda already understood and had forgiven him. But she would never admit that, because Griffin was a chef and his way of trying to win her over involved bringing baked goods.

"I brought something for you." Nikki set a large box down on the kitchen table.

"Cake?" Amanda guessed, looking at the size of the container. Last week had been cookies and a couple of freezer meals.

"Better. Check this out." Nikki opened the flaps and pulled out a microphone, speakers, a laptop computer, and some device she didn't recognize. Would she have known prior to her head injury? She sometimes got the nagging feeling she was missing out on some bits and pieces of cognition.

"I don't need any of that," she said.

"You do. I got you a job."

"If it's telemarketing, you're talking to the wrong person." She'd been fired from the one telemarketing job she attempted. Apparently, the calls were timed, and chatting with the lonely person on the other end of the line for a half hour meant she never made her sales numbers.

"No, better, this is something you'll love. Remember when we were kids and you wanted to be an actress?"

"Every kid wants to be an actress."

"Not me, I wanted to be a ballerina firefighter real estate agent."

"Yeah, I remember. Too bad you didn't go into real estate; you'd make good money."

"Actually, I've been doing the certification course. I'm thinking I'll make a bigger commission on houses than I do selling engagement rings." That was news. Had Nikki already told her? Maybe she had, but Amanda hadn't been paying attention. Her fatigue made it difficult to concentrate sometimes.

"So you finally get to follow your dreams? When does firefighter training start?"

"I'm following my dreams *within reason*. And you are, too. You remember when you recorded yourself reading a book for great-grandma, so we could go party in Mexico for a week?"

"A mystery set in the Bahamas, I think. Gran liked the descriptions of male bodies on the beach."

"Yeah, that one. I played it for a friend of Griffin's who writes young adult novels. He wants to convert them into audiobooks, and he thinks you'd be perfect. The protagonist is a young girl in Texas who is fighting against demonic forces to protect her small town. They aren't quite as terrible as they sound."

"He wants me to record the audio?"

"Yep. I picked up all the equipment you need—don't worry, I convinced Kenny to fund my shopping spree. The author will pay the standard industry rate. He's going to call you tomorrow to chat about details and send you a contract. You've got a couple of weeks to work on it, so you can record when you're awake enough. This is basically voice acting. And you can do it on your own time. It'll keep you busy while you heal."

"I'm never going to heal."

"Me-me, don't say that. You will. You know it takes time, and you've never been one for being patient."

Nikki's optimism served to exhaust Mandi. But she felt a tiny kernel of hope developing. She wasn't going to be able to hold down a regular job, not for months at least. Reading out loud though, that was one of her favorite things anyway. A chapter at a time, during her waking periods ... that could work.

Chapter Forty-Eight

Midland, Texas, December 2016

Amanda closed the novel and turned off her recording equipment. Not bad, a solid two hours of work. Her endurance was improving. Plus, this mystery was much better than the horror series she'd been working on earlier this week. She needed a break though, for both her voice and her eyes. If she tried to do much more, her near-constant headache would return.

When she emerged from the soundproof curtained booth that Danny constructed for her in the corner of her bedroom, she found a note slid under her door. Even from a distance, she could tell by the distinctive spidery left-slanting handwriting that it came from her grandmother.

Mandi—when you finish your work, come downstairs for coffee. But for heaven's sake, brush your hair, and put on a decent shirt first.

She sighed. Grandma always pushed her towards doing more for her recovery. And she tried, she really did. But the headaches and fatigue could strike at any moment, making it hard to do much besides sit around, depressed and alone. That was her life now. She just needed to get used to it, as did the rest of the family. At least her headaches kept her from drinking. Alcohol would make everything worse.

Although she no longer cared about her looks, as a courtesy to Grandma, she did run a brush through her hair and sniffed her shirt to make sure it was clean. She even splashed some water on her face to wake herself up and try to look refreshed.

When she made her way down the stairs, she heard voices talking quietly. Grandma and someone male. Since Dad was out golfing, it was probably one of the boy twins, come by to harass her again about providing babysitting services. They seemed to think she needed to get out of the house more, and the best way to do so involved providing them free labor.

But the shoulders of the man sitting across from her grandmother were far too broad to be either of her brothers. Her heart stopped. No. It couldn't be him.

"Grandma, why didn't you tell me we had company?" she asked, her way of announcing her presence. The man stood and turned towards her, and her stopped heart kicked into high gear. All the blood rushed from her head.

"It's good to see you, Mandi," he said.

"Have we met?" He looked so much like Everett, but she couldn't let herself believe it was him. His formerly shaggy I'm-in-a-band hair was neater, trimmed back with almost military precision. There were different lines on his face, and he looked almost as though he lost weight. He was still huge, but somehow tighter, leaner.

"I . . . you don't remember me? I'm Everett, we used to . . ." His voice was more tentative than before, and laced with pain.

"Amanda Jean!" Grandma's harsh voice cut right through Everett's stumbling words. "Stop pretending to have amnesia. That stopped being funny months ago!"

Everett let out a relieved chuckle. "Nikki warned me you might do that, and I still fell for it."

Amanda crossed her arms over her chest to hide her bra-less state. A little forewarning would have been nice. Grandma's note just said put on a decent shirt, it certainly hadn't warned her that her ex-boyfriend was sitting in the kitchen with a coffee mug and plate indicating he'd eaten some of Griffin's cookies. Had she known, she would have put on the cute little black dress she'd purloined from Nikki's suitcase and cracked open her makeup case. Let the man see what he was missing.

"I wasn't joking. I know who Everett Ryan is. He lives on Whispering Pines Island and wants nothing to do with me. If he had cared, he'd have tried to contact me at some point in the past three months. So, I don't know who you are, sir, but I can only assume this is one of those body-snatching situations and any moment now your alien overlords will try to steal my body as well."

"You are the most ridiculous child. I'll let you two catch up. That pot of coffee is fresh, if you want a cup." Grandma gave Amanda a reassuring pat on the back as she left the room.

Everett started to speak, but Amanda lifted a finger to her lips. "Shhhh." They waited, staring at each other for a moment. After counting to twenty in her mind, Amanda called out "I know you're eavesdropping. And I know you have me on speakerphone."

"I'm sure she doesn't ..." Everett started, but Grandma peeked around the doorway.

"Sorry. Blame Kenny. After he dropped Everett off, he made me promise to call when you woke up." She ducked away again.

Amanda turned back to Everett. There were a thousand questions swirling in her mind, first and foremost among them, "What did she mean about Kenny?"

"He was the one who picked me up at the airport. His kids sure have a lot of energy. They did this weird sing-shouting thing the entire ride over here."

"He says that was only the twins. Graci was quiet." Grandma's head appeared again. "I'm hanging up on him now."

Amanda sighed. This would never work. "I don't normally invite strangers into my private space, but since you're wearing the skin of someone I once loved, I'll make an exception for you. Let's talk upstairs."

She gestured for him to go ahead of her up the stairs. She couldn't bear the thought of him watching her walk, seeing how weak and pale and thin she had become. The vibrant woman he'd temporarily loved was long gone, and she wasn't coming back.

"This is my room. Ignore the mess." It was embarrassing to see him again, to talk to him in a room cluttered with empty water glasses and piles of clothes that she hadn't been able to bring herself to put away, the old homecoming mums still hanging on the walls as though she were back in high school and showing off for her friends. This room did not reflect her personality, it was just a place she slept to heal.

"I like your set-up." He scanned the room, and, as she would have expected, fixated on the soundproof booth in the corner. The little square of space, much smaller than his drum room, had exactly enough room for her equipment. She liked the slightly claustrophobic nature of it, the way the thick curtains hung around her, protecting her from the outside world.

"Danny made that. I got a job recording audiobooks."

"I know. I listened to *Houston, We Have a Demon* on my flight. The writing is terrible, but the narrator sucked right me in." His familiar grin caused her actual physical pain. How could he still look at her like that? Perhaps he'd gone blind in the intervening months.

"I've done better ones since then. I recorded a billionaire meets Texas debutante trilogy that hit the charts. How did you ... how did you know?" This was the confusing part. He'd been having coffee with her grandmother, her brother picked him up from the airport, he name-dropped her twin so lightly. Yet he had avoided her entirely.

"I've missed you." He was just as adroit at dodging questions as always. "Your hair looks pretty like that." He reached out as though he wanted to touch her, and she stepped out of his reach and patted the side of her head awkwardly. She'd had to move her part and comb her hair over to cover up the shaved spot from her surgery. There was a patch of three-inch long hairs hidden there. If she ever went out in public, she wore a hat so the new growth didn't stick out oddly and draw attention.

"It was this or a pixie cut. I don't feel like myself with short hair. Everett, why are you here? What the hell do you think you're doing, showing up like this?"

"I wanted to talk to you."

"I have a phone." One that never rang.

"No, I had to see you, for real. Live and in person. Mandi, last time I saw you, you were dying in a hospital bed. I couldn't just call you. I needed . . ." He reached for her again, and again she stepped back. If he touched her, she would cry and wrap her arms around his massive chest and let him break her heart again.

"Last time you saw me, I was wearing a rather fashionable garbage bag, or so I'm told."

He ducked his head in embarrassment. "Sorry about that."

"Sorry about what? Making me a plastic shroud?"

"Sorry about everything. I just . . . please, can we talk?" Uninvited, he sat down on her bed.

Everett Ryan was on her bed. For a second she flashed back to July, when the idea of Everett on any bed made her want to be there as well, stripping off her clothes and doing dirty things to his body. But he didn't want her now, worn down and broken as she was. She sat on the floor instead, back against the wall.

"Talk, then. Why are you here?"

"This is my grand romantic gesture. It's not working, is it?" He frowned. "Amanda, what were you going to tell me, the day of the attack? You came to my band practice looking for me. Why?"

Her stomach twisted in pain. It was too late for this conversation. But she may as well tell him. "I'm not quite certain of how I was going to phrase it. Rose helped me practice the words, supposedly, but I can't remember that. But I think I was going to give you a year." During a painful phone call, Rose filled her in on the details of their last visit. Things might be so different now if she'd sought Everett out at the ferry rather than band practice.

"What does that mean?"

"One year. One winter, one more summer. I was going to offer to stay for a year, if you'd agree to go when the time was up."

Everett briefly covered his face with his hands, rubbing his clean-shaven cheeks. She missed the scruff. "You were going to stay."

"But that doesn't matter now, does it?"

"No, I suppose not." His words were a knife to her heart, and here she'd thought she was over him. "Things have changed."

"They sure have."

"I got a new tattoo."

Amanda bit her tongue to keep from demanding he take his shirt—or pants?—off to show her immediately. It had better not be her name.

He watched her for a moment. "Want to see?" he finally asked.

"Depends on where it is."

"Fair enough." He was wearing a button-down shirt—another change—and he slowly undid the top buttons to reveal a new crow on his chest. This one had undertones of red rather than gray, and was much smaller than his others, but done with the same skilled hand.

"Another crow?" She wanted to touch it, to run a finger along the lines and absorb the heat of his skin underneath. Damn him for bringing these feelings back. It would have been easier if he'd stayed away.

"My third crow," he said and raised an eyebrow, as if waiting for her to say something. "Do you want to know why I got it?"

"Sure."

"Because I finally realized what you meant when you said you'd consider moving to New Jersey. That's where Coast Guard boot camp is. I didn't understand at the time."

"You would have been an excellent ... what do they call themselves? Sailor? Soldier? Coast Guardian?"

"Seaman. Stop giggling, it's not funny."

"It kind of is. You'd have been an excellent seaman, Everett." She gave him a jaunty salute, even though she wasn't sure if they did that in the Coast Guard.

"Yeah. Honor Graduate, top of my class, the whole works. Numerous awards."

"You have quite an ego." He was right though; she was sure of it. Hell, he would probably be a general or an admiral or whatever the top rank was by now, if he'd joined up right out of high school. She could picture him, in uniform, standing at the bow of a ship, commanding his underlings.

"It's not ego, it's the truth. Mandi, I joined the Coast Guard."

Her heart leapt. He'd done it. He'd moved on in his life.

"You're a seaman?"

"That's not as funny as you're trying to make it sound."

"When do you start training?"

"Mid-October."

"Next year?" Unless she'd really been missing something—which was possible, given her memory issues during her recovery—this was December.

"No. Mandi, I graduated yesterday. On Wednesday, I report for duty. I've been assigned to Station Maui."

"You actually did it? You left Whispering Pines?" Why now? Why couldn't he have made this decision in August, before her injury? Life would have been much better, for both of them.

"I did. Every time things got difficult in boot camp, do you know what I did? I put my hand to my new tattoo and pictured your face, to remind me of why I was there. This crow on my chest, it's you, Mandi."

"I'm a crow to you?"

"One for sorrow, two for mirth. Do you remember the next line?" She shook her head, and he continued. "Three for marriage."

"What?"

"This is it, Mandi. I told you, I'm making my grand romantic gesture. This is me, coming to you and begging you to not only take me back, but come with me. I got us a warm island. Imagine it, sandy beaches and sunshine, and you and I sharing a real big bed for a change."

"Everett, that's a lovely fantasy, but you don't know me anymore." Everything in her was screaming that she needed to say yes, she needed to launch herself into his arms and kiss him for the rest of her life, but she couldn't burden him with her neediness and physical issues now.

"I know you well enough."

"No, you don't. I've changed. I'm not your Mandi anymore. My head . . . I'm still recovering, but I may not ever be quite myself again. This dizziness and fatigue will reduce, over time, but might not ever go away. I'm also at greater risk of developing seizures and depression." The depression was already present, the unwelcome side effect of knowing her life was going to be slower and sadder than she had planned.

"So, what you're saying is I'll have to work harder to take care of you? Mandi, I messed up by letting you go once. I'm not going to do it again."

"Everett, you don't want me. I'm an alcoholic."

He gaped at her in astonishment. "That's the first time I've heard you admit to it."

"It's true. I learned it the hard way. You know what I did the morning after you broke up with me? I sat outside a liquor store until it opened, and I bought the largest bottle of vodka that would fit in my bag. I showed up at work drunk, and Sam threw me in the lake to sober me up."

"That's why he did that? I heard rumors, but I assumed you insulted his cooking."

"He wouldn't drown me for that."

"I don't know, it could have been the proverbial straw that broke the camel's back." His endearing grin appeared again, and she crossed her arms over her chest to hold herself in place. *Do not leap into his arms, Mandi. You'll only get hurt.*

"You don't seem as upset about this as I expected. That was your deal breaker, remember? You wouldn't be with a drunk?" This was the part that killed her. She pulled the typical O'Connell move, sabotaging herself, so she'd have an excuse as to why she couldn't get her man back. Even back on the island, before Aubry's attack, she already burned that bridge.

"It was my deal breaker before I fell in love with you. But once I got to know you, how could I let that get between us? Especially now that you've acknowledged the problem. I'll support you no matter what, Mandi."

"But you shouldn't have to. I'm worse than an alcoholic, I'm an alcoholic with a head injury. You're a gorgeous hardworking seaman, you can do better than me." Even though she was trying to be serious, she still couldn't help but giggle like a middleschooler every time she said seaman. And wait until her brothers heard—they'd drop it into every conversation. *Hey, Mandi, I hear you like seamen. How's your seaman doing? Had any seamen on your bed lately?*

"I don't understand why you think I can do better than you. You're my inspiration. If I hadn't met you, I'd still be going back and forth over the same gray stretch of water. I'd still be empty and cold on the inside. You give me life, Mandi."

"That's a good speech."

"I told you, I'm making a grand romantic gesture." He slid off the bed and went on one knee right in front of her. He reached into his pocket and pulled out a small ring box. "It's not much. I sent Nessie some very specific requirements, and she tracked this down. It's not a giant diamond, but I thought you'd like it."

When he opened the box, she gasped. The antique white gold ring with filigree that matched her camphor glass necklace was the most perfect engagement ring she could have ever imagined. Even Nikki couldn't have chosen better for her.

"Oh, Everett," she sighed. "What makes you think we can do this?"

"Easy. We go down to the courthouse Monday. There's usually a waiting period, but I'm active-duty military, so we can get it waived. We'll do the legal ceremony there and celebrate afterward. I'll fly to Hawaii on Tuesday and start doing whatever I need to set up our housing, while you pack your things. Then you join me, and we spend the rest of our lives together."

"You make everything sound simple. But I can't just up and get married." Men never understood all the logistics involved.

"Sure you can. Nikki is coming down from Austin this afternoon, and she's bringing her wedding dress for you to borrow. She said she was having the hem taken down so you can wear heels if you want. Kenny offered to host a reception at his house. His and Danny's kids have been making decorations; I'm skeptical as to how well they're going to turn out. Amy and Cara can't be there, but Danny said he'll video chat them into the ceremony."

"You've talked to everyone in my family about this?" And they all kept it a secret? How long had they let her wallow in loneliness and sorrow all the while knowing Everett was working his way back to her?

"Mandi, I love you. But I'm not a stupid man. I knew I needed everyone's support before you'd consider saying yes. You're not the only one I had to prove something to."

"And you think I can drop everything and move to Hawaii with you? And do what, sit around while you do seaman-type things?"

"I'll reassemble your recording studio there. You can record your audiobooks while I work, and we'll have more time together than we ever had before. Plus, Mandi, you turn twenty-six next month, and you'll get booted from your parent's insurance. With me, you'll be on Tricare, and we can find you a neurologist right away."

"Ah, yes, insurance. My goodness, Everett, you certainly pick the most romantic reasons for marriage. Is that what you think of me? I'm so desperate for health insurance that I'll marry the first man who comes along to seduce me with a fancy healthcare plan?"

"If I thought you'd marry the first man that came along, I'd have been here months ago. But I wanted to prove myself first, show you that I was making an effort for you."

"Aren't you worried it might be too late? You spent all this time conspiring with my siblings, but you never once asked what I wanted, or what I needed. You never tried to talk to me about any of this."

"You're right, I didn't. Don't you understand? I had to earn the right to talk to you again. I already know I'm not good enough for you!" He stood up and began pacing the room. "I let you go. I walked away from you. And after you were injured, instead of following you to Texas to care for you and help you heal,

I stayed behind like a coward, because I was afraid you'd reject me again. I wasn't brave enough to try. And do you know what my mother said to me? I mean, besides that I'd made the biggest mistake of my life? She told me she knew from the moment she met you that you'd be the one to take me away. You'd be the kick in the ass I so desperately needed to get out there and make something of my life. And I let you go!"

"Sugar Pie . . ."

"No, let me get this out." He stopped his pacing right in front of her and took her hands, pulling her to her feet. She let him, feeling a warmth stir deep inside her at his familiar touch. "Mandi, losing you destroyed me. You showed me what life would be like if I were happy, and then you were gone. And I know you, you need drama and excitement, and you want your life to be a grand and wonderful story. So, I enlisted in the Coast Guard, for you. To prove to you that I could move on and do something significant. And I requested Hawaii for you, to give you the climate you deserve—though, forgive me, it won't be a permanent station, I may end up in Alaska or back on the Great Lakes someday. All of this, Amanda, is me trying to win you back. I'm trying to be the hero in your love story."

He paused in his speech. "Wait, did you just call me Sugar Pie?"

"I did. Sugar Pie, you had me at Hawaii."

"Really?"

"No. It's not that easy. Yes, I want a love story, and yes, I want my story to be with you, but there's something very important you're missing."

"What? Tell me, anything, I'll do it."

"You showed up here with a sparkly ring and a plan. You even arranged my dress for me. You've got a wedding ceremony and a reception all lined up. But Sugar Pie, you never popped the question."

"I didn't?"

"No, you flashed a ring at me and told me your plan, but you kinda skipped an important part."

He immediately dropped back down to his knee and fumbled with the ring box. "Amanda O'Connell, would you do me the honor of becoming my wife?"

"Finally." She smiled down at this gentle giant who promised her so much. The months of his absence fell away. This was right, this was what she always needed. He was her man. "Yes, Everett Ryan, I will marry you."

Before she could fall into his arms and give him the great big sloppy kiss he so deserved, before she could rip his shirt off and taste his new tattoo, before she could do any of what she wanted, her bedroom door opened.

"Sorry, we didn't hear her answer," Nikki said, with Grandma looking over her shoulder somewhat sheepishly.

"My answer was both of you need to get the hell out and lock the door behind you! Me and my Sugar Pie have some catching up to do." She heard the door click shut as she wrapped her arms around Everett and sank into his embrace. He was exactly as perfect as she'd remembered.

Did you enjoy what you read?

I sincerely hope you enjoyed reading this book as much as I enjoyed writing it. If you did, I would greatly appreciate if you left me a short review on Amazon or Goodreads. Reviews are crucial for any author, and even just a line or two can make a huge difference.

About the Author

Sara LaFontain is usually in Tucson, but you can find her more easily at www.saralafontain.com or www.facebook.com/saralafontainauthor

Acknowledgments

Writing is hard.

But it's worth it. It's worth the headaches and the frustration, and criticisms. When inspiration hits and the words flow, it's magical. And when someone reads my words and feels something, when they laugh or cry or smile, that's what makes all of it worth it.

But I can't do it alone.

If it weren't for the love and support of my husband, Ryan Williams, Whispering Pines Island wouldn't exist. He graciously allowed me to use his first name for the Ferry family, and he didn't object when I used this book to mock his footwear choices.

I need my fellow writers, too. Women's Fiction Writer's Association members helped out throughout this process. Thanks especially to Brooke Dorsch, Naomi Lisa Shippen, and Y.M. Nelson for reading my book in whole or in part and providing feedback.

I also love the Every Damn Day writers, who keep me accountable. I've never met any of you in person, but you hold a special place in my heart.

In real life, Llyana Smith is my biggest supporter. She patiently reads everything, and helps me make it better.

Speaking of making it better, thank you Amanda Slaybaugh for your awesome editing. I, promise, I, will, learn, how, and, when, to, use, commas, someday.

Leigh McDonald, thank you for creating yet another beautiful cover.

And last, but not least, Rowan and Willow, thank you for occasionally letting your poor mama get some work done.

Read the entire **Whispering Pines Island Series:**

That Last Summer: A Love Story

Say the Words
A Short Story Sequel to That Last Summer

No Longer Yours

Cherry Christmas, Baby!
A Short Story Sequel to No Longer Yours

If This Were a Love Story